TRACEY BARSKI

The Alternate End of Cassidy Marchand

Book One of The Alternate Chronicles

Third edition

ISBN: 9781961707009

This book was professionally typeset on Reedsy.
Find out more at reedsy.com

To my husband: I would not be where I am without your support, love, and constant prayers. You are a blessing from above.

Contents

Content Warning

Hello friends! In caring for those who read my stories, I want to be forthcoming about what you'll find in my book. Cassidy has lived a hard life. As such, she reflects on, discusses, and experiences flashbacks to her experiences of abuse and abandonment. There are discussions about a serial killer, his modus operandi, and instances of stalking. There is also a violent scene in which she faces a murderer. Take care of yourself and make sure this is something you could handle before jumping into reading!

With love,
Tracey

1

Caught Redheaded

Pickpocketing required a bit of finesse. Sleight of hand, misdirection, an accomplice or two. But I didn't have as much to work with at a small coffee shop in a dinky town—solo, short on time, and a tad desperate. After watching the mark stammer his way through a brief conversation with the female barista, I decided that robbing him might be easier than I thought.

I figured I'd go for what Callum always called the Smash and Grab. It was less violent than the name would suggest. It turned out my pretty face made a fairly decent weapon.

I slouched in my chair at the back of the cafe, waiting as the mark settled himself by the window, cracking his knuckles for the third time since entering. He set his crumbly pastry and sizable manila folder on the table. I slid out of my seat, eyes glued to the jacket he slung over the back of his chair, the left side sagging with the weight of his wallet.

He opened the folder, the stack of papers revealing charts and spreadsheets that meant nothing to me. He noticed my approach and looked up. I smiled and lowered my lashes slowly, shaking out my long, red hair. His Adam's apple bobbed with the force of his swallow. *Smash.*

"I don't suppose you have change for a twenty?" I asked, lowering my voice to a purr.

His cheeks flushed. "I-I'm sorry. I only have twenties. I just went to the ATM."

I smiled again, brushed a hand over his shoulder as I leaned down. Of course, I knew he'd gone to the ATM. It was the reason I'd chosen the cafe. I had a good view of those who used it, could tell when someone needed a quick twenty or if they were making a larger withdrawal. I'd watched him get his cash across the street and walk into the cafe as if pulled by my will.

"That's all right," I said. "It doesn't hurt to ask." I slipped my hand into his jacket and palmed the leather wallet I'd seen him stuff into a pocket. *Grab.*

My hair fell in a fragrant curtain across his face, and he looked momentarily stunned. I dropped the wallet into my handbag as I straightened and made my way to the door.

I cast one last look backward and smiled again at the man I'd just robbed. He dragged his eyes from my swinging hips to my face, his mouth slightly agape, but he managed to give me a dazed grin.

As soon as I heard the tinkling of the bell over the door, I made my unhurried escape. The air was crisp, the new autumn chill nipping at my cheeks as I headed around the corner. The town was quaint, but I'd lingered longer than I should have.

Half a block later, I pulled my hair into a messy bun and took a pair of big sunglasses from my purse to cover my eyes.

I cut into the alleyway behind the cafe down to the next block over, and the junker of a car I called "home for now" waited indolently between two buildings. It was identifiable by the olive green paint—chipping—and the bald tires.

I skidded to a halt as a uniformed police officer sauntered into view, his eyes skimming over the boat of a car, his lips pursed. The helmet was a dead giveaway for motorcycle cop, as were the knee-high boots he used to kick the passenger side tire. If I wasn't suddenly juiced on adrenaline, I might have been offended at the violence toward the Beast.

The radio attached to his shoulder squawked, and I jumped. There was no way of knowing if it had anything to do with me, but I didn't want to chance it and spun on my heel to escape in the other direction.

"Hey!" the cop barked.

I pretended not to hear and hurried toward the other end of the alley.

"Hey, I'm talking to you!"

I stiffened at the sound of footsteps pounding the pavement. I couldn't act like I hadn't heard him as he splashed through puddles left over from yesterday's rain. I would have to run or face him. All I wanted was to get away, be on that open road. Safe.

Just as I was about to break into a sprint, another man stopped at the mouth of the alley in front of me. He wore jeans with a tucked-in, blue button-down. But it was the badge and gun he wore on his hip that caught my eye. I froze mid-step, gripping my purse tighter, nails digging into the faux leather. The footsteps behind me slowed.

The dark-eyed plainclothes officer in front of me crossed his arms over his chest. He was a slender, athletic man, long and lean. Young despite the parentheses that framed his mouth and the lines that fanned from his eyes. He must have been a squinter by nature.

"Going somewhere, miss?" His voice was gravelly but friendly, like a polite cowboy. I decided the description fit.

I shrugged, flashing the smile that usually got me out of scrapes. "Is it a crime to take a shortcut?"

He half-smiled and waved his hand at the officer behind me.

I glanced backward in time to see the motorcycle cop head back toward the Beast. I turned to face the cowboy again.

He tucked a hand into his pocket. "I just got a report about a redheaded woman who pickpocketed an unsuspecting patron inside the cafe. Almost $200 missing."

"Ah." I concentrated on not shifting my purse out of view. "So you're profiling all redheads?"

"I'm sure we could clear the whole thing up if you come back to the cafe for the victim to ID. Then I can go back to getting my afternoon coffee."

"Or?" I smiled hopefully.

He tilted his head. "Or I can take you down to the station. Clear it up there."

"And if I give the wallet back?"

He full-on smiled, perfectly straight teeth nearly blinding. It was amazing what a smile could do for an already handsome face. "That all depends on whether the victim wants to press charges. Either way, you'll have to come with me."

I walked forward, and he slid a hand around my arm to keep me from bolting. "He's not a victim. I lifted his wallet. It's not like I assaulted him."

"Semantics." He shrugged, and there was humor in his tone. "I won't cuff you, but you'll have to ride in the back of my cruiser."

"Semantics," I tossed back, letting him pull me to his unmarked vehicle.

He opened the door for me and smirked. "The wallet?"

I sighed and stuck my hand into my beat-up purse. The feel of the wallet's genuine leather after a cheap imitation made me reluctant to hand it over.

"I'll keep in mind how cooperative you're being." He looked down at the billfold. "I bet you need this more than he does."

He shut the cruiser's door before I could reply, and I sat back against the worn, lumpy seat while he walked up the street toward the cafe. I wasn't sure what I was going to do now. If the guy pressed charges, I wouldn't have enough money to get myself out of jail, let alone out of town.

I stared sullenly out the window. My mistake was probably talking to the guy. He might not have connected me with the crime if I hadn't brought attention to myself. Go unnoticed. Wasn't that Callum's motto?

A body passed in front of my view, the gun distracting me as the cop moved to open the driver's side door. He slid in behind the wheel, dark eyes catching mine in the rear view mirror.

"He's thinking about pressing charges," Squinty Cowboy said. "I have to take you to the station. Just in case."

"Great," I muttered, sitting back again. Maybe. . . I sucked my teeth and appraised the man in the front seat. My self-condemnation was momentarily forgotten as the allure of an attractive cop hinted at the possibility of weaseling my way out of a sticky situation.

He pulled away from the curb. "You're not from around here."

I smiled at the non-question. "You don't remember me from high school? Dang. There were only ten of us."

He squinted at me in the mirror. "Yeah, make fun of the small-town guy. Just remember, I'm the one who could probably use my charm to get you out of charges."

"You'd do that for a hardened criminal like me? I'm sure I'm the worst you've come across here in Mayberry."

He pursed his lips. "I wish that were the case. We don't have the crime rates of Chicago or New York, but we have worse offenses than jaywalking. Sometimes Mr. McGregor escapes from the nursing home and wanders through town naked."

I grinned and sat forward, resting my forearms against the back of his seat. There was promise in his joking manner. "So, are you Andy Griffith?"

He laughed lightly, mostly air huffing through his nose. "Not quite. That would be a pay raise. Drew Seward. Detective."

"Ah."

He waited a beat. "And you are?"

I hesitated, a twitchy sensation creeping through me.

"I have a feeling that if I check the database, your name will come up anyway. You might as well be straight with me."

"Cassidy Marchand." My name stumbled stiffly through my lips.

"So tell me, Ms. Marchand. What inspired you to steal from an innocent, if socially inept, man?"

"The thrill?" I tossed out.

He gave me a skeptical look.

"Just trying to get out of town," I said with a sigh.

"Any particular reason?"

Not a reason I was willing to share. I'd been down that road before. Didn't do me a lick of good. I shifted in my seat, looking down at my scuffed-up boots.

"C'mon. We're old friends now."

"It's not important."

"Well, apparently it is if you had to steal from someone to accomplish it." His dark eyes shifted from the road to the rear view mirror.

I sat back as if by the force of his gaze. That lazy, squinty stare made it easy to imagine him on a ranch in Montana with dirt-smeared jeans and scuffed boots, eyes narrowed against the sunlight. He even had that leisurely walk, like he wasn't in a hurry about anything.

He looked away, and I forced myself to focus on the business district as we drove through. Quaint little shops and boutiques lined the street in a four-block square. During my short time here, I'd heard the district simply called "the Square."

The police department was on the corner, located in the middle of the Square. Across the street was the library, a one hundred year old building whose brick facade had that weathered but sturdy look of turn-of-the-century architecture.

Detective Seward pulled into the parking lot behind the police station. I watched him unfold his long frame from the car and open the backseat door for me.

He blocked any chance of escape with his body. "You're not going to run are you?"

I grimaced. "I doubt I would get far. You look like a sprinter."

"All State, four years in a row," he announced proudly, stepping aside. "I'll spare you the indignity of handcuffing you."

"You're *so* kind."

"Honestly, I think I can convince the guy not to press charges." His tone was conversational as he took my arm like he'd done when we left the alley. "I think he's only considering it because he's embarrassed. I don't think pretty women hit on him very often." He half-grinned. "He's gonna be suspicious of any woman who flirts with him from now on."

"I psychologically damaged a man by stealing his wallet?" I tsked as we entered the station. "Are you trying to guilt me straight, Officer?"

"Detective," he corrected good-naturedly as he marched me through the front desk area and into a small room. "Creedy," he said to a thin man behind a desk.

The man looked up, curiosity lighting up his sharp green eyes. He had a mop of curly hair over a boyishly handsome face. His eyes stayed glued on my face for longer than I was entirely comfortable with.

"Can you print her, get the process started?" Seward nodded in my direction.

I whipped my head to look at him. "Wait, wait. Can't we hold off, just to see if we can talk him out of charges?"

"Sorry, Red. Gotta go by the book. I'll hold off on the rest for a bit while you sit in a cell, and I can get this figured out."

I sighed and submitted to the process, again hoping my cooperation might play in my favor.

Once he fingerprinted me, Seward brought me back into the main section of the station. Desks were lined up in rows of two all the way down the room. Several doors lined three of the outside edges. Offices, conference rooms, interrogation rooms. One door boldly proclaimed it was the office of the head of homicide, Captain Patterson.

Despite its relatively small size, the station was bustling with activity. "What happened?" I asked with a smirk. "Did Mr. McGregor escape from the nursing home again?"

The detective had lost all his good humor; every plane of his face hardened almost immediately.

"Seward!" a uniformed woman called. She sat at a desk near

a window, a phone pressed to her ear.

The detective's head snapped in her direction, and he nodded his acknowledgment of her frantic wave. He continued marching me forward. "Sorry to do this to you, Ms. Marchand."

I started to dig my heels in. "Do what?"

We were headed toward a heavy door tucked into the back corner.

"You may have to sit for a while longer than planned. It looks like something came up." He ran a key card over the lock and yanked the door open.

The uniformed officer just inside the door stood from his desk, his name badge catching the light, and I made out the name "Keener." Keys jangled against the belt tightened around his bulbous waist.

I turned to watch the door cut us off from the inner office. "But—"

Seward grimaced. "I really am sorry. I'm sure this will be cleared up soon enough, and you'll be on your way."

I clenched my teeth. Would sitting in a quiet cell for a couple of hours really hurt anything now that I was already here? If he was busy with something else, he wasn't digging into my life any more than he'd already tried to. I needed some time to figure out how I was going to get myself out of town anyway. Officer Keener unlocked an empty cell and held the door for me.

I made a show of stepping inside willingly. If my helpful attitude didn't get me extra good girl points. . .

Keener stepped inside to collect my purse and sunglasses. I relinquished them without a fight and barely caught sight of the detective's back as he headed toward the main area of the station.

I released a loud breath as Keener locked me in.

He offered a sympathetic look. "Must not be that bad if Seward didn't handcuff you."

"Yeah, lucky me."

He gave me a grim smile. "Hang in there. Name's Officer Keener if you need."

I rolled my eyes as he shuffled off to his desk.

With nothing else to do, I sat on the uncomfortable wooden bench, splaying my legs in front of me and slouching against the concrete wall at my back.

Time passed without any excitement. I shifted my position at least a hundred times, read some pleasant messages carved into the bench about giving Rhonda a call or to eff off. The concrete floor stained by God-knew-what made it seem more like the place was used for people to sleep off whatever high they were riding instead of any actual criminals. It was amazing that, with all the hard surfaces, it still had a *smell*. Something like moldy socks, stale beer, and unwashed bodies. I wasn't keen on thinking too much harder on it.

I was lying on my back with my knees up, staring at the ceiling tiles while an old boombox spat oldies from the desk by the door. The sound was slightly warbled like the speakers had been blown, but I could appreciate Marvin Gaye, even if a little distorted.

The broken speakers didn't hide the sound of footsteps heading toward my cell.

I turned my head to look at him but made no other move. There was a tightness, a serious intensity about his face that hadn't been there before. And he'd changed his shirt.

Seward leaned forward against the black bars. "How you holding up?"

"Oh, having the time of my life."

One corner of his mouth turned up, but the tightness around his eyes remained. "You hungry?"

I sat up and squinted at him. "I could eat," I said slowly.

The thick officer who'd locked me in shuffled down to Seward, handing him a bag. "Thanks, Keener."

I could smell the food from where I sat and tried to ignore the ravenous growl my stomach threatened to unleash.

The detective slid the bag between the bars and raised a brow. "I hope you like Italian subs. The bad breath from the pastrami is always worth it."

"I have no plans to kiss anyone, so I think I'll be fine."

He smirked.

I stood to take the bag. "Wouldn't this be considered, like, aiding and abetting or something?"

He tipped his head. "I've turned many a criminal back to the path of righteousness with a well-made sandwich."

I opened the bag and looked inside. "Smells pretty heavenly, but only the taste test will determine if this sinner will be repenting any time soon."

"The real sin would be letting this supremely built sandwich go to waste."

I sat down and unwrapped it to take my first bite. I almost groaned in ecstasy, but I refused to give Seward the satisfaction.

But when I looked at him, his gaze was far away. The seriousness he'd come in with had tightened his expression again. Something big must have happened.

As if he sensed my eyes on him, his attention returned to me. "So, in between questioning witnesses today, I was able to stop by your vehicle."

I lowered the sandwich before I took another bite, tensed for what would inevitably come next.

"You've been living in your car."

There it was. "Yeah, because I have high standards." When he didn't smile, I took a deep breath. "I get motels if I can afford them."

"Which you accomplish by stealing." He raised a brow.

"Only when I have to," I insisted, working at casual. "I try to find work when I get to a new town, but not a lot of places will hire me temporarily."

"You keep yourself pretty clean for being pretty much homeless."

I set the sandwich aside. "I'm *not* homeless." I hated the label almost as much as the fact that he was basically right.

"What would you call it?"

"Temporary."

He shook his head. "That doesn't sit right with me."

I bristled. "Well, you're not in charge of my life, are you?"

"Listen," he said, an edge to his voice, "this is not a safe place to be 'temporarily' homeless. We've got a guy on the loose kidnapping women and carving them up with a frigging kitchen knife. He targets your type."

The blood drained from my face. "My type?"

"Redheads."

I waited for my thoughts to stop wheeling. "Wait, plural?"

"Today's murder was number three."

I battled back the shiver that danced down my spine. "I appreciate the concern," I said, glad my voice was strong and controlled. "But I'm perfectly fine."

"For now. I've arranged for you to stay here tonight. I'll have one of the guys fill your car up so you can get yourself out of town in the morning."

I sat up straighter. "I don't need charity."

He continued as if he hadn't heard me. "I know it's not much, but you'll be safe here tonight." He pushed away from my cell to head back out.

"Hey!" I stood and marched over to glare at his retreating form. "You have no right to keep me here! Where's my phone call?" I gripped the cold, metal bars with desperate hands. The desk cop didn't even look up as Seward disappeared behind the door again.

I growled my frustration and whirled around to go back to my bench, now serving as my bed. As much as it sucked that the decision had been made for me, there was a tiny part of me that was relieved.

A killer who—what had he said?—*carved up* women like me. Fear was a living thing inside of me, slithering and cold, and this cell suddenly didn't seem so bad. Part of me wanted to hide here forever. Hiding was something I was used to. It had been my life for the last six months.

"I'll find you, Cass. I always do."

I shivered at the memory. His breath, hot against my face, the flat darkness in his gaze. The police dragged him away a year ago. They'd had him on some petty charges, so he'd only been in for half a year. As soon as Callum Gallagher's old pal told me he was out of prison early, I'd packed up and run.

Losing my mother to cancer as a child and my father to abandonment probably sealed my fate for having bad taste in men. And Callum played the bad boy with a heart of gold like an Oscar winner. Of course, like an idiot, I'd fallen for it. He was manipulative, and he really enjoyed having people under his thumb. Once he had a grip on me, there was no way he'd let me go.

His threats that he would always find me didn't deter me from trying. But twice found and twice punished had a way of taking the fight out of you. At least with him in prison, I could get a head start.

A slow-moving song came on the radio, and I matched my breathing to the tempo, willing my mind to focus elsewhere. At least I had good music to keep myself distracted.

But that didn't last as long as I would have liked.

"Hey, Red." Officer Keener's voice came to me before he appeared in front of my cell. "End of my shift. This is Devereaux if you need something." He gestured to the younger cop, a beanpole of a man who looked like the marathon running type.

I gave Keener an imploring look. "A new DJ? Please tell me he has good taste in music."

Keener winced. "Sorry."

I blew out a breath.

Devereaux smirked and gave me a little salute before they both headed off. He changed the radio station to country, and I curled my lip when the twang floated down to me. At least he kept the volume low.

My efforts to tune it out opened the door to thoughts I was working to ignore. But everything the Detective had told me about the serial killer reminded me how much fear ruled my life, and the unease made me jumpy. I flinched at the sound of the desk chair scraping against the concrete floor. The door opened and shut, and the stillness in the air assured me I was alone.

It was getting late; the sky, long-ago darkened and laden with stars, was visible through the tiny window above me. It added to the jitters, the chill that skittered down my spine. So when the song on the radio was interrupted by fuzzy static, my heartbeat accelerated. It was stupid to be afraid of something so innocuous. The static continued cutting in and out, like someone trying to figure out the perfect frequency on an old dial tuner.

I rose from the bench and walked toward the bars of my cell, feeling as if I was moving through water. I slid my fingers around the rough metal of the bars and peered toward the door separating the cell block from the rest of the station. I couldn't see anything through the window cut into the door, but as I stood there, the lights began to flicker.

"This is like a bad horror movie," I muttered. I imagined a grotesque creature walking through the walls and clawing my eyes out.

The lights flickered faster, and a ringing started to fill the room. At first, it was just another unnerving sound added to the racket made by the static, but it quickly progressed to an unbearably painful level.

My hands flew up to cover my ears almost of their own volition as the ringing grew louder, more powerful. One by one, starting by the door, the light bulbs burst, glass raining down onto the floor in a glittering deluge, dousing the light in the room.

The one closest to my cell shattered, and I spun away to protect myself from the shards. The overwhelming pressure of the noise forced me to my knees, and I squeezed my eyes shut, pressed my fingers tighter into my ears. Through gritted teeth, I moaned, trying to drown the sound out with my own voice as everything faded around me.

2

Parallel Hangover

I didn't remember falling asleep. It was a wonder I had been able to at all. Sunlight streamed in through the high window above me, and I woke to find myself staring at the wall. I was lying on my side, my hip aching from being in that position too long.

I groaned, feeling like a freight train had run me over and dragged me for several miles. A hangover without the fun of drinking the night before. I pushed myself up cautiously to a sitting position, wondering how I'd gotten from the floor to the bench or how I wasn't deaf after that horrible ringing—the last thing I remembered.

"Hello?" a voice called out from down the hall, and it rattled in my head like a handful of pennies in a tin can.

I blinked several times, trying to get my eyes to open properly. I pressed an unsteady hand to my temple.

Cautious footsteps sounded as someone made their way toward me. I glanced up in time to see Keener peering into the cell. His eyes narrowed on me, brow wrinkling.

"What are you doing in there?"

I dropped the hand rubbing my temple, and it made an audible *plop* into my lap. "What kind of stupid question is that?" Irritation lanced my tone.

"Who put you in here? I haven't had any reports or paperwork for any holds." He glanced behind him. "Is this some kind of joke? Did they sneak you in here when I went to get my coffee?"

I squinted as if it would help me better understand what he was saying. Was he playing a joke on *me*? "You were here when Detective Seward brought me in yesterday."

He looked as confused as I felt. "Detective Seward," he muttered as he turned to head back toward his desk. The door opened into the main part of the station, voices cutting into the cell block momentarily, then I was left in blessed silence. Good riddance.

I stood, flexing my leg muscles to dispel the stiffness, and shut my eyes against a sudden, fierce pounding in my head.

What the hell happened?

Even though the sun was shining audaciously through the window, the lights on the walls burned as brightly as if it were night. I froze, staring at the bulbs. Whole. I looked down. No glass shimmered on the floor.

The door down the hall opened again, and I jerked my head in that direction, immediately regretting it.

". . . messing with me, Keener?" Seward's voice demanded. "I'm telling you I didn't bring anyone in yesterday."

Detective Seward's wiry frame came into view first, and he stopped abruptly when he saw me. Keener held out his hands to keep from bowling him over.

Seward's eyes went huge, disbelief evident on his face. "What is this?" he demanded, his voice taking on an emotion

I couldn't place. "What *is* this?" he said louder, the sound clattering inside my skull.

"That's what I'm asking you!" Keener responded, slightly panicked.

He didn't take his eyes off me. "Unlock the door." When Keener didn't move, he barked the order: "Unlock the damn door!"

Keener twitched into motion and yanked the key ring from his belt. Right as the lock clicked, Seward yanked the door open so hard, he knocked Keener back.

Seward rushed in so quickly that I took a startled step back. At my movement, he froze, his breath coming out in short gasps, hands clenching and unclenching.

"Cass?" His voice almost broke on my name.

Something in my chest tightened. The tone was intimate, but it carried more of a weight, like he hadn't seen me in years. My brain fumbled for a word to classify it. It was almost like. . . grief. It had been a long time since I'd acknowledged it in my own life, but it was recognizable now—a heaviness that you never got rid of, that was nearly debilitating if you let it be.

I swallowed, unable to find the words to respond.

He reached out to touch my face as if he wasn't sure I was real.

I flinched. I wasn't used to such gestures, let alone ones without violence behind them.

It seemed to jerk him out of whatever daze he was in. His mouth snapped shut, the muscles in his jaw working as if he were struggling for control. He straightened and backed out of the cell. As he marched stiffly down the hall and away, he raked shaking hands through his hair.

Keener stared after him, holding the cell door open. He

looked at me, his eyebrows up in question.

"If you're expecting me to explain what's going on, I'm sorry to disappoint. I have no freaking idea."

He didn't respond. He pushed the door closed and locked it with halting movements like he was unsure it was the right thing to do.

I turned to sit down as Keener walked back toward his desk scratching his head. I wasn't sure what was going on, and I wished I didn't have to stick around to find out. Seward had promised to help me get on my way today, and I was more than willing to take him up on it.

The door at the end of the hall opened again and someone stomped in my direction once more. I heard Keener scrambling to get up.

"Stay put," Seward said behind him as he came into view again. His expression had hardened in the five minutes he'd been gone, and there was a flinty look to his eyes that had my muscles jumping. He leveled a look at me. "We're going to figure this out."

Unable to contain myself, I responded coolly, "What's this 'we?' You're the detective."

His mouth tightened. "What's your full name?"

Naturally, I'd have to make this harder. "I already told you my name. Yesterday."

Through his teeth: "Tell me again."

"Cassidy Jean Marchand."

His eyes narrowed. "Date of birth."

I huffed a sigh. "February 16th, 1989"

"Where do you live?"

My cheeks flushed red despite my best efforts. "In my car."

His eyes flickered at that answer but only for a second. "Your mother's name."

Anger was a sudden beast inside of me, clawing for control. "What is this?" I demanded.

"Your. Mother's. Name." Each enunciated word made me flinch like I was being slapped.

"My mother is *dead*," I snarled. "What does her name matter?"

This time, his own anger flashed like a flame in his dark eyes. "Answer the question."

"I thought we'd already cleared this up. Am I in trouble for something else?"

He slammed his hands against the bars so abruptly, I yelped. "Who the hell are you?!"

"Seward!" Keener's voice rang through the room, suddenly authoritative. "Back off."

Detective Seward released his death grip on the bars and backed away from the cell slowly, and it was the first time I'd seen danger in his eyes, the kind that I'd only seen in the gaze of a man who had cruel hands, one I'd been running from for months.

Refusing to cower under that look, I forced my back straight and lifted my chin a fraction of an inch.

The look of defiance didn't affect this man the way it did the other. Seward broke eye contact and looked down as he settled back against the stone wall behind him. For Callum, it would have been a challenge. One he'd have to conquer.

I swallowed the ghost of fear and fought to hold in a sigh of relief. Seward's fingers raked through his hair. It seemed like he was trying to get a grip after receiving the worst news of his life.

"Unlock the cell, Keener," he said, low, quiet.

"I don't know if that's the best idea."

"Just do it." He lifted his head. Again, the hardened expression was in place, but the danger was gone. The flinty look seemed more like protection now. From me. He pushed away from the wall as Keener came forward to unlock the door once more. Seward stood beside him, statue-like.

"Come with me," Seward said.

When I didn't move, he worked to soften his expression.

"Please."

I bit my lip and pushed myself to my feet. I looked at Keener as I walked out of the cell, but he was watching Seward.

Seward took off toward the door, and I had no choice but to follow him. He led me through the maze of desks outside the cell block. It wasn't a flurry of activity as it had been yesterday, but it certainly wasn't operating at a leisurely pace. Phones still rang incessantly, and there was always a handful of people weaving around the desks from one end of the room to the other.

I followed Seward down a hall to a big, gray door. He yanked it open and ushered me inside. It was an interrogation room like I'd seen on TV. Plain gray walls, cold metal table, two uncomfortable-looking chairs. The light flickered on, barely making an impact even in the small space.

"Have a seat."

I waited a beat, took in his serious expression, and walked to the chair that faced the two-way mirror.

He shut the door and made his way to his own chair, but he seemed to be gathering his thoughts. The cop mask was still in place—that steely look. This was definitely not the easy-going man I'd encountered the day before.

As he sat, shifting his weight, he pulled out a recorder and set it on the table. He made a show of pressing the *record* button. "State your full name."

I decided not to argue again that we'd been through this already. "Cassidy Jean Marchand."

"Date and place of birth."

"February 16th, 1989. Evanston, Illinois."

"Parents' names."

The sound of my breathing filled the room as I hesitated. "Patrick and Amelia Marchand."

"Where were they born?" he asked, leaning forward a bit as the hand he rested on the table clenched.

I sighed, trying to dredge up those memories, faded and distant. "My dad was born in Massachusetts, I think. My mom was born in Wisconsin." All information I'd memorized from the handwritten book my mother had made when she was first diagnosed. Things about her life so I would never forget her. It was one of the few belongings I'd taken with me when CPS picked me up.

"Tell me how you got into one of our cells."

I snapped back to the present and allowed my irritation to bubble to the surface. "Oh, you know. I just walked in." He continued to stare at me. "Dude, you arrested me yesterday." I held up a finger. "Well, technically that's not true. I haven't been booked on any charges. When the call came in about the murder, you left me in the cell."

His eyes narrowed. "*I* brought you in?"

I tossed my hands in the air. "Do you have amnesia or something? I pickpocketed this guy at the cafe. You happened to come in for your afternoon coffee or *whatever*. You so kindly decided to keep me overnight in that jail cell, which, by the way, is less comfortable to sleep in than my car."

He placed an elbow on the table and rubbed his forehead above his eyebrows, then leveled a squint at me. "*I* brought you in on pickpocketing charges? Yesterday?"

"Do you want it in Spanish this time? *Si. You* brought me in *yesterday*."

He sat back and exhaled loudly through his nose, eyes still narrowed.

"Come on, you really don't remember? I called you Andy Griffith. We had adorable repartee." I raised a brow. What kind of weird joke was he playing on me? Or did it have anything to do with what happened to me the night before? Was it possible that whatever it was that nearly popped my eardrums had actually altered his memory? Or worse, *mine*? Was this a crazy coma dream?

No, not possible. I shook my head as if someone had said it out loud.

He held up his hands in mock surrender. "It's not that I don't remember. I *know* I didn't pick you up. I got the call for the murder while I was still waiting on my coffee. I went straight to the scene from the cafe."

I rolled my eyes. "Come *on*."

He pressed his lips together, shrugging.

I squinted at him then sat back. "I get it. You're messing with me." I tried my best to force out a laugh because he *had* to be kidding, and I was being paranoid about a trip to the Twilight Zone.

But he just stared at me.

"Seriously." I placed my palms flat on the table. "Are you messing with me?" *Please, please be messing with me.*

He looked at my hands and frowned, then seemed to come to a decision. He shut off the recorder. "Come with me."

I rose and followed him once again. He led me out of the room and down the hall further, bursting through the door into the little lab where I'd been fingerprinted the day before.

The same man stood behind the desk. He looked up, and his eyes narrowed on my face like he'd seen me before and was trying to place me. I couldn't remember his name, but I lifted my brows as if it would help him, hope igniting within me. If he recognized me from the last time I was in this situation, maybe he could help me out, but the look in his eyes died as he shifted his focus to Seward.

"I need you to run her prints," Seward said.

"Again," I muttered. He ignored me.

The man raised a brow but shrugged. "Sure."

Seward gestured for me to step forward as the other man waited for my hand, which I offered and he flipped palm-down onto the tiny scanner. His gaze flickered back and forth between my face and what he was doing. He was trying to be discreet about his appraisal of me for whatever reason. Made it no less strange.

He released me. "Other one please."

I placed it on the scanner myself this time, trying to ignore his subtle scrutiny.

After a moment, he smiled at me then looked at Seward. "All set. It'll take a bit to run through the system. I'll let you know when it's finished."

"Great." Seward pointed a finger at me. "You. With me."

Once again out in the hall, he led me toward the front door.

"Um, where are we going? Did that guy decide to press charges? Because if this weird charade is your way of trying to scare me into giving up my life of crime, you succeeded. I might even join a convent."

He didn't answer me. Instead, he led me to his vehicle, the same beat-up Dodge Charger. He went around to the driver's side, and I waited.

He yanked his door open and looked at me. "What's the problem?"

"Should I sit in front or the back?"

He rolled his eyes. "The front is fine."

I opened the door and climbed in. "There's no need to get mad at me. I don't know what the hell is going on."

"Join the club," he muttered as he started the car and shifted into drive. The vehicle lurched away from the curb before I had myself buckled.

Instead of wasting my energy trying to figure out where he was taking me, I focused on the town as we drove through. I noticed the character of the buildings as we passed, the stamps of individuality in the way owners painted their storefronts. A used bookstore was painted in soothing earth tones, reminding me of worn, old books. The toy store down a few doors was framed in bright blue and white with a red front door.

After a few minutes, we emerged from the business district and entered the neighborhoods that surrounded it. Quaint little houses were stacked on small lots, one after the other. I appreciated the Victorians thrown in with the Tudors and colonials. Occasionally, we came across some that had been redone in deco styles, a jarring contrast to the others. From what I'd seen, the oldest houses and neighborhoods spiraled out from the main district. The larger, newer homes surrounded those like a circular band on the outside. I preferred the older homes since they tended to have more character. The new ones were all prefabbed, same shapes and sizes, no originality.

I was admiring a small colonial when I realized the car had

slowed in front of a home that looked like a farmhouse, the color a sunshiney yellow.

"Do you recognize this house?" Seward asked.

I glanced over at him. "Should I?"

He didn't answer. Instead, he leaned forward to look at the house and chewed on his bottom lip. The sound of his phone ringing startled us both, and he fumbled into his pocket to pull it out.

"Seward," he answered.

I watched his face as whoever was on the other end spoke. He must have been aware of my gaze because he kept his expression even.

"Thanks." He hung up.

"News?" I asked.

He slid a glance in my direction before he checked the mirrors and pulled away from the curb. We drove through more of the neighborhoods, out further into the newer developments.

In the distance, I saw that the houses parted to make way for a small cluster of boxy buildings and warehouses.

"Where are we?"

"Technology center," Seward replied.

"And what are we doing here?"

Again, he didn't respond as we pulled into the parking lot in front of a row of three buildings. A sign for the first one, the building directly in front of us, was a medical lab.

"Listen, you're the cop here, so you're in charge. That's fine. I've been more than cooperative. Maybe against my better judgment, considering you've been acting weird all morning and there's a murderer on the loose."

His eyes narrowed at the last part, but he didn't interrupt.

"I need to know what's going on or else I'm out of here. You said you were only going to hold me overnight then let me head out of town. We're looking at unlawful holding or whatever you want to call it."

He shifted into park, and looked at me. "You didn't recognize that house we went to?"

I threw my hands in the air. "You think the answer is going to change? Like I'm lying to you? I've been in town for three weeks. My first, and hopefully my last, time here. God knows this has been weird enough that I'd prefer not to have a repeat experience."

His nostrils flared. "I can't explain what's going on because I don't actually know. But I'm really trying to figure it out."

"A little communication goes a long way." I shoved my door open.

He climbed out of the car and led the way into the building. It was like walking outside after a snowstorm when the sun was shining. Everything was immaculately white, the brightness stabbing into my eyes.

Seward flashed his badge at the front desk and made his way down a bland hallway, not bothering to look at the signs on the doors. It was clear he had been here before and knew his way around. We passed four doors in the empty corridor before he pushed through one, ushering me in with him before I got a chance to read the plaque on the outside.

3

Circus, Meet Monkeys

"Skylar!" Drew barked, and I jumped at the sound in the small space. Beakers, tubes, small refrigerators, and glittering equipment were all neatly stacked and gleaming around the room.

A short woman around my age walked out of a smaller room tucked back in the corner. Her lab coat looked several sizes too large for her, and she yanked a pair of large reading glasses from her face. I read irritation in the pinch of her eyes.

Her gaze transferred from Seward to me, and her expression morphed as she placed a hand on a nearby table to steady herself. Her eyes widened, lips parting as she took several quavering breaths.

I checked for the detective's reaction, saw a raw grief in his face and the way his chest heaved with sudden emotion, and realized there was something very strange happening.

"I need you to run some tests," he said, his voice rough with barely controlled emotion.

"Tests?" I squeaked.

They stared at each other, no acknowledgment that I had

even said anything.

She shook her head but not in refusal. More like she was trying to clear her thoughts. "How?"

He pressed his lips together. "I think the first question we need to answer is 'who?'."

"Have you run her prints?"

He tilted his head, his expression communicating something I couldn't understand. I might as well have not been there at all for all the attention they were giving me.

I raised my hand. "Do I get a say in any of this?"

He turned toward me slightly, and his tender expression hardened again. "It's only a blood and DNA test. But we do need your consent."

Skylar shook her head again and brought her fingers to her temples. "This can't be real." She looked at him again, questions in her eyes.

He met her gaze, his lips becoming a tight line.

"All right. What the hell is going on?" I demanded.

They both looked at me, but neither answered.

I folded my arms over my chest and raised a brow. "I won't give my permission until I get some answers."

Skylar finally spoke. "It's. . . complicated. But I'll do my best. It won't take long," she assured me.

I stabbed a finger in Seward's direction, pent-up frustration making it violent. "You said the guy wasn't pressing charges, but even if he was, this seems a little over the top."

Seward's body was tight, clenched against whatever invisible onslaught assailed him, but his words were soft, deflated. "You're not being charged with anything. We just need some answers."

I snorted. "Answers for what?"

He sucked in a breath, snapped his mouth shut, and shook his head.

The raw emotions that oppressed him softened me enough to consider it.

This is probably a bad idea. I grimaced. *Or my ticket out of here.*

I narrowed my eyes, folding my arms across my chest. "So if I do this, I can go, right?"

The idea seemed to strike a match in his eyes, and Skylar inhaled softly.

"If that's what you want." The gravelly voice was so low, I almost didn't hear it. I got the distinct impression they weren't thrilled with the idea of me leaving.

I sighed. "Is it important?" I knew it was a stupid question. The pained expressions on their faces, the struggle in their eyes told me it was, even if I didn't know why.

Skylar swallowed hard, large brown eyes still on my face, tracing my features in a way that made me shift in discomfort.

"Very," she responded when Seward said nothing.

Even the power of the conviction in her eyes didn't make me eager to agree to anything. But if it meant I could leave and put as many miles between me and this insanity as possible, I was willing to submit.

"All right. But then you're taking me to my car, and I'm getting out of this crazy place."

They exchanged a tight glance.

Then she nodded slowly and turned to him. "Why don't you make a coffee run? This will take a little bit."

Without glancing in my direction, he walked toward the door, lips pressed together. I watched her watch him and took in her petite frame, her heart-shaped face framed by the short, curly hair. And there, in her eyes, was the same mark of grief.

She shifted her focus back to me and smiled weakly. "You can have a seat over here." She gestured with a small, child-size hand to a metal stool.

I glanced at it but didn't move.

"Have you ever had your blood drawn?" she asked.

"No."

"You'll want to sit down. You never know how you might handle it. Even the toughest guys get queasy."

After thinking it through, I moved toward the stool to sit, adjusting my wrinkled shirt for want of something to do with my hands.

"Cassidy."

I lifted my eyes to her, an automatic response to my name.

She tilted her head, and I could tell she had only said it to measure my reaction. "Would you roll your sleeve up for me?" She opened a drawer nearby. Something rattled against the sides. She pulled out a small cloth, removing the plastic protector to lay it flat on the table next to me.

She then walked across the room to a supply cabinet and retrieved several plastic packages that she stuffed into the crook of her arm as she added to the pile.

"So. . . what am I missing here?"

She gave me a sideways glance as she stuck her hand in for more. It was a long time before she responded. Her focus remained on rearranging the supplies so that she could carry them back to the table.

"You both reacted very strongly to seeing me," I prompted.

She seemed to be unnecessarily careful as she walked, keeping her eyes on her hands as she laid the supplies out on the table. Her exhale was tremulous. "A friend of ours died a few weeks ago."

I let that sit, waiting for it to click, but it still didn't connect to anything. "What does that have to do with me?"

Frowning, she adjusted her lab coat and sat. "We're trying to find out," she said after a moment. Her dainty hand pulled open another drawer. After plucking two latex gloves from its depths, she shut it and yanked them on.

I waited, watching her calculated movements. "I don't understand."

She pressed her lips together as she ripped open packages, setting a needle, plastic tubing, and a vial on the cloth. "You look like her." Her voice was feather-soft. "So much that it's like you're a clone or something."

"She must have been drop-dead gorgeous then." I pulled out my slow smile, waiting for the joke to catch.

Her eyes flickered to my face then away.

Okay, probably bad form if she'd died so recently. But there was more to it than that. I sensed it in the air between us.

"Come on." I laughed. "It's a coincidence."

She pressed her lips together.

Realization dawned on me. The way she'd said my name moments ago and the fact that Seward had never said in front of her.

"Her name was Cassidy," I guessed.

She didn't say anything, and there was a deep, painful sadness in her eyes. She pulled the protective cap from the needle. Attaching the pieces only took her a few seconds. She removed a small square package, which she pulled apart to reveal the tiny alcohol wipe inside.

"Your arm?" She held her hand out, and I hesitated.

I'd agreed to be helpful, but how much did I really know about these people? What if she was about to shoot me up with heroin?

I narrowed my eyes at her open hand, thought about how fancy the equipment in this room was, how put together she appeared, and slowly offered my arm. She tied a rubber tourniquet around my bicep, then wiped the crook of my elbow. Just underneath the thin sheath of skin, purple veins were visible.

"I'm not her."

"We're just making sure. Especially since—" She stopped herself.

"Since what?"

She shook her head and held the needle above my pulsing vein. "It's not worth speculating about until we have results."

"I'm not her," I insisted. "I've never met you in my life. And she's gone. And, you know, there's the fact that it's impossible."

She stopped moving for a moment and looked at me hard. "Your name is Cassidy Marchand, isn't it?"

I nodded once, slowly. It was too weird. To look so much like someone that her closest friends mistake me for her *and* to have her name. And if that was the case, why had Seward reacted to me so differently this morning than the day before? My faint headache reminded me of what had happened the previous night, and I wondered if it had done some serious brain damage. Was I remembering a yesterday that never even happened? Or maybe this was a *really* vivid, whacked-out dream. That sounded like a better, more plausible option. Definitely preferable.

She pressed the needle into my skin, and I jumped at the sharp, unexpected prick of pain.

"Sorry," she muttered.

We watched the dark liquid fly through the tube and pool into the vial. After a moment, she released the tourniquet and picked up a cotton ball, pressing it against the injection site. She pulled the needle out and continued to hold the cotton against the tiny hole to staunch the blood that would bubble up.

I took over holding it at her prompting so she could clean up and place a cap on the vial. She then replaced the cotton ball with a bandage.

She walked across the room to a machine, turned it on, and placed the blood inside. After pressing some other buttons, the machine settled into a gentle hum.

"That's going to take some time." She moved back toward me to collect the supplies she'd used and tossed them and her gloves into a trash can with a hazardous waste sticker on the front. She cast an anxious glance toward the machine behind her.

"How long did you know her?"

Skylar stiffened and looked down at her small hands. "Almost 15 years." She lifted her eyes and gave me a sad smile. "We grew up with her."

"We?" I asked. "As in you and the detective?"

She nodded, though her eyes slid away from mine as she shoved her hands into her pocket. "I figure I can use the blood for the DNA instead of doing a cheek swab. Saves time."

I shrugged. "Hey, this is your circus. As long as we get it done, and I get to go." I let my gaze rove the room that looked remarkably like my seventh grade science classroom. I half-expected to see Mr. MacDonald come in wearing goggles and carrying a Bunsen burner.

"Where will you go?"

I looked at her, noting the way she was wringing her hands together. I shrugged. "I'm into the small town thing. Easy to navigate, hard to find on a map."

"You don't like it here?" Wheedling.

I squinted at her. "Well, it's quaint, but things have gotten a little weird. As much fun as this has been—" I gestured between us—"I don't stay in one place for long regardless."

"I suppose I could understand that." Her gaze wandered around with the caress of familiarity. She looked rather childlike in the oversized lab coat, and all I could think of was a little girl playing with toy science equipment. "I wonder when our coffee's gonna get here," she mused, trying to fill the silence.

I didn't respond, the tension coming off of her making me jittery.

The machine beeped.

She expelled a breath and looked at it for a drawn-out moment like she expected it to get up and walk out of the room if she watched it long enough. Slowly, she walked toward it and woke up the computer next to it.

"It's a match." She whispered it.

4

Stranger with My Face

"What?" My voice dropped to match hers.

"I'd have to do more testing to get fuller results. But from the sample we had of her blood. . ." She raised her eyes to mine. "Same blood type."

"That doesn't mean anything." Why did I sound so panicked?

"It's the rarest type. Like, less than 1% of the population have it." Very earnest expression.

I stood as if that could deflect her words. "So?"

"They ran your fingerprints at the station. They were a match."

"It must have been a mistake," I insisted.

"The official DNA test is going to take longer to do." She moved around me to get to the samples she'd taken.

"What do you expect to find from that?" I spun to face her. "It's literally impossible. A weird coincidence."

She stopped and turned to me. "What is your father's name?"

"I don't see—"

"Your father's name, Cassidy."

I had refused to speak it aloud for a long time, and now, twice in one day, I'd be forced to give voice to the name I'd treated like a curse word. After he left, I'd tried to scrub him from my memory, pretend he'd never existed.

She waited, not knowing what kind of war was going on inside of me.

"Patrick."

She sucked in a breath. "And your mother?"

This name I also rarely spoke, but for the opposite reason. It was sacred, too precious to share with others. If it meant this ridiculous testing would be over, I would breech that sacrosanct line again.

"Amelia. She died when I was—"

"Eight," she interrupted. "She was sick, right? Cancer."

I snapped my mouth shut, felt a weight tug inside my rib cage like my heart was being pulled down to my toes.

"And your father owns a hardware store," she continued, confident in the statement.

But anger flared, hot and stinging. "He what?"

She looked at me as if she'd been struck by the weapon in my voice. "Does he not?"

"I don't know what he does, other than abandon his family. He left after my mother died. I spent almost ten years bouncing around the foster system." It was a struggle to fight the bitterness back, for that was the biggest, ugliest monster inside of me. The one I had fed and let fester all these years.

She stared at me, frozen. "I didn't mean to—"

"There's your proof." My tone wasn't kind. "I'm not her. Aside from the fact that it is, *literally*, impossible, her life experiences are different. This is one huge, super freaky coincidence."

She pursed her lips and turned to remove the vial from the machine, unconvinced. With careful movements, she pulled out a sharpie to label it.

I fought the urge to snatch it out of her hands and fling it against the wall. "I am not your friend," I insisted, fingernails digging into my palms. "I'm sorry she died, and I know it must be hard. But it is impossible—never mind the names, my mother's death, the fingerprints, my stupid face that looks like hers. It's impossible!"

She turned her eyes on me, defiant in the face of my increasing animosity. "Do you have a scar on your left knee? In the shape of Africa?"

I clenched my teeth.

"On the outside, by your kneecap." She gestured to the spot with the marker.

I shook my head. "Coincidence." I wasn't going to let her drag me into the mire of her delusions.

"You slipped on ice," she said. "You were wearing a dress because your class was going to the symphony that day. While you'd waited for the bus that morning, you and the other kids were playing tag, and you fell."

The lump that formed in my throat was surprising. And infuriating.

"It was the day your mother was diagnosed," she continued softly.

My breathing was loud in the quiet room, my heart beating so hard against my ribs as if it was trying to escape.

She looked down at the vial in her hand, the permanent marker poised in the air, then set them down, lifting her eyes to me. "You always said every detail of that day was burned into your mind. Like it was a movie you could watch over and over again."

"I ripped it. Of all my dresses, that one was her favorite," I breathed.

She nodded. "The blue one with sunflowers." Her tone matched my own.

My breath hitched. I had never told anyone about that before. Not a soul. That kind of guilt was a lot for an eight-year-old girl. I'd messed up her favorite dress, and that had defined my behavior throughout her entire illness.

"How?" I whispered.

"You're her. You have to be." The tears glistened in her eyes, magnifying the hope that ignited there.

I shook my head and backed up like she had some kind of disease. "This has to be a super weird, messed up dream."

"Well, maybe—maybe they were wrong about the victim. Maybe it wasn't actually you. What if you never actually died?" Before I could argue the point, she shook her head. "But, I saw you. In the morgue." She took a shaky breath and looked at me.

"So, what? I clawed my way out of the ground like some kind of zombie?" I scoffed.

"How else would you explain it?" she demanded. "Maybe you have amnesia and you don't remember."

"If I have amnesia, there'd be gaps in my memory, not an entire alternate version of my life."

"There has to be some way to trigger the memories." She spoke as if she hadn't heard me. She snapped her fingers at me suddenly. "Your sixteenth birthday. We went to the Sadie Hawkins dance and stayed up half the night telling scary stories. We freaked ourselves out and had to sleep with the lights on. I remember because we got up to get pop tarts in the middle of the night, and Jane came down the stairs and scared us half to death."

"I don't know who the hell Jane is," I said, narrowing my eyes, "but you want to know what actually happened on my sixteenth birthday? I got arrested for shoplifting. My foster parents let me sit in the cell for a full day before they bailed me out."

"What about the time-"

"Just stop!"

She stiffened, gaze snapping to my face. There was desperation there; she badly wanted it to be the truth. And I had to admit that that life sounded blissful compared to my own.

I waited until I knew I could speak calmly. It still came through clenched teeth: "There is some other explanation." But I wondered again if maybe it *was* me, if whatever force had blown through the police station shorted out my brain. How could something like that erase memories and put in other ones, experiences that still felt real enough to touch? Was I going crazy? No, it had to be some sort of dream. Or nightmare.

She watched me work through it all with barely contained anticipation. As if she thought I would concede, tell her she was right. That I was her dead friend resurrected.

I shook my head. "No, there's some other reason. I'm dreaming."

"You're definitely not dreaming." Her voice was forceful.

"You can't prove that," I said, though this didn't feel like any dream I'd ever had before. Usually the second I recognized it as a dream, I woke up. And everything was too vivid to my senses; it was all too real. My dreams always had some off element beyond whatever crackpot storyline my brain played out. My hair was the wrong color, people were driving boats on land, I lived in the wrong house, or—the worst—I couldn't scream, no matter how hard I tried.

This situation definitely made me want to scream.

She was silent for a long time, but behind her eyes, her brain was visibly working. She tilted her head, considering whatever idea she had come up with. "Have you ever watched any science fiction shows?" she asked slowly.

I blinked, thrown off balance. "What?"

"You know, like Star Trek, the X-Files, that sort of thing?"

"No. Not really." My voice was flat. Where was she going with this?

"My ex-boyfriend liked them, so I got caught up watching them sometimes." She seemed to gain momentum despite my passive expression. "Anyway, there are several episodes of Star Trek where the characters are thrust into an alternate universe. One in which their lives are completely different. They run into other versions of themselves."

"Sounds fascinating."

She didn't even mind my tone. "I read an article about it not that long ago, too." She continued, her tone academic, more like a teacher than someone speculating: "Basically, the idea is that with every decision you make, there are multiple outcomes, which branch off into innumerable directions. Meaning that there are literally billions and billions of different versions of your life that exist on separate, yet parallel, planes."

I worked through her words. "So," I began, "you think that I'm an alternate version of your friend."

She nodded. "Or, from your perspective, this is an alternate version of *your* life."

I snorted. "That's ridiculous."

"Is it?" Her small hands gripped the black counter top in front of her. "In your world, your father left you, thrusting you on an entirely different path. You know what happened in this version?" She waited. I didn't prompt her. "Your father remarried. You all moved here when you were eleven."

"Isn't that lovely?" I replied, rolling my eyes. "What a pleasant explanation. Not to mention convenient. "

I was only momentarily regretful at the hurt that flashed into her eyes before she turned to hide it, putting the marker back in the drawer.

I folded my arms over my chest, my mouth twisting wryly. "No, really. Looks like it's a happy ending for everyone. You get your friend back, and I get the family I never had."

She squinted up at me, wary.

"Too bad for the fairy tale, I'm damaged goods. I can't fit into that little hole your Cassidy left. I've had completely different experiences. I am a completely different person, even if we have the same name, even the same DNA." I smiled, and I knew there was malice there. "And that's assuming I believe your theory, which I don't."

Her expression closed off, and she stood up straighter. She probably only reached about five foot four, and that was with heels on. But I had to give her credit for maintaining dignity in the face of my scathing tone.

"You wanted some other explanation," she said in defense, "so I gave you one."

The door opened behind me, and her eyes shifted there.

A man cleared his throat from behind us. "How are the, uh, tests going?"

I refused to whirl around to look at Detective Seward, though the stubbornness was reaching a level of absurdity that even I acknowledged. I reminded myself there was nothing to prove to either of them, no reason to fear a weakness was visible. They were the vulnerable ones in this scenario, not me.

Skylar looked at me, then back at him. "The blood was a match. It'll take me a couple of days to complete the DNA test."

He was quiet a moment. "So. . ."

"It appears, from all evidence," she said, sighing, "she *is* Cassidy."

He blew out a shaky breath, and I finally turned to look at him. His naturally tan skin seemed to lose its color. His dark eyes met mine.

"Alternate Reality Cassidy," I corrected with acid in my tone.

I caught Skylar's quick glare from the corner of my eye.

Seward blinked. "What?"

"According to your friend, here, I'm from an alternate universe."

He narrowed his eyes at my mocking tone, then turned his attention to Skylar as she folded her arms across her chest. Irritation pinched her expression.

It barely masked the grief, but she managed to look reproachful. "You don't have to be an ass about it."

I snorted. "What do you expect after that theory? A hug?"

"I didn't hear you coming up with anything better. In fact, you've been pretty bull-headed about everything." She hurled the words at me.

I gave a mirthless laugh, looking toward the ceiling. "All things considered, I've been pretty cooperative. If this oaf didn't have my purse and keys, I'd be long gone by now, and none of this would even be a problem."

I was surprised to see the moisture that formed in Skylar's eyes. Seward brushed past me to reach for her. He pulled her close, and she looked so tiny tucked against his towering frame.

A twinge of envy whipped through me, but I clung to frustration and leaned back against one of the counters, waiting for it to be over. I had to remind myself she was grieving the loss of a friend, and to have me show up must be like salt on a still-fresh wound.

Seward said something to her, but all I made out was the rumbling sound of his voice. I glanced over in time to catch her nodding in response.

He released her and looked at me. "The cup on the left is for you." He nodded to the counter behind me.

I turned to see the two to-go cups that I'd missed earlier. "Thanks."

He walked toward the door and beckoned me to follow.

I plucked the cup from the counter and tried not to look at Skylar. I didn't want to make it worse. I wasn't ready to apologize, so it was as good as it was going to get. The guilt washed away most of my anger. As I followed Seward back out to his vehicle, crack-brained as it was, I found myself grudgingly considering her theory. Amnesia didn't seem to fit, even with the craziness of what had happened the night before. And I had basically ruled out the possibility of it being a dream.

"Where are we going?" I asked as we emerged into the glaring sunlight. I squinted against the sudden brightness and sipped my coffee. Which turned out to be a chai latte—my favorite. I skidded to a stop in front of the car and stared at the cup in my hand.

"What's wrong?" he asked.

I met his gaze. "It's chai."

Recognition softened his features. "You like it better than coffee."

A lump formed in my throat, but I swallowed it down. "But you didn't even know the test results."

"That call I got on the way here? That was the result of your fingerprint scan." He looked at the keys in his hand, shaking them as if searching for the right one. "I thought I'd take a chance."

5

Batshit

After a few minutes of driving back the way we'd come, I couldn't stand the silence anymore.

"What do you think of Skylar's theory?"

Dark eyes flickered briefly to my face. "An alternate version of you? Sounds pretty far-fetched."

I snorted. "I think the word you're looking for is '*batshit.*'"

He allowed a quick smirk. "Fair enough. But I don't know what else could explain something like this."

"I'm in a schizophrenic hallucination?" I tossed out.

He tilted his head. "From your perspective, that would certainly seem more plausible. And I suppose there's no way for me to prove that I'm real."

"Yeah, I've seen *A Beautiful Mind.* For us crazies, it's hard to distinguish between what's real and what's not. I'd prefer not to do shock therapy."

He huffed a laugh. "They don't even do that anymore."

"Heavy meds, then."

"Well, I can guarantee that if you go to a psychiatrist's office and tell them this whole story, they'll put you on those heavy meds. But, if you remember from the movie, they pointed out that the people from his schizophrenic visions never once show themselves or interact with anyone else in the world. You saw me interacting with Keener and Creedy at the station."

I winced. "Good point. Unless I have much more elaborate hallucinations than Russell Crowe."

"John Nash," Seward said.

"What?"

"Russell Crowe is the actor. John Nash is the actual schizophrenic."

I lifted a brow. As if it mattered.

He shrugged. He was one of *those.*

"So, alternate reality is looking most likely, then. At least more appealing." I picked at a fingernail for a minute before looking up at him. "I guess this means you're not taking me back to my car like you promised."

He glanced at me. "Do you think it would even be there?"

I shrugged, trying to hide how vital it was that we find out. "Maybe we should check? It has my clothes, and I could really use a shower," I added to make myself sound less desperate.

He sighed. "Where did you park it?"

"By the cafe on Main."

The ride was silent, but the tension built on the air, vibrating against my skin. If the car was there, it would be the one truth, the only tether to the life I remembered. It would validate my very existence.

I pressed my hands into fists as we came upon the Square. People were walking around, untouched by the absurdity of what was happening. I leaned forward as the cafe came into view, the same hand-painted advertisement about pumpkin-flavored drinks splashed across the front in gaudy neons.

We turned the corner, and only the shiny, metallic finish of a luxury sedan glinted in the sunlight. Seward slowed, the muscles in his jaw working overtime.

"I don't suppose you own a Mercedes," he said, trying for levity and failing.

"I wish," I breathed, my chest tightening. "Someone could have towed it." I couldn't suppress the desperation that bumped my voice up in pitch.

He gave me a skeptical look but pulled out his cell phone. "I'll see what I can find out." He gunned the engine, heading back out of the Square.

I stared out the window at the buildings flying by, then the houses, willing this to be some sort of mistake. A crazy dream, an elaborate prank. Anything. None of what he said registered in my mind until he ended the call.

I looked at him, took in the white-knuckled grip he had on the steering wheel and the tension in his shoulders. He wasn't as calm as he'd like to pretend he was.

Dread solidified in my blood. "Nothing?"

He shook his head.

"Stolen then."

He winced, doubtful.

"It's the only proof I'm not her." I swallowed the sob that was building in my throat. I pressed the heels of my hands to my eyes. "God, this whole thing makes me feel like I'm insane. Makes us all look like we're out of our freaking minds."

"It does," he agreed. He looked at me as I took steadying breaths, his eyes hard. "But I saw her. Her. . . body. I know for a fact that she's gone. There's no mistaking that."

He was dancing around something, and it had my pulse jumping. At least it kept the tears at bay. "How'd she die?"

He turned down a residential street, a different way than we'd gone before. "She was murdered." His voice was flat, as if saying it like that would make it less of a bomb.

But it exploded all over me. I waited while the dust settled, until the scorching heat of the words lessened to a slow burn within me.

"I'm really sorry, Detective."

"Me too." He gave his head one quick shake. "And just call me Drew."

We fell silent again as we drove past the older homes and into a newer, fancier development. The houses were huge with sweeping gardens clearly kept up by professionals. Hand-laid brick driveways trailed up to three- and four-car garages. Why would anyone need that many garages? Or that many cars, for that matter?

Toward the end of the block, the expensive mansions gave way to open space, golden weeds springing out of the ground in scrubby tufts. It was a depressing scene against the gray autumn sky.

The road curved and crested a hill that overlooked a small valley. Up ahead of us, a black wrought-iron fence rose up, claws gouging the sky. I sucked in a breath when I saw what it was protecting. Why cemeteries had to play to stereotypes, I couldn't fathom. I half-expected an other-worldly fog to cling lazily to the headstones.

We pulled into the parking lot, and Drew turned off the engine. But he didn't move. He simply sat, staring at his hands on the steering wheel. I understood his reluctance and almost told him to turn around, take us far away. The last place in the world I wanted to be was here, reminded of that moment I'd lost my mother and my father all at once. But maybe I needed to see it, too.

He set his jaw and shoved his door open. He turned to me. "You don't have to come with me."

I stared through the open gate, at the gray tombstones, so meticulously lined up. I shot him a look and opened my door by way of answer.

He nodded as if I'd spoken, and I snatched my tea from the cup holder as I got out, needing to do something with my hands. The heat seeped into my palms but didn't help the chill that settled into me as we walked through the stones.

Drew led me toward the back, his eyes focused ahead, no regard for the names as we passed. But I couldn't ignore them, the sentimental words lashing at me. I gripped my cup tighter and hunched my shoulders against the onslaught.

Finally, he turned down a row and stopped. The ground still had that fresh look of recently churned dirt. But it was packed down, perfectly even with the earth around it, new squares of sod placed over it like a blanket. Wreaths and flowers decorated the grave, but it was garish against the bleak surroundings.

I shivered in the breeze and from the unease of being in that place. The realization that I was practically standing over my own grave sent tingles down my arms and into my fingertips. I almost dropped the tea. The tombstone was one of those temporary deals, a simple marker at the head of the plot. My name was carved neatly into the plaque, and it screamed at me, shouting out the truth that I had yet to accept.

Drew looked at me, his chest moving forcefully, and I knew he must have heard it too. This was harder for him than he'd thought it would be. He ran a hand over his mouth and chin, an attempt to get a grip.

I wanted to reach out to him, to offer comfort, but I was

rooted to the spot. This was all wrong. This was not my world, and I didn't know how to reach out to people in pain. I knew how to run. And it was a step that I hadn't bolted already. To be standing there at all was some kind of miracle.

"It looks the same," he whispered.

"What were you expecting?" I asked, trying to be gentle.

"I guess. . . I hoped maybe. . . it wasn't true. That maybe you could still be. . ." He wasn't quite crying, not yet. But there were tears when he looked at me. "It was stupid."

Hope *was* stupid. Crushed every time. I didn't want to tell him that I'd been hoping the same thing. "I'm sorry," I said. "I really am. I probably make it worse just being here."

He shook his head and took a deep breath, eyes glued to the ground where she'd been buried. It was like he expected it to change, maybe to see that, yes, it did look different. But it remained undisturbed.

He stood there a moment longer, as unmoving as the statues around us. Reluctantly, he turned, and he seemed to deliberately avoid eye contact with me. He walked back toward the car, and I jogged to keep up, stumbling along on numb legs.

6

The Wrong Question

The ride back was stifling, but I dared not break the silence. I had no sarcastic remarks to protect myself from the pain that radiated off of him in waves. I did my best not to cringe as each one crashed over me, but as I stared out the window, I realized that his pain was not the only one that filled up the car and stole the air from my lungs.

Because I had just looked at my own grave. I had seen what my fate could have been, could *still* be.

It helped when he pulled to a curb and I was distracted by the small house. It was quaint, painted robin's egg blue with a bright red door. In front of the small porch was a flowerbed, filled with dormant plants that danced in a slight breeze.

"Am I supposed to recognize this house too?" I asked.

He frowned. "No, I guess not." He opened his door and got out. "But I suppose if you need a shower and a change of clothes, this would be the best place to get it."

So it was the other Cassidy's house. I waited only a moment before I decided to follow his lead. I joined him on the sidewalk and looked the place up and down. It was definitely older and was almost as small as an apartment. But it was cute, and it showed the other Cassidy's fastidious nature in the perfectly manicured lawn and updated paint job.

Idyllic, I thought with acid in my mouth.

Without looking at me, Drew led the way to the porch steps. I followed after a moment's hesitation. While he was unlocking the door, I looked to the left where a weathered but sturdy-looking porch swing was swaying. My throat tightened. Some dreams didn't change, no matter what your life looked like. I resisted the urge to go sit in it right then, to see if it was as calming as I'd always imagined it would be. It was a little too chilly, but it would be easy to enjoy the view of the neighborhood beyond the postage stamp front yard, pretend this was where I belonged.

But Drew opened the door. Seeing the outside of the house made me more curious about the inside, to know what I could have had. What I might now have. There was no telling if this was a permanent arrangement. Could I simply pick up her life where she'd left off?

That felt wrong.

I reminded myself that I didn't have to stay. I could say *sayonara*, hit the road, and never look back. Never have to see what had been denied me. It would definitely be a relief to escape the insanity I'd walked into.

It was dark, blinds and curtains drawn. The air was stifled inside, more than just lightless. It was like the whole house was grieving. Maybe the people who had been there left traces of the despair and sadness when they were inside. The anguish seeped into the walls like poison.

I stood right inside and shut the door while Drew strode across the room to open the curtains and twist the wand on the blinds to let some light in.

Instead of looking at what the house contained, to find clues of my other self, I watched him take it in. He was stoic, much more composed than he had been earlier, now that he'd been able to collect himself. But he swallowed hard as his gaze traveled the space.

Even though he was controlled, I still felt as if I was intruding on a private moment and turned my attention to the small living room. It was reasonably spacious and opened to the kitchen and dining room. It gave the impression of airy and light with spring colors. The walls were painted a light gray, and there were accents around the room in the robin's egg blue and a soft green. Pictures were everywhere. On the walls, on the bookshelves, tucked between thick books.

"This is probably hard for you," I said, pretending it wasn't hard for me too. "We don't have to stay. I'll buy clothes somewhere."

"With what money?"

I shrugged.

He rubbed the back of his neck and shook his head. "I still can't seem to wrap my head around this." He sat heavily on the couch, pulled by some unseen force.

To give him a moment, I walked to the nearest photo hanging on the wall. I—or rather, Cassidy—was radiant, smiling broadly between Skylar, so tiny next to her, and Drew on the other side. They were younger, maybe high school age, faces rounded with youth. It was jarring to see myself, posed so perfectly in these pictures that I never took.

"Skylar said you all were friends for a long time." I worked to detach myself, keep my tone neutral.

He saw me by the pictures. "Since you—uh, Cassidy—moved here."

I moved on to the next one. It was a bowling alley. Skylar and the other Cassidy were posing very seriously with bowling balls raised in the air as if in tribute to something. So many of the pictures that followed were similar. They had the same feel. Friendship, camaraderie, a sense of belonging.

Evidence of a life that didn't seem real, that never existed at all. But, no, here was proof. *She* had existed, had touched the world with a warmth I didn't possess. I was the intruder here. It was verification that I had been an ass to Skylar. She'd offered the only explanation that could make these pictures make sense. It was a crushing weight to know that there was a life I could have had, one brighter than the dingy existence I'd scraped out.

To loosen the tightness in my chest, I focused on the photos, Drew's arm around her shoulders.

"Was there. . ." I trailed off, the heat burning into my cheeks. "Was there anything between you and her?" I turned to look at him.

His smirk was humorless. "No."

It was the only explanation I was going to get, apparently. It wasn't as though he said it too quickly to cover something. But the answer felt incomplete, and I was sure there was more to it.

The picture next to it was of the other Cassidy with a young man I didn't recognize. Not that I should know everyone in her life, but up until then, I knew all the faces in the photos. He was turned slightly inward, his face directed at the camera, but his eyes were on her face.

"Who is this?" I tapped the glass of the frame with a fingernail and glanced back to Drew.

I thought he would wave dismissively about some other friend, but the color drained from his face. I had asked the wrong question. But the look on the guy's face was alien to me, and I wanted more desperately to know.

"That's Evan," he said slowly, getting to his feet with a grunt. He walked over to stand next to me, his eyes on the photo. He wrapped his arms around himself as if warding off a blow. "My cousin. He came here for his residency."

"A doctor," I filled in.

He nodded, frowning. "He and Cassidy were supposed to get married next spring."

I sucked in a breath, though I had known something like that must have been the answer. The way this man was looking at her, how he was turned toward her like she was some sort of magnet. And she was, this version of myself. She exuded strength, confidence, and warmth. All things no one would ever say of me. These were things she learned from having a family that loved her and had been there for her. The opportunity I'd never been given.

I shook myself from the introspection. "God, it must be hard on him," I said, my throat thick.

Drew nodded beside me. "Hard on everyone." Even the words seemed difficult for him to get out.

I could imagine. The grief from my mother's death was an old pain, like a weight I'd been carrying around so long that my muscles had gotten used to it. But I remembered how heavy it was at first, how hard I had to work to lug it around. Some people didn't get stronger. Sometimes they broke. I imagined that's what happened to my father. At least in my universe. He'd broken under that weight.

Thinking of him must have drawn my attention to the picture

tucked in between some textbooks because there he was, staring back at me. Dust had gathered on the frame, but I picked it up anyway, my grip unsteady.

He was older. There were lines in his face that hadn't been there before; his hair was mostly silver. Even his blue eyes had become a faded denim color. But I knew it was him. It was the smile. The one I'd inherited.

I couldn't help the anger that rose at the sight of him with the woman who must be his new wife. She was Asian, her straight, black hair shining in the sunshine they squinted against. She was lovely, and they both beamed at me, tanned and happy.

"Your relationship with your father isn't good," Drew said.

I glanced at him. I'd almost forgotten he was there. "How could you tell?" I replaced the frame.

"Aside from the look on your face a second ago, the way you hesitated when I asked you for your parents' names earlier."

I squinted up at him.

He was smiling grimly. "Cop, remember?"

"Detective, no less," I added. "Our relationship isn't good because we don't have one. He left not long after my mother died."

He pressed his lips together and shook his head. "It's hard to believe Pat would do that to you. Not the one I know, anyway. But after seeing how Evan has been handling your—Cassidy's death, I can't say I wouldn't understand."

"Right," I said, moving toward the living room.

"Hey, I'm not saying it's okay." He held up his hands as if in surrender. "My dad left too. It's crappy. But grief does something to people."

"Yeah, I'm aware."

He closed his mouth with an audible click, realizing what

he'd said.

"It's fine," I said, even though it wasn't. All of a sudden, that weight seemed heavier again. I turned to peek into the kitchen as a distraction, noted that it was neat, perfectly coordinated with the decor of the living room. I figured I'd give myself a little tour and continued down the hall.

The first of the two bedrooms had been turned into a tidy office. The computer screen was dark and sticky notes with neat handwriting—recognizable as my own—were placed around the desk, certain colors in certain spots. No doubt some kind of system. That was definitely not a recognizable trait.

The next room was the bedroom. Not large, the walls were painted a calming brown. A teal bedspread brought color to the room. It looked well-lived in but was also very orderly. This version of me was either very tidy or someone had picked up after she'd died.

I came back into the living room. Drew had given me my space by letting me wander around. I found him sitting on the couch, a picture in his hands. His fingers were clenched around the frame, and it looked like he wanted to crush it.

Again, I felt like an intruder. This grief was not mine, and I had no right even to witness it. Everything about this place screamed that I didn't belong here. "Why don't you drive me to the bus station or something? Forget this happened, that I ever existed."

He jerked his head up. "That's not likely to happen. Besides, where would you even go? You don't have any money, and you don't know anyone but us."

"I'll make it work." I shrugged it off, even though his words blistered me. I didn't know anyone. I was alone. More alone than I'd ever been, even that day my father had left me waiting at school for hours, never to be seen again. Or sitting in that God-awful room outside the social worker's office. Because at least I existed there. Proof in the fact that those people knew this version of me.

"No. I want you to stay." His words were soft, more a reaction to the look on my face than his own emotions. Or maybe something else, because he cleared his throat. "How else are we going to figure this out?"

I leaned against the wall and stuffed my hands into my pockets, pretending that his words wouldn't make me do whatever he asked. Because I wanted to feel wanted. I ignored the ache in my chest. "Are you going to tell Evan about me?"

He sighed. "I don't know. It's a lot to handle. And he's kind of a mess right now."

I nodded, looking at my feet, the scuffed toes of my black boots. "But we don't know if this is permanent or not. How long until he finds out?"

He scrubbed a hand down his face. "I don't know," he said again. "There's also your parents."

"No." That one word was edged like a knife.

He lifted his eyes to me.

"They are not my parents." The pain in my chest sharpened. I reached up and pressed my fist against it. "I do not want to see them."

He swallowed. "All right. You don't have to."

"How would we explain my presence to them anyway? 'Hey, remember how your beautiful, perfect daughter was killed? Well, here she is, spat here by an alternate dimension. The catch is she doesn't know you or care to and probably sucks by comparison anyway.'"

His expression tightened. My joke had taken a bit of a sour turn, and even he was burned by the bitterness.

I turned away. "It would hurt them more than anything. It hasn't been an easy thing for you to deal with."

"That's true." His voice was very soft. I felt compelled to look at him. "Still, it would be difficult to keep your presence here a secret." Several thoughts seemed to cross his mind, emotions flickering across his face in quick succession. A resolute firmness settled across his features. "They're not the only ones we'd need to hide you from."

My brow furrowed. "What are you talking about?"

"Cassidy's killer."

My mouth went dry as I watched him stand abruptly. I thought about what the other Drew had told me the night before. A serial killer who targeted girls *like me*. No, not *like* me. He *had* gotten to me, this other version of me.

"A thing for redheads," I breathed.

Drew heard me, turning slightly, his eyes worried. "There's no real discernible pattern, other than the redheads. They've been different ages, different socioeconomic backgrounds, different locations, no connections between any of them."

My stomach roiled just imagining it.

"This means you're in danger, and we need to keep you safe. Aside from the fact that he'd be really confused that you're here, I'm sure he'd come after you a second time. It's like you're the one who got away, taunting him."

"So, how do we handle this?"

Our collective attention snapped to the door as the knob jiggled. I leapt away from the wall as Drew surged to his feet, his hand automatically on the gun at his hip. He looked at me and held a finger to his lips as he moved toward the door.

The knob twisted, and my stomach climbed toward my throat.

7

Grief In Contrast

His eyes were hooded, dark circles deepening them. He was thinner than in the picture. He looked at me as if I weren't even there. Just another piece of furniture in the room.

But even obviously unwell, Evan was a good-looking man. Golden curls against a gilded face that was square and strong. A perfectly straight nose. If Hercules were real, Evan would be exactly how I'd imagine him. The picture hadn't done him justice.

Where Drew was leanly muscular, Evan was thick. If I'd had to guess, he'd been a football player. Drew probably pushed six-four. Evan maybe hit six-foot-one. Even their coloring was different. Drew was dark-haired, dark-eyed. It was like looking at a night sky and the sun. I had a hard time believing they were related.

Evan looked at Drew, his eyes stopping at the hand resting on the butt of his gun. "You going to shoot me?" he asked. The ghost of a smile played on his lips. There and gone.

Drew didn't respond. And judging by the look on his face—like he'd been caught in a lie—he wasn't sure how to.

I simply stood frozen, just as uncertain about what to do. But Evan hadn't even acknowledged me, though I could've sworn he'd looked right at me.

"W-what are you doing here?" Drew asked, slowly taking his hand from his weapon. It was as if he were afraid to move too quickly, like Evan was an injured animal he didn't want to scare.

Evan looked at me, a wild look growing in his eyes, like maybe he was realizing I wasn't a figment of his imagination. My heart kicked up an uneven rhythm.

Drew looked at me too, and I knew that would be the giveaway.

Evan's eyes wheeled to him, then back to me. "Drew, can you see her?"

"Let me explain," Drew started, taking a step forward.

"Can you *see* her?" he said, louder.

"It's not what you think, Evan." Drew lifted his hands as Evan marched over to me.

I backed away as he came closer; the grief marking his eyes made him look dangerous, unstable. My heart stuttered inside its cage.

"Evan!" Drew shouted as his cousin lifted his hand.

Very gently, he brushed it against my cheek, and all three of us froze.

"Cass," Evan whispered, his eyes fluttering shut for a moment. His breathing eased as if he were in physical pain and my name was his morphine.

I looked at Drew, the panic written in bold letters on my face. Every muscle in my body was tight; my hands were clenched so hard, my nails were digging into my palms.

Drew's face changed, hardened. The cop was back, and he stepped forward, covering the distance Evan had walked in one long stride. He placed a firm, careful hand on Evan's shoulder.

Evan's eyes flew open, revealing an ocean of unfathomable pain that made my bones ache looking into them.

"Hey, man," Drew said, his gravelly voice gentle. "I'm going to need you to sit down." Drew pulled him away.

Evan went willingly, but his eyes stayed glued on me.

Drew guided him to the couch.

Evan's eyes finally left my face to find Drew's. "Is she really here?"

My heart no longer beat so wildly, but his words, the tone like a lost child's, almost made it break. The guilt over my very existence almost buckled my knees. I should have left the second Skylar finished that stupid blood test, to save this poor man the resurgence of grief. Sadness clawed at me, and I hated it—the hate gave me a distraction, that black emotion directed toward myself, toward Drew and Skylar for bringing me here. If I'd simply left, been allowed to leave, everyone would be a lot better off.

My heated gaze went to Drew, but he wasn't looking at me. His attention was on Evan.

"No, she's not. . . This is. . . God, how do I explain this?" Drew turned to me as if for help but seemed to understand my antagonistic glare and returned his eyes to Evan. "Something weird happened. I mean, we don't even know what or how, but that is a *version* of Cassidy."

Evan's eyes narrowed at him.

"But not our Cassidy."

Evan surged to his feet and shoved Drew backward. I jumped when he shouted, "You think this is funny?"

Drew was as shocked as I was. "No, I—"

Evan shoved him again.

My heart rate spiked as I watched him step forward again while Drew worked to keep his balance. Evan had compact muscle on his side and a lower center of gravity.

Jittery, afraid of what he could do if he didn't stop, I pushed away from the wall. "Evan!"

He froze, but his glare remained on Drew. After a moment, he looked at me again, his chest heaving with the force of his breathing. Abruptly, he sat, his hands fisting into his hair. "I can't do this anymore."

"Hey," Drew said gently, putting a hand on Evan's shoulder.

Evan jerked away from him. "Don't touch me."

Drew snapped his mouth shut, covering his hurt pretty well. But it was there in his eyes when he turned to walk toward me and give Evan some space. "I'm going to call Skylar to come." He kept his voice low. "I think she would be able to handle this situation better."

"If you think so," I replied, my palm against my chest, feeling my heart's rhythm slowing.

"I'm sorry." He turned his gaze on mine and the earnest look in them made me reconsider my earlier anger.

I didn't respond, and he stepped away a couple of feet to pull out his phone. He spoke so softly again that the rumble of his voice was all I could make out. I didn't even try to listen in. Instead, I focused my attention on Evan. The sag in his shoulders, the bags under his eyes broke my heart. I didn't blame him for being angry, for thinking this was some cruel joke. It certainly felt like one to me.

As Drew hung up and joined me, I thought about how I might have felt in a similar situation. If my mother had shown up after she'd died. But not really *my* mother. A different version who didn't know me. It would have crushed me.

It didn't take long for Skylar to get there. When Drew opened the door, she brushed past him to get into the house and seemed to shrink once she got inside. It was as if the memories that existed in this house pressed in on her. She licked her lips as she glanced around, deliberately not looking at me.

When she saw Evan, she joined him on the couch and put a small hand on his arm. He looked at her, his eyes red.

Drew was chewing on his lip as he moved back to join me. "I think we should probably give them space. You hungry?"

My stomach growled as if in response.

"I'll take that as a yes." He gave a half-smile, though the humor was short-lived. He touched my arm and led me to the door and outside.

I hadn't noticed in the house, but as soon as we were out in the sunshine, I could breathe normally. The air had been too heavy inside. Even Drew sighed in relief once out in the fresh air.

"Is he going to be all right?" I asked.

Drew glanced back at the house as if the answer were written on its walls. He frowned. "I don't know. But I feel like Skylar would be able to explain things better than I could. In some ways, I think he blames me."

I stopped next to the car as he walked around to the driver's side. "Why would he blame you?"

He didn't look at me, just opened his door and climbed in. I had no choice but to do the same if I wanted the answer. As soon as my door was shut, he gunned away from the curb.

"Why would he blame you?" I asked again, this time more gently.

He exhaled loudly. "Because I'm the detective. I should've caught the guy beforehand."

"That's not fair."

He shook his head. "I was the one to tell him what had happened. I think he associates the bad news with me."

"It's still not fair," I said, though I felt a twinge of guilt, knowing I had directed some of my own blame toward him.

"It happens a lot, actually. People don't have the answers they want, so they take their frustrations out on whoever's convenient."

I frowned, touching the lid of my forgotten chai tea in the console. It was probably tepid by now. I thought about my earlier anger at Drew. But then I thought about how he hadn't even gotten an explanation, hadn't even gotten proof yet of who I was, and he'd brought me a chai tea.

I looked at him, watched him scrub a hand over his mouth and chin, noticed that even though he was trying to brush it off, he was bothered by it. Bothered to shoulder the blame that he didn't deserve. Or maybe because he blamed himself too.

"Where are we going for breakfast?"

He glanced over. "Well, I don't want to risk having you out in public. But I figure you probably want something a little better than McDonald's."

"Hey, I live in my car. McDonald's is pretty close to gourmet for me."

It was meant to be a joke, but he didn't laugh. "Why are you living in your car?"

I turned away to look out the window.

"Are you in some kind of trouble?"

"It doesn't matter. The trouble didn't follow me here."

"No," he agreed. "Instead, you walked into a whole new

kind of trouble."

"That's not your fault, Drew."

He looked at me, a little startled. "I never said it was."

I met his gaze, the dark depth of his eyes. "You didn't have to."

He turned away from me, pressing his lips together.

I traced a finger on the glass of my window and watched the movement. Which was worse? Being here, possibly the target of a murderer, or being there, always on the run? Hiding from someone either way.

"How do you think this happened?" Drew asked. "I mean, you being here?"

I shrugged. "Skylar seemed to have a better grasp on the whole thing. She would probably know where to start."

He shook his head, dissatisfied. "Did anything weird happen recently? Meet somebody strange? Anything out of the ordinary?"

I started to shake my head. But in all the craziness of the morning, I'd forgotten the weirdness of the night before. "Last night."

He glanced at me.

"I was in the cell block, alone. The radio was on some God-awful country station."

"Must have been Devereaux," he commented.

I smirked but continued: "But then the music started getting fuzzy, kind of like driving through a tunnel. And the lights were flickering. Then this ringing sound started. It got so loud, I thought my eardrums would burst, and the light bulbs exploded one-by-one."

His brows drew low over his eyes. "Did it stop?"

"It must have, eventually. The only thing I remember

afterward is waking up with Keener demanding where I'd come from."

"And that was when he went to get me." He pursed his lips. "I didn't see any burnt out light bulbs this morning. And I haven't heard anything about a ringing sound."

"Maybe it only happened on my side of. . ." I waved my hands, grasping for the right concept, and didn't succeed. "Of whatever."

"Maybe. But the question is how?"

We entered the outskirts of the Square. Drew drove past the police station to pull up in front of a lavender-colored corner building that had a pastel sign with the words "Dell's Cafe" hanging above the door.

He parked in the no-parking zone, turning to me. "Stay here. I'm going to run in and get you something to eat. Don't talk to anyone, don't make eye contact, don't draw attention to yourself."

I huffed out a breath. "All right. I got it. I'm not stupid. Just hungry, so get going."

He sighed and opened his door, unfolding to get out. He scanned the street in either direction as he loped around the front of the car.

I slid down lower in my seat. My earlier irritation from his overzealous instructions dissipated once I was left alone. A murderer was on the loose, and judging by Drew's barely contained frustration, they had no clue who it was. And a serial killer, no less. I'd watched enough crime shows to know that most murders were not premeditated but committed out of some extreme passion, which meant that they made mistakes. But serial killers were calculated and methodical, more careful about clues they left.

Not many people were out walking, but I found myself scrutinizing any person on the street. I quickly dismissed a woman pushing a stroller, but lingered on a man dressed in a black wool coat on the corner. He was staring in the direction of the Charger, his hands in his pockets.

The urge to bolt from the car and join Drew inside was strong. I didn't know for sure if the man was even looking at me. But I could guarantee that if I ran now, he would definitely notice me.

I clamped my hands on either side of my seat cushion, willing myself not to slide any lower in an attempt to hide myself as my heart started an uneven pattern for the zillionth time that day. I tried to slow it, to even out my breathing and minimize any movement that would draw his eyes.

After a moment, he began walking in my direction, his gaze still pointed at the car. His eyebrows were pulled low over his dark eyes, mouth turned down. I sucked in a breath as he came closer, fingers screaming from how tightly I was gripping my seat.

But right when I thought he was going to yank the car door open and drag me away, I caught the other person in my peripheral vision who met him right next to the car. They shook hands and headed around the corner together.

I was still trying to relax my muscles when Drew came out of the cafe holding a white paper bag. He got back into the car and set the bag on my lap.

"What's wrong?" he asked as he turned to pull his seat belt over his shoulder.

I was still trying to pry my fingers from my seat. "Well, all your 'don't even breathe' talk has me all paranoid."

"Why? Did you see something?" He grabbed my arm.

"Ease off, Iron Fist." I swiped his hand away. "Talk about paranoid. It's fine. I was overreacting."

"You're sure it was nothing?"

"Positive. Now go before we both get so paranoid you lock me in a safe house."

He tilted his head, considering.

I jabbed a finger at him. "No."

8

Crime and Counterfeit

We parked in front of Other Cassidy's house again. I'd scarfed the fresh-made egg sandwich in classic unladylike fashion on the way over, but now we both sat in silence, unmoving. I was pretty sure Drew was just as reluctant to walk back into the emotional hailstorm as I was.

"How long do you think we can avoid going inside?" I asked, my eyes glued on the cheery front door.

"I could last through the first snowfall." He glanced at me. "But I'm guessing you don't have your winter coat."

I snapped my fingers. "Dang. Forgot to grab it before I was sucked into an alternate dimension."

He laughed, and I was reminded what a smile did to his face. "Guess we're going in then."

We both got out of the car, and he walked behind me up the path to the porch steps. I stopped at the door and looked back at Drew. His pinched expression didn't bolster my confidence. Ignoring the flip in my stomach, I opened the door.

Evan raised his eyes, but it was his only reaction. He was sitting on the couch, elbows on knees, chin resting on top of his fisted hands. He looked calmer, but his gaze was intent on me as I walked into the living room, like he still wasn't sure I actually existed. He didn't even shift his attention to Drew as he came in behind me.

Skylar walked out of the kitchen holding a steaming mug. She glanced over as she walked to Evan, handing him the mug.

He accepted it with a frown and only held it in his hands, finally taking his eyes from me to look at whatever was inside like it held the secret of life.

I waited right inside the door, the heaviness of the emotions settling on me again like a too-warm blanket. Drew moved past me to join the other two. A unit. A fractured one, but one that could survive. The twinge of envy hit me again and left an awful taste in my mouth.

Skylar looked over at me standing awkwardly by the door. Her mouth tilted, and she walked over. Drew placed his hand on Evan's shoulder. It took a moment, but Evan looked up at him calmly and patted the hand. The tension between them dissipated, unspoken apologies accepted, and I felt like I'd been deposited into a world I would never fully understand.

"Rough morning," I commented as Skylar came to stand next to me, crossing her arms over her chest.

She grimaced. "Not the worst."

"I don't imagine so." I brushed a lock of hair that had fallen from my bun behind my ear and gave myself an internal pep talk for an apology. "Listen, I'm sorry about earlier. I was a jerk."

She lifted one shoulder and let it drop. "I don't really blame you. It's a tough thing to swallow. I suggested the theory, and I still have trouble believing it."

"I hope Evan handled it better than me."

She sucked in a breath through her teeth. "Once you were gone, I think it was easier."

"I thought I was finally going crazy." Evan's voice was soft enough that I didn't realize he was talking to us. But he looked directly at me.

I tried to swallow the dryness out of my throat, but it didn't help.

"Join the club, buddy," Drew said.

I was desperate to change the subject. Or at least shift it. "Drew and I were speculating about how it happened."

He took the hint and looked at Skylar. "We figured you'd have a better idea of where to start as far as looking into understanding it."

She winced. "I'm not sure how much of a help I'll be. Anything I know is based on Star Trek episodes. Not any real evidence."

"But science fiction has some basis in reality," Evan said. "String theory is a respected hypothesis. And black holes are scientific fact."

We all looked at him as if for the first time.

"That's true," Skylar conceded after a moment. "I guess we could start by looking into some of the theories the shows used. I think a lot of them attributed these kinds of situations to wormholes."

"Except that's out in space," I said.

She shrugged. "Gotta start somewhere."

"Well, while you start there," Drew said, checking his phone. Whatever he saw there changed his expression, hardened it. "I have to head to the station. Crimes to solve and whatnot."

Panic clawed up my spine. I was so off-balance that any change in the dynamic could set me over the edge. It was bad enough that Evan was there, the one whose hooded gaze made me feel like I was a criminal for even being there.

My hands fisted at my sides of their own volition. "When will you be back?" I worked at keeping my voice even.

It was obvious the cop in him sensed my nerves. He offered a reassuring smile and touched my arm. "It won't be too long. Couple of hours to get some stuff done." He looked at Skylar. "I figure we can rotate. You can babysit her while I'm gone. Then we'll switch."

"Hey," I protested, though it was half-hearted.

"Yeah, sure," Skylar said, shrugging.

I snuck a glance at Evan, worried that he might volunteer his services, but he was staring absently into the depths of his coffee cup again.

"Call me if you need anything." He yanked the door open, and his dark gaze fell on me briefly before he left.

"Evan, you don't have to stay." Skylar's face was soft, sympathetic. It was amazing to me how much she could express in those large eyes.

His head snapped up like he'd forgotten we were there, and his eyes settled on me again, as if there was some sort of magnet pulling them there. "I'd actually like to if that's all right." They shifted to her.

Skylar's expression told me she wanted to argue, but she nodded. "All right."

I wished she would have fought it, but I wasn't in charge and didn't have the energy to work up an argument I was willing to defend. I didn't realize the events of that morning had drained me so much. Skylar glanced at me before heading over to Evan.

"You done?" She held out a hand for the mug, which he relinquished.

As tired as I was, I didn't move away from my perch by the door. I couldn't shake the feeling that this was sacred ground with Evan there. Like I might offend him if I moved freely within the home of his dead fiancée.

He watched me from the couch, hands clasped loosely between his knees, and I was reminded again of the comparison to Hercules. The stillness only added to the effect, making him look like a statue of the Greek hero.

"You can sit down," he said after a moment. "I won't bite."

I didn't move right away, not wanting to confirm that I was a little afraid of him. But I gave in and moved toward the couch, sitting as far away from him as I could. He smirked but made no comment.

Skylar came out of the kitchen and stood in front of us on the couch, fisted hands on her hips, lips pursed. "Well, what should we do now?"

"I don't know," I said. "But one of the reasons Drew brought me here was to take a shower." My voice trailed off uncertainly.

Her eyes traveled over my greasy hair, still in the messy bun I'd thrown it in the day before and my grungy, well-worn clothes. "Well, I guess we won't have trouble finding clothes that will fit you."

I threw a glance at Evan, whose whole body seemed to clench.

"I don't need to wear her clothes," I said quickly. "I can just put this back on."

"No," he said. It was almost a whisper. "You can wear her stuff. We were going to donate it anyway."

Skylar caught her top lip between her teeth, the uncertainty fluttering in her eyes. "If you don't mind."

He shrugged, not looking at us.

I stood, and I was fairly certain her reluctant expression was mirrored on my own face. But she led me down the hall to the other Cassidy's room, and the oppressive feeling that I was an intruder abated a little.

Skylar opened the door to a walk-in closet and flipped on a light. Clothing was organized by color; shoes were stacked on racks along the walls. Not one thing was out of place, and I wondered again if the other Cassidy was freakishly neat or if someone had come to organize after she'd been killed. I suspected the former.

Skylar regarded me passively as I scanned the contents, but she seemed to be working hard at it. I contemplated the pastels and cheery brights. It was an impressive array of choices and colors.

This could have been my life, I thought.

I stepped inside tentatively and ran my calloused fingers over the soft, textured materials. "What did Cassidy do? For work, I mean."

Skylar leaned against the door jamb. "She was a nurse. Pediatric unit."

Of course. How much more perfect could she be? No doubt a saint, the pride of her family, engaged to a doctor. Radiant. I spotted the white garment bag tucked in the corner of the closet and knew immediately what it must be. I hesitated, but I really couldn't keep myself from reaching out to touch it.

"When were they going to get married?"

Skylar was quiet a moment, a million emotions stumbling over each other in her eyes. A pain so deep lashed tears into them, but she didn't let them spill. "April."

"Did they meet at the hospital where she worked? Drew mentioned Evan came here for a residency."

She nodded, folding her arms across her chest as if to ward

off an attack. "They met at a party Drew had, but they did end up working at the hospital together."

I had a hard time imagining Hercules, built like a football player, being a doctor.

"See anything you like?" She straightened, and I knew it was her way of saying she was done talking about it.

I frowned and turned my attention to the clothing again. I selected a pair of jeans and a fitted white t-shirt. Skylar showed me the dresser where I could find underwear and left me to myself. I walked into the small master bathroom with trepidation. I don't know what made me so reluctant. Maybe it was knowing I would be going through the motions this other me had on a daily basis. This room was where she began her day. Where she had probably stared at herself in the mirror, nitpicking the parts of her body society had taught her to be dissatisfied with.

I paused to appraise myself, naked, in the mirror as the shower warmed up. Did we dislike the same parts? I ran my slender fingers over the bones that poked out, the freckle just to the left of my belly button, wondering if she'd always liked that beauty mark as I had.

I touched the dark circles under my eyes, wondering if those were a result of the harder days of my life that she'd never seen or if she'd had them too, so visible against our pale skin.

The steam building on the mirror broke my trance, and I turned to the shower, relishing the anticipation of the stinging heat of the water.

I wasn't disappointed, and I was grateful that the shower head had settings for water pressure. I turned it up to pound against my face, my back, and cranked the knob so that the water was nearly scalding, turning my skin pink.

Years of grime seemed to sluice away with the water, like layers of tension peeled off. In some ways, I wished I could wash away the memory of my life and slide the other Cassidy's in its place. Be the woman they were all wishing I was. Hell, that *I* wished I was.

I opened the shampoo bottle, smelled the glorious scent, and hesitated. Not only was I invading her home, but now I would smell like her too. Would it be too much? I debated the virtues of having clean hair against the grief that hung on the people around me. It was like a spider web, thin and sticky, trapping them together, forever connected. And I'd walked right into it, snared in its clinging grip. But I was already going to be wearing her clothes. What was one more thing?

I knew I couldn't draw the shower out for too much longer, especially when the water started to cool. So I shut it off and toweled dry in the humidity of a bathroom I'd turned into a sauna.

It was an odd thing to put on someone else's clothing and find that they fit so perfectly. They were not exactly my style, but definitely closer than the pastel button-downs and cashmere sweaters that made up a good portion of her wardrobe. At least I wouldn't worry too much about ruining a basic tee should it come to that.

I braided my thick hair, still damp and threw on some of her mascara on a whim. My skin was still rosy when I stepped out of the bathroom. I slid on a pair of socks and raided her closet for a pair of black boots that would go well with my own staple black, faux-leather jacket.

Skylar and Evan were talking when I opened the door, and I hesitated. I wasn't sure if I should make my presence known or try to be unobtrusive. I had no way of knowing what they were talking about, or if I'd be intruding. I was about to shut the door loudly to alert them when Evan spoke.

"I still might go crazy."

"Evan—"

"When I walked in the door and saw her, I thought it was a really good hallucination. I mean, I see her all the time. I haven't slept in days because all I do is dream about her. Every time I close my eyes. It starts out where she's whole, well. Then my brain reminds me that she's gone, forces me to relive that moment, seeing her. . . all cut up." He paused, breath ragged. "This is like one of those dreams. Thinking she's back, alive. But then she turns into this other version, this counterfeit." He said the word like it was poison in his mouth. It stung me. "It's like my waking nightmare. We have to get rid of her."

"Just because she's not our Cassidy doesn't make her any less valid as a person," Skylar said. Her tone was soft but defensive. "I don't even know if we can find a way to send her back even if we figure out how she got here. I can't—won't make her leave."

"She can't replace her," he said tightly. I swear I could hear the tears in his voice. "She's not your best friend."

There was a rustle of movement, like she'd drawn back. "I know that." It was softer, like a whisper.

"You don't understand," Evan started. "I can't have her here."

"I'm sorry, but this is not all about you. I told you to go home, and maybe you should if it bothers you so much." The pain was so evident in her voice. "You're not the only one who lost someone you loved."

It was quiet for a moment. It was odd how Evan's words hurt

me even though I'd gotten used to being unwanted long ago. It wasn't like his opinion should have mattered. I'd just met him. It would probably be better for everyone if I did leave.

I slipped back into Cassidy's bedroom, closing the door quietly, and leaned against it for a moment. I was worse off than I'd been before. I had no car and no money. I didn't exist in this world.

But *she* had. An idea sparked in my mind, and I lurched into action. I moved to the dresser, digging through drawers full of clothes. Then I spotted the purse hanging from the post on the bed.

With a glance at the door, I made my way over. There was the usual nonsense inside. Receipts, lipstick, odds and ends. But I found her wallet easily enough. I plucked her driver's license, debit card, and checkbook out and slid them all into my pocket.

Resourcefulness in a tight spot. Or rather, petty crime to get me by. Probably one of the only good things that came from my relationship with Callum, though that was debatable. Hopefully, no one had started the process of closing out her accounts.

I crossed the room to the window, dragging the heavy drapes back. These old houses tended not to have screens on every window and were often designed in a way that made climbing out—or in—easy. I gritted my teeth as I pulled the window back, praying it wasn't as noisy as I felt like it was.

"Cassidy?" Skylar's voice and simultaneous knock on the door startled me, causing my hands to slip along the window frame. A splinter slid into the tip of my middle finger.

I sucked in a breath between my teeth, pulling my hand back to inspect it.

"Are you okay?" Skylar asked.

"Fine," I said back, hurrying to slide the window closed again.

The door opened slowly as I spun away from the window.

I plastered a sheepish smile on my face as hers came into view. "I was snooping a little. Sorry."

She half-smiled, shaking her head. "I'm sure you're curious about her."

I pressed my lips together, nodding, hoping the guilt wasn't obvious on my face. Or the frustration that my plans had been thwarted. I'd wait until tonight, when everyone was asleep. Give myself a head start. With some funds and her license, I could be halfway into the next state by the next morning.

"I was thinking of doing some research. To see if we can figure out what brought you here." She walked all the way into the room, but she kept her hand on the doorknob, her eyes roving the space like she thought a ghost might pop out.

I wanted to respond that it didn't matter, that I was going to leave anyway. But I clamped my mouth shut against the urge. Common sense told me that she wasn't going to approve of my means of escape.

And there *was* a small part of me that wanted a reason to stay, even just to understand what had brought me here. I wasn't sure I cared one way or the other about how to send me back. Starting over, without the consequences of my past to follow me was appealing. I could finally, truly be free. But what did a small delay hurt? At least some effort to figure out how I got here wouldn't ruin my new possibilities, and damned if I wasn't curious.

"All right. Where do we start?"

9

Google Expedition

Skylar's version of research was Google. While she clicked around on the computer in the office, I tried to focus on what she was doing in an attempt to ignore Evan. He was slouched in the Papasan chair in the corner, his eyes on me. When I grew restless, I settled for examining the pictures around the room. They boasted of the life I never knew could have been possible. It was obvious the other Cassidy valued the memories captured in these pictures more than decorative art or sculptures.

The room was full of moments frozen in time ranging from elementary school through college and beyond. Some of the earlier photos I recognized, remembered posing for. Blowing out candles on my fourth birthday, my mother crouched behind me with a broad smile on her face, the mane of red hair cascading over her shoulder.

Somewhere through the vicissitudes of life, I'd lost a lot of those pictures. I'd forgotten about this one, and I traced my finger over my mother's smiling face. I looked a lot like her, and it was startling to see now, after all this time. Tall and willowy like she had been, and the unmistakable red hair, a trait I'd always been proud of.

Evan stood and walked across the room, shoving his hands into his pockets. The muscles in his shoulders were pulled tight like he couldn't fully relax.

I stepped away from the photo, nervous that I would offend him by looking at her things. Even though he'd given me permission, I sensed that it bothered him to see me wearing her clothes, that I smelled like her. It was written all over his face every time he looked at me, when his eyes would travel up and down my body, and his hands would clench.

As much as that had my nerves dancing, had my hands itching for something to keep them busy, underneath all of that barely concealed hostility, he was bone-tired. The kind of tired that went deeper than poor or no sleep. The heavy weight of what he'd been dealing with settled like a mantle on his shoulders, threatening to flat-out knock him over.

"Google has some interesting articles," Skylar said. She spun around in the desk chair, her enthusiastic expression dampening a little upon seeing Evan and me, but she didn't let the smile falter.

"Google is your idea of research?" Evan scoffed. "That's about as reliable as asking someone on Main Street."

She sniffed and lifted her chin slightly. "It's a place to start. Don't pretend like it's not your first step when you want to find something out." She spun back around before he could respond.

Evan decided it wasn't worth it and moved closer to me, glancing over my shoulder to see what I'd been looking at. I went rigid as he drew near, and it was hard to keep myself from pulling back. His gaze flickered to mine, and there was a frozen moment where his eyes traced over the planes of my face. For an instant, he looked like a confused little boy, and I felt myself softening despite how his earlier words had made me feel.

Before he could say anything, I touched the picture of my mother and me again. "It's been a long time since I've seen this one."

His eyes narrowed like he was trying to figure out if I was messing with him. "Why?"

I turned my gaze to the picture. "When they put you in foster care, basically all you get is a plastic trash bag to put your stuff in. You can only take so much." I didn't work very hard to keep the edge from my voice.

"Foster care?" he asked.

I realized he hadn't heard this part of my story. And no matter how long it had been, how tough I pretended to be, it still took a lot of energy to talk about it. "My dad left after my mother died. We didn't have much family, and the distant relatives didn't want the responsibility of an eight-year-old. So it was the system for me."

"He just left?" Evan asked, and that flinty look in his eyes seemed to soften ever so slightly.

I shrugged. "Skylar figures that's the catalyst for the different path my life went from the other Cassidy's."

He turned to look at Skylar who was watching us instead of reading the article she'd pulled up on the computer.

"I can't believe Pat would do that." Evan said it almost to himself, but it had the sting of derision in it.

I had to swallow the sudden ball of anger in my throat, the knife that was attached to the words that were slinking to the forefront of my mind. Ordinarily, I'd let them loose. Especially after the things he'd said. But the ghost of grief hung too palpably about him, and I was feeling sympathetic. Instead, I clenched my teeth and turned stiffly back to the picture of my mother and me. I studied the floral dress I was wearing. The faint stain of the ketchup I'd spilled on myself earlier that day was visible even though the picture was grainy, and it nearly blended into the flower print. Maybe I could see it because I knew it was there. I remembered crying after I'd watched the glob splatter onto the skirt as if it was the worst thing that could have ever happened to me.

"This article I'm reading says that, theoretically, parallel universes exist one on top of the other. Like another plane within our midst."

"So, what?" I asked, turning to face her. "Some kind of door opened so I could step from mine into yours?"

"Kind of. I think that's the basic idea." Her face was scrunched like she was still trying to understand. "Gosh. This is way over my head. Quantum mechanics, theoretical physics, cosmology." She shook her head, grimacing. "And it's focusing more on the Big Bang Theory than anything."

Evan nodded, though he didn't seem even remotely interested. "String theory."

Skylar squinted at the screen and slowly started to nod. "Yeah, that's mentioned here." She tapped the screen with her finger. ". . . and supergravity?"

I blinked. "What's that supposed to mean?"

"There was some argument about how many dimensions there are. But now they agree? And are the same thing?"

Evan laughed, but it was dark and humorless, almost mean. "Sounds like research is paying off. Really clarifies what the hell happened here."

Skylar's head jerked in his direction. Hurt and sadness flitted across her delicate features, but she lifted her chin. "Evan, you should go." I was impressed her voice didn't shake, but she was firm and gentle.

His eyes flashed to me for only an instant. Without the slightest shift in expression, he turned and walked out of the room. I didn't realize how mad he was until I heard the front door slam shut.

Skylar released a breath. "I'm sorry. I know he's struggling, but that doesn't give anyone the right to be a jerk."

"As an expert at being a jerk, I'd say he's doing as well as can be expected, given the. . ." I waved my hands in the air. "Situation."

She sniffed. "It's not an excuse."

It was hard to come up with an argument. As she'd pointed out to him earlier, he was not the only one who'd lost someone he loved. Did he have more right than the rest to be angry, to let his emotions run ragged over everyone around him? It's not like there was some sort of rule book or hierarchy for grief.

But everyone coped differently, and my presence was a complication no one could prepare for.

I decided changing the subject was a better plan than speculating about it. "So, the research."

She grimaced and spun back around to the computer. "I'm not sure I can even get a good grip on this stuff."

"What about the library?"

She shook her head. "It would probably be more of the same."

"So, then what?"

"Conjecture?" She held up her hands. "Like I said, we gotta start somewhere."

"Doesn't seem like much of a start."

She frowned, pensive.

So maybe I wouldn't get my curiosity satisfied before I left. Not that it mattered that much in the grand scheme. There was no guarantee that we could send me back if we *did* manage to find an explanation.

I snuck a glance at Skylar as an irrational fear that she would somehow figure out what I was planning crept into my mind. I didn't want any of them suspecting that I would leave. Most particularly my means of doing so.

She tapped a finger against her chin, no suspicion in her expression. What I did see in her face was speculation, an idea apparently forming in her mind. "Do you remember that article I mentioned earlier?"

"Sure," I said slowly, not remembering at all.

She dismissed that with a wave of her hand. "Not that long ago, a magazine interviewed this professor from the college about something like this. I'd thought it was a satire at first, but he was absolutely serious. They kind of ripped him a new one in the article. He's supposedly an expert."

"An expert on what, exactly?"

"Physics or something." She spun back to the computer, squinting. "Let me see if I can find it."

I came to stand behind her as she typed into the search bar and perused the links.

"Here." She clicked the link and scanned over the article. "Eli Thibald," she said.

I read the excerpt over her shoulder and raised a brow. "So this whack job is our expert? It says right there that most people think he's insane."

"He's still teaching at the college," she insisted. "I don't think he'd keep his job if he's as crazy as everyone thinks he is."

"Come on, the dude thinks magnetic fields and the stars make some sort of parallel universe magic."

She gave me an exasperated look. "We've been entertaining the idea of you being from a parallel universe all day, and you want to disparage this guy's theory because it sounds ridiculous?"

I rubbed my arm. "Fine. But just because he's an expert doesn't guarantee he can control and make whatever happened the first time happen a second time."

"Don't worry; I'm not getting my hopes up. But he might be our only shot at getting *some* answers or an idea, so I think it's worth a try."

"All right. You're running this thing."

She spun back around to look him up in the college's directory page, and I turned to stare through the gauzy curtains over the window to the backyard. I didn't register any of what I saw. Some part of me still wished this was a freaky dream even as it got weirder by the minute. It was an effort to reconcile the dichotomy in my mind: there was no way this could be real, but there was nothing to give me hope that I would wake up any moment, find myself in that jail cell or even my junker car.

"Well, I emailed him," Skylar announced, pulling me from my thoughts. "I'm getting hungry. How about I order pizza?"

I shrugged, only now becoming aware of my growing hunger. My egg sandwich earlier had not made a lasting impression on my digestive system. As I checked the clock that ticked unobtrusively in the corner of the room, I realized it probably shouldn't after this much time. I hadn't paid attention to how long it had been.

"What do you like on your pizza?" She asked, standing and

pulling out her cell phone.

"Black olives and pineapple."

She froze in the middle of dialing and slowly looked at me.

It didn't take much to guess what had gotten to her, but I asked anyway. "What?"

She shook her head. "I should have expected it, I suppose. I mean, you're not really the same person. But you kind of are."

"She liked her pizza that way too," I guessed.

She shrugged, focusing on dialing again. "I wouldn't have noticed normally,but not a lot of people like that combo and only that combo."

"Odd how some things are the same," I commented quietly.

"I think it makes sense," she replied. "Circumstances don't necessarily dictate your tastes."

"It does in some cases, I think. I mean, her clothing choices are not exactly my style."

Skylar laughed, and the sound was like sunshine, warm and invigorating. I found myself smiling in return. "I won't disagree with you on that front," she said. "She tried to make herself look more professional and erred on the side of middle-aged soccer mom."

"Well, for a middle-aged soccer mom, she was looking pretty good, if I do say so myself."

She laughed again and pressed her phone to her ear. She walked out to order the pizza, and I was left to peruse the other pictures in the room. From how many there were, it was clear that either Cassidy had been a fanatical photo-taker, or someone she hung around with was.

She was always perfectly posed in each of the photos. Knees slightly bent because she towered over most of her friends, head tilted just so, smile wide and brilliant. Perfect. The word echoed in my head again.

In comparison, everything in my life seemed broken and disjointed, with sharp edges and dark pits.

I picked up a photo album to avoid going down that train of thought. I touched the cover cautiously, the worn edges familiar. This was the one I'd taken with me from foster home to foster home, the only thing I'd had that was really mine. I'd outgrown my clothes and toys, and everything else was transient. Yet somehow, as I'd passed into adulthood, I'd still ended up losing it along the way.

I opened the cover to see a baby picture. I was small, bundled in a pink blanket, my tiny hands balled into fists. Page after page of images, dates scrawled underneath to commemorate milestones, birthdays, happy memories. But this book continued where the one I'd known stopped. There was a gap in time after the age of eight. When my mother died. But it picked up after a year or so. The other Cassidy and my—no, *her* father—at Disneyland. There was a shadow under his eyes, a grimness to his face. But as I flipped through pictures, it grew less pronounced over time.

Then the picture of his wedding to the Asian woman. She was petite and beautiful in her white dress, and my father was smiling brightly. Cassidy was between them, holding both their hands, a crown of flowers holding back the flame of hair. I stared at that picture for a long time, so enraptured by the looks on their faces. I studied their hands all clasped together in a chain like I could somehow will it to be my truth.

10

Don't Trust the Pizza Guy

"Pizza's on its way," Skylar announced, walking back into the room. Her eyes zeroed in on my face, and she stopped.

I grappled to find an explanation for whatever she saw there, to shrug it off, joke, anything. But I drew a blank; I had no armor to protect myself.

"It's weird seeing pictures of events I've never experienced," I finally said. That small admission gave me an exposed feeling, and I wrapped my arms around myself.

She slipped her cell phone into the back pocket of her jeans. "Can I ask you a question?" Her voice was softer, more gentle.

I braced myself. "Okay," I said, even though I wasn't sure at all if it was.

"Do you think it's possible," she started, but the pause stretched as she gathered courage to say the rest. She tried again: "Do you think that maybe whatever brought you here wasn't some freak accident? That maybe someone or something wanted you—wanted us—to have a second chance?"

I sucked in a breath. I hadn't expected this to be the question she chose to ask. And maybe it was the child-like innocence in her eyes and the fact that someone had genuinely asked me my opinion on something like it mattered that had my throat constricting and my eyes burning.

It took me a moment to be sure my voice wouldn't betray the sudden emotion. "If it was intentional, it seems more cruel than anything. I'm not her, Skylar. I can never be what she was to you, whether this is permanent or not."

As badly as we all wish I could be. The brutal thought ghosted through my mind.

Her expression fell a little, but she smiled faintly. "You're right; you're not our Cassidy. But there is some of her in you. You really can't be as different as you think. It's hard to not bring up wedding plans or say 'remember when. . .'"

The words raked across my heart with talons of bitter jealousy. "Yeah, and it's hard to look at my father's face and not light this damn book on fire." I shook the photo album I still held in my hands.

Inspiration lit in her eyes. "Well, what if you *used* this as a second chance? Knowing that here, your dad didn't abandon you? Maybe you could give him the benefit of the doubt."

My fingers tightened around the book. Logically, I knew this was a different version of my father. But seeing what my life could have been if he'd been there, if he'd stayed, made me angry enough to shut out any version of him, no matter how much of a saint he was.

I set the album back on its shelf even though I really wanted to fling it across the room. Skylar's question had been asked in innocence, but I didn't trust myself to answer her without vitriol. And, right then, I needed space, air, away from any of the disappointed hopes that I could be the perfect version of myself.

She must have seen the pain in my face. "I'm sorry," she murmured.

"I just need a minute," I said through my teeth as I brushed past her.

I didn't know where I could go to escape, to gather my thoughts, to chain my bitterness back up because it had shown up too many times already that day. All it did was leave a stinging ache in my body, an acrid taste in my mouth, and words thrown out that I couldn't take back. But anywhere in the damn house, I was face to face with the life I could've had, should've had, in pictures of the beatific smile undarkened by the struggles I'd experienced.

I yanked the front door open and let the crisp air hit me. The shock forced me to suck in a sharp breath like I hadn't gotten enough oxygen. But as I stood, looking at the tiny front yard littered with golden, crunchy leaves, I realized I had nowhere to go. At least not yet. That was a detail I'd deal with later.

With no direction, no ideas, the burst of emotion leeched out of me, and I settled into a deflated gloom. I spotted the porch swing to my right and, even though the chill in the air made goosebumps prickle over my skin, I decided this was my moment to test out something I'd always dreamed of having. Maybe I could clear my head, start getting a plan in place.

I brushed the fallen leaves from the cushion on the swing and huffed out a breath as I sat. Drawing one leg up, I wrapped my arms around it to keep as much body heat in as I could while I used my other foot to push myself back and forth. The motion soothed my nerves.

I wouldn't admit it to anyone else, but I acknowledged that part of the reason I didn't want to see my dad was that I probably *could* forgive him, given time. Because this version hadn't left. He'd mustered his strength to be there for his daughter. And, honestly, I understood that other version too. In some ways, I could believe that losing my mother had destroyed him to the point that he didn't think he could recover. But the bitterness was comfortable, familiar. I'd lived entrenched in it long enough that I didn't know exactly how to live my life without it.

"What are you doing out here?"

I started at Drew's accusatory tone.

He was striding up the walkway, the authority hanging around him like a cloud.

I was automatically defensive. "I was getting some air."

There was no sympathy in the hardened planes of his face. "Are you crazy? Sitting out here, in the open for anyone to see?" He grabbed my hand and pulled me to my feet.

My anger was quick to cover the hurt that he didn't seem to care what I was feeling. "What? Am I some dirty little secret now?"

He rolled his eyes as he steered me toward the front door and inside the house. Once he'd shut the door behind him, he turned to me and the heat of anger was in his own eyes, a slow burn. "Do you remember what we were talking about just this morning? Serial killer ringing any bells?"

I crossed my arms over my chest. "You think he's going to hang around the house of a woman he's already killed?"

It was an odd thing to see Drew angry. Unlike most people, myself included, his anger made him eerily still, his voice a low growl. It was almost more unsettling. "You never know. Sometimes they like to revisit scenes from their crimes. Gives them a little boost. This guy is a stalker, likes to track his victims first. He knew where Cassidy lived, and he may come back here because it gives him some sort of thrill."

I didn't want to give Drew the satisfaction of seeing me shiver. But I realized I hadn't been paying attention, didn't even hear his car pull up. The killer could have driven down the street to look at the house and seen me sitting outside, moping like a petulant child, none the wiser. That thought was a cold bucket of fear that doused my anger and silenced me.

"That's what I thought," he said with a sigh.

"Is everything okay?" Skylar asked, shrouded in the shadow of the hallway. She stood between it and the living room, hesitating.

"Fine." He didn't spare her a glance. His eyes were on my face, maybe to make sure the point had really settled.

When she shifted to me for an explanation, I shrugged. "Poor life choices."

Drew's mouth tilted up at the corners, but he shook his head, running a hand through his hair—a signature trait, it seemed. The humor was short-lived as his gaze settled on me again, sober and heavy.

He said nothing, maybe because he didn't want to bring it up in front of Skylar. I wasn't sure. But it was all there in the look: be more careful. I gave a short nod at the same moment there was a knock on the door.

Drew stiffened, his hand automatically going to the gun on his hip.

"It's probably just the pizza guy," Skylar said, her quizzical gaze following his movement. She strode forward and reached for the doorknob.

Drew pivoted behind her, his hand not moving from the weapon, and squared his stance. She pulled the door open to reveal the delivery guy in all his pizza-scented glory. The smell made my mouth water. The kid's eyes widened at the sight of Drew's defensive posture.

"Ignore him," Skylar told him, accepting the steaming boxes he held out to her, which she passed on to me so she could pay him.

I moved past Drew, who didn't relax his stance at all. I set the boxes on the table as Skylar finished paying and closed the front door. She gave Drew a questioning look as he finally removed his hand from the gun and folded his arms over his chest.

I opened the top box, the heat washing over me in a pleasant wave. The cheese was still bubbling. Skylar went to get plates.

"Are you going to have some, Drew?" She paused in the process of reaching for the plates.

He narrowed one eye at her.

"C'mon." I smiled, hoping to chase the brood away with lightheartedness. I lifted the pizza box and held it in front of his face. "Carbs and cheesy goodness!"

He grunted and turned to Skylar. "Fine."

She grinned and pulled three plates down.

Our hunger made for a silent meal. I focused on my slice, trying to pretend the quiet wasn't awkward and probably failing. Still, the pizza was a comfort after such a surreal day.

"I was thinking," Drew said, leaning back in his chair and rubbing his still-flat stomach appreciatively. "You need somewhere to stay while you're here."

"I wasn't actually planning on staying at all, so. . ." I returned my gaze to my pizza, picking an errant pepperoni off.

He exhaled through his nose, and I looked up in time to catch the ire in his expression. "Right. Well, I was hoping we could do some investigating, try to figure out what happened. At least for a couple of days, maybe you could stick around. If it's not *too* much trouble."

I ignored the sarcasm in that last part and shrugged, dread settling into me for whatever arrangement he was going to suggest. A sick fear settled in my stomach that he would insist I stay with Cassidy's father and his wife.

"It's not safe to stay here, and I'd prefer that you weren't alone much. If it's okay with her, I think you should stay with Skylar."

She looked surprised but not unhappy. "That's fine with me." She tossed her napkin onto her empty plate.

"Whatever," I conceded.

I almost missed the relief on Drew's face, but it was visible as the single vertical line between his brows disappeared. "Good. Anyway, since we can't really have you out and about much, she has cable to keep you occupied."

"Jump back everybody," I said, holding my hands up in mock surprise. "Cable? what is this, the Ritz?" I reached into the pizza box for another slice.

Drew's mouth twisted into a wry smile.

Skylar's phone chirped from beside her plate, and she lurched forward to check it. Her eyes lit up. "It's a good thing you're staying because the professor wants to meet with us tomorrow morning."

"What professor?" Drew asked, expression tightening.

"Skylar emailed a crackpot to see if he could shed a little light on our situation. He's supposedly an expert on alternate dimensions."

He raised a brow. "What time tomorrow?"

"Ten," she replied.

"Then I'm coming with you."

11

Professor Helpful

"Stop wiggling so much," Drew said. His arms were folded over his chest, and he narrowed his eyes at anyone who walked by us in the hallway.

I stilled my bouncing legs, admitting to myself that his appraisal of passersby made me more jittery than the prospect that we might have answers to what brought me here in a matter of minutes. From yesterday's experience, I knew he was being extra cautious. But it was that in combination with the fact that I was uncomfortable. The black slacks I wore, the soft button-down shirt, the professional look of the peacoat. This was the other Cassidy. The educated, classy one who worked at a hospital, not the one who lived in her car and resorted to petty crime to get by between jobs. But it served Skylar's purpose.

One student looked at me and smiled as he passed, but it faded when Drew gave him a powerful glare.

"Will you knock it off?" I said. "You're freaking me out, and I'm not even on the receiving end of your Clint Eastwood stare-down."

He turned to look at me.

"Never mind. I'm in the club."

Skylar returned from the bathroom, looking completely at ease in her khakis and turtleneck. She raised a brow as she sat. "Am I interrupting something?"

"Just a staring contest," I replied at the same time he said, "No."

She suppressed a smile and settled the notebook she'd selected as a prop into her lap. I watched the pen she tapped against it, the only outward sign of her anxiety. Drew continued to glower.

A girl walked out of the good professor's office, slipping her psychedelic backpack onto her shoulders, and gave us the once-over before heading down the hall.

"We're up," Skylar said, standing.

Drew rose, towering over me.

I didn't stand right away. Something made me reluctant. Some weird fear of whatever we might discover, that whatever this man said would prove that this wasn't a dream like I was still trying to convince myself it was. I stood to follow them into the office. I was immediately accosted by the heady scent of incense, the lazy smoke drifting from the top of a filing cabinet in the corner. Large prints of multi-colored fractals decorated the walls and a hand-woven tapestry of a lotus flower hung above the dark-haired man sitting behind the desk before us.

"I'm Eli Thibald," he said, standing. He was compact and fanatically fit, but a tension hung on him like a string pulled too tightly. "You must be Skylar Morris." He shook Skylar's hand, and his sleepy eyes took us in. "And friends?"

Drew offered his own hand. "Drew."

The professor took it and nodded his acknowledgment. Then his eyes fell on me. "And you are?"

I took my turn shaking his hand. "Cassidy."

He settled back into his seat, but the tension remained. "I'm sorry I don't have enough chairs." He gestured to the two across the desk from him.

"That's all right," Drew said. "I'll stand."

Eli Thibald was a handsome man, maybe in his forties. Silver peppered the dark hair at the temples only, and his face was smooth. His eyes held the knowing look of life experience and higher education. Certificates and degrees from Harvard and MIT gathered dust on bookshelves. Despite my earlier skepticism, I was certain now that I would have a hard time discounting anything the man had to say.

Thibald's eyes followed us as we took our seats. "I don't get many visitors these days."

"Yes, it was difficult to get in to see you," Skylar commented.

He pursed his lips and the sleepy eyes sharpened. "Well, I understand you read the article."

She nodded.

He sighed. "Since its publication, I've received quite a bit of criticism and harassment. I'm a little more selective about who I meet with. I usually only allow students."

I was impressed Skylar didn't squirm under the appraising look he gave her. "Well, we appreciate you making an exception for us."

He leaned back in his chair, a picture of ease, but the vibration of apprehension pulsed through the room. "I wasn't aware when I agreed to the meeting that you would be bringing guests."

She gave him an apologetic look. "I didn't mean to mislead

you. These are my colleagues. I assure you they're trustworthy."

He waved a dismissive hand. "Well, we're here now. What exactly are you wanting to know?

"Well." Her eyes darted to the folded hands in her lap. "As you know, we read the article about parallel universes. You believe inter-dimensional travel is possible."

"Yes, I do," he answered, cautious.

"Well, if it's possible," she started slowly, "how might that happen?"

He pursed his lips, debating something. "Well, let's start with this: how much do you know about string theory, parallel universes, and things of that ilk?"

Her cheeks grew pink. "Not much. I tried to do some research, but a lot of it is over my head."

He nodded, having expected that. "Well, some theorists posit that there are multiple dimensions sitting right on top of each other. But they're in separate planes. If that's the case, then it really shouldn't be that difficult to, at least temporarily, connect the planes."

"Okay. So, what might connect them?" She leaned forward a bit.

He scratched at his chin, warming to the topic. "There's a lot of speculation about that."

"What do you, personally, believe?" Drew spoke up for the first time.

The professor's gaze narrowed on Drew, and the cautious look was back in his eyes. "You're not recording this, are you?"

Drew held up both hands as if to show that they were empty. "I swear I'm not."

The professor nodded slowly. "I believe it has everything

to do with how the stars are aligned and magnetic fields. The energy generated by the field and the celestial alignment could cause a disruption large enough to be felt across the earth's atmosphere."

Drew raised one brow.

"Stick with me here," the professor said, raising a placating hand. "I mean that the cosmos and its position has an impact on our planet. Maybe more than we realize. And that ties into naturally occurring magnetic fields all over the world. I believe that's what we see when we look at the Pyramids of Ancient Egypt. People seem to think they were built as tombs or religious monoliths. But their purpose could be very different. Based on their age, which appears to be a lot older than originally thought, and their positions, they had significant connections to the heavens." His speech picked up speed. "All those idiot scholars and the Egyptian government try to pull the wool over our eyes, misdirect anyone who tries to study this theory in more depth. A man I went to Harvard with was—"

"What does that connection mean?" I asked, trying to keep the topic focused.

He blinked. "Ah, yes, sorry." He shook his head. "Where was I?"

"The true purpose of the Pyramids," I reminded.

"Yes, yes." He thought for a moment. "The Pyramids were positioned in certain geographical locations based on where certain stars were located at that time. Originally, it was believed they were placed where they are for the proximity to the Nile, which has since moved due to erosion over the last few thousand years. Back then, cultures always developed around major sources of water, especially in arid climates like

Egypt."

"But the Egyptians *didn't* build the Pyramids around the Nile?" I asked.

"Not because of it, no. From geological research and the erosion patterns left by the Nile, the Pyramids were built *nearby*, but facing an entirely different direction. And based on some of their hieroglyphs, the ancient Egyptians had a much higher understanding of mathematics, physics, and cosmology than anyone has given them credit for."

"So, what does that have to do with magnetic fields?" Skylar asked.

"Well, according to some, the Pyramids were made to be conduits of energy. Based on some of those theories, the energy from the magnetic fields could conceivably be harnessed for any number of purposes. I believe it's one way to jump between universes."

Surely it couldn't be that simple. "So how would a person harness this energy?" I asked. "Go to Egypt?"

He looked at me and steepled his fingers, tapping them against his chin. "I don't think you would have to go to such extreme measures. Magnetic fields are found all over the world. Besides, it's unlikely the Egyptian government will allow you to get so close to their sacred monuments."

His bitterness didn't dampen the anticipation that tingled in my fingers. "If that's the case, could someone stumble into one of these fields and accidentally travel from one dimension to another?"

He pulled his focus back to the conversation and shook his head, smiling a little. "I'm not sure that would be possible. I rather imagine you would have to deliberately harness the energy and focus it exactly in order for it to happen. That requires machinery the average person wouldn't have access to. And that's on top of doing very precise cosmological calculations."

I sat forward and placed my hands on his desk. "So someone else could set all of this up and pull another person to another dimension without their knowledge?"

He took in my expression, Drew squinting at him, Skylar's anxious hands. His eyes narrowed. "That's more likely than it happening by accident." He reluctantly turned to Skylar. "What sort of research did you say you were doing?"

She shifted under his scrutiny. "We're writing a science fiction novel."

"Ahh." His expression fell. No doubt a fiction novel was not exactly something a man of his caliber would find savory.

I forced myself to relax, to sit back in my chair and pretend everything he said was just helpful information, not my one last hope of understanding what I was doing here.

Drew folded his arms across his chest, covering his skepticism remarkably well. "If something like that enabled a person to jump between universes, would the exact same conditions be necessary for them to get back?"

Thibald thought about that, his eyes traveling heavenward for a moment. "Not necessarily. They could be *similar* conditions. There only has to be a series of cosmic alignments. The universe around us is always moving. If someone jumped dimensions last Tuesday, for example, the alignments are already different. To get back to the same place they left, he or she would have to figure out where that field is *now* and whether they can access it. Otherwise, they'd have to wait for it to appear back where it started."

"So how could we predict when and where?" I worked hard

not to scoot forward in my seat again.

Again, he seemed to pick up on my intensity.

Skylar shot me a look of silent communication. *Take it easy.*

"I mean, the characters, of course," I said, stumbling to cover my mistake. "Getting back is essential to the resolution of the plot."

He blinked slowly, absorbing my weak attempt with dubious acceptance. "Well, as I mentioned, you have to find a magnetic field to give off a significant amount of energy, and you'd have to pay close attention to the movement of the heavens."

"So what kind of things would the characters be looking for in the stars?" Skylar asked, trying to take over.

The suspicion didn't quite leave his eyes.

"We just want to be thorough and as believable as possible," she assured him. "Maybe if we knew what we were looking for ourselves, we could give a realistic representation in our novel."

"Maybe even a demonstration," I added.

His eyes brightened with excitement, and his skepticism melted away. "Well, if you're really that interested, I'll have to do some research, figure out exactly when the right conditions would be observable."

"That would be really great!" Skylar grinned.

I was relieved that her level of enthusiasm matched the moment and hoped I looked as convincing.

"Let's set up a meeting in a few days," Thibald said, standing. "I'll email you when I have some information, and we'll set one up then."

"Great, thanks," Skylar said. We all moved toward the door as a unit and the professor held it open for us as we filed out.

"What a load of crock," Drew muttered once we were halfway

down the hall. He walked ahead of us, his long legs carrying him away.

Skylar was nearly running to keep up. "I don't hear you coming up with anything better."

Drew stopped abruptly, and we almost ran into him. "Come on, Sky. Magnetic fields? Stars aligning? Were we talking to a physicist or a friggin' magician?"

"It's the only lead we have, and I'm not going to simply let it go." She put a hand on her hip, but her tone was mild.

I watched them silently, chewing on the questions I felt had yet to be answered. Part of me agreed with Drew, but maybe we hadn't asked the *right* questions. Had I missed my opportunity because I'd been too eager already and drawn suspicion? Or would it be worth it to lay out the whole truth? His conviction about traveling between dimensions might help him believe me.

"No wonder he's people-shy. That scathing article was right," Drew muttered. "He's a walking fortune cookie. Next thing you know, he'll suggest we hop on one foot and rub our heads while he tells us our horoscopes."

"This really must be an alternate dimension," Skylar said, tone dry. "You're starting to sound like Cassidy."

I held up a hand. "Whoa. I think I'm having an out of body experience. You're *both* starting to sound like me."

Drew rolled his eyes and spun to continue walking toward the exit.

"Just keep an open mind," Skylar suggested, chasing after him. "We have some time to think it over. He'll get back to us. It was worth a try."

I nibbled on the edge of my thumb nail, anxiety buzzing through me. I glanced back toward Thibald's office, wondering if we'd left too soon. I wasn't sure I could wait very long for him to set up our next appointment.

Skylar stopped. "Shoot."

"What?" Drew asked, glancing back at her.

She patted her hands over her body. "I left the notebook in his office."

It was like fate, and I was not going to miss the opportunity. "I'll get it," I offered.

Skylar waved her hand. "I'm the one who left it."

"My legs are longer so I walk faster," I insisted.

She gave me a petulant look.

"It's true," Drew said. He nodded at me. "Go ahead. We'll wait for you in the car."

I spun on my heel and hurried back to Thibald's office, moving through the crowd of students that came pouring out of classrooms.

Thibald grunted his welcome when I knocked.

"Sorry," I said, poking my head in. "We left our notebook."

He nodded to the one sitting on the edge of his desk. "I picked it up a moment ago." He had his feet up and was leaning back in his chair, fingers interlaced to support his head.

I took the notebook and turned to go, losing my nerve. No, I needed to know. I stopped and whirled to face him again. "Sorry. I have one more question."

He raised a brow but said nothing. I took it as his permission.

"If our character got pulled to another dimension without her knowledge," I began. "What would she experience? Some sort of energy surge?"

He leaned forward, intrigued. "Well, that level of power could blow out lights, windows, maybe. The pressure alone could possibly burst a person's eardrums."

I gripped the notebook so hard my fingers screamed in protest. "And frequencies? Like radios?"

"I'd imagine they would cut in and out if the surge didn't blow the power circuits." He zeroed in on my expression. "Where exactly is your character when this energy surge takes place?"

"Um, a police station. The jail, actually."

He sat back, considering. "Sturdy buildings, usually. And you said your character is the only one pulled into that other dimension?"

As far as I know. "Yes."

"Well," he said, pensive. "I suppose it could be contained within the walls in the jail since they're typically concrete." He turned his attention back to me. "That would be a very interesting addition to our experiment." He nodded, then leaned forward to scribble something in a notebook in front of him. "Very interesting! Anything else we should consider?"

I shook my head and tried to force myself to smile through my sudden lightheadedness. "Thank you for answering my questions."

I rushed out and back down the hall, praying my legs wouldn't give out from under me. The chill wind outside nipped at my face, and I hoped it would whip some color back into my cheeks. Drew started the car as soon as I gripped the door handle. I slid in and handed the notebook to Skylar without looking at her.

"Are you okay?" Drew asked, his eyes on me through the rear view mirror.

"Fine," I said, breathlessly. "We had to look for it. Skylar must have kicked it under his desk when she stood up." I hoped the lie wasn't obvious on my face.

He said nothing and backed out of the lot.

12

Ineffective Incognito

A glutton for punishment.

That's the only thing I could call it as I Googled information on Cassidy.

Her social media pages were set to private, but there were still random photos available for me to peruse. It was like a movie of the way my life should have been.

She had probably been the perfect teenager before transitioning into this respectable young woman, working in the local hospital's pediatric department as a nurse. Pictures of her posing with her sorority sisters in college, in her cap and gown at graduation, in scrubs, holding up her stethoscope as if it were some kind of trophy—plenty to envy. A magazine-worthy engagement photo of her and Evan served as her profile picture.

His page hadn't been set to private, and of course, I skimmed through his entire photo library. The typical college party nonsense, but then an unusually mature focus during medical school. Posts about his residency transitioned to picture upon picture of him with Cassidy. Hiking, game nights, dinners out.

He was tagged in pictures of some youth outreach program for at-risk kids that he volunteered for. There was the prototypical picture with their initials carved into a tree surrounded by a heart.

I rolled my eyes and clicked back enough times to get to the original search results. I seized up at the sight of one headline under *News*:

SLAIN COLORADO WOMAN THIRD IN FRIGHTENING STRING OF MURDERS

I swallowed, clicking on the link, lured by the morbid impulse to know more.

It was an early article, stingy on details, for which I'm sure her family was grateful.

Someone had snuck a picture of Evan at the scene. He stood in profile, bustling cops around him, crime scene tape slashing violent yellow across the image. His hand was raised to cover his eyes, shoulders slumped. It was a stark contrast, his motionlessness obvious next to the blurred forms of the police on the scene.

I remembered his words back at Cassidy's house. *All cut up.*

I shivered.

After that, I needed something less gruesome, though I suppose no less emotional to learn about. I read about my father. I had to remind myself that he wasn't my father; he was hers. I had no claim to him.

I didn't find much. Only that his business often gave back to the community. He backed little league teams and 5ks. His wife, Jane, was quoted in an article about the local high school where she taught English.

My chest tightened from an old sorrow. I thought the jealousy would have lessened or at least become familiar, but it stung every time it burned through me. To alleviate the pain, I steered away from researching them further.

I snooped on Drew and Skylar instead, though I didn't find much there either. Both went to the local college, as did most of the kids who graduated from their high school. I thought back to my own high school days, grimacing as no name or face came to mind as a particular friend. I'd gone to several different schools in my stays with various families, so it was no wonder. There were some articles about cases Drew worked as a beat cop and then as a detective, proving that he'd earned his spot and climbed the ladder quickly.

I rested my chin in my hand, my finger tapping against the desk. I stared at the blinking cursor in the search bar of Google. Forty-eight hours after meeting with the professor and being cooped up had birthed uncertainty. My detour into cyberstalking didn't mitigate the jitters.

Just hitting the road and leaving it all behind was starting to appeal again. If only to feel like I was actually *doing* something, even with Professor Thibald's theory rattling around in my head.

It was clear that he wasn't as crack-brained as we'd all initially thought. If what he said was true, it *was* possible to send me back.

Back home. Where I belonged.

I rubbed my palms against my thighs, trying to use the friction to get warmth back into my hands. If only I could dispel the chill that settled into my bones when I thought of going back. Because what home was there to go to?

Still, it wasn't like I could take up the other Cassidy's life. I would never be what they wanted; my face was a match, but I was a poor substitute for what they'd lost. And I could never live under the pressure to be something I wasn't.

A steely resolve drew me out of my wavering thoughts, and I clicked into online ads for crappy cars. I couldn't commit to anything without knowing how much money I might have access to. I couldn't exactly ask for that information, not with a dead woman's ID and debit card burning a hole in my pocket, evidence of my habit of deceit and delinquency.

Shame sliced at me. I didn't want to start a new life by relying on old habits. I always claimed I settled for petty thieving to fill the gaps in desperation to keep moving. But was I making excuses?

One last time, a voice in my head insisted. *Then never again.*

Technically, I *was* Cassidy Marchand. If I took her name and ran, I was simply seizing my opportunity to start fresh, be anyone I wanted. My very presence would no longer be a source of pain. But if I took money out of her accounts and snuck away, I wasn't starting fresh at all.

I growled in frustration, slamming a fist against the desk.

I shot out of the chair but had nowhere to go. So I walked to the window. The empty sidewalks that made up the courtyard of the apartment complex were deserted except for the fallen leaves fidgeting in the intermittent breeze.

I craved the feel of that brisk wind on my face, the way it grabbed at my hair, how it would slink through my clothes to caress my skin. Maybe I was going stir-crazy. I'd never thought of wind so longingly before.

All I knew was that I needed to get out, do something. Clear my head or make a plan. Anything. Drew had been very serious about me not going anywhere, not letting anyone see me. I hadn't even been allowed to go with Skylar when she stopped at Cassidy's house to grab me new clothes.

He was the one who'd said the town wasn't so small that everyone knew the other Cassidy. But I was sure the murders had been splashed all over the news. I couldn't walk out the door and expect no one to notice me on the street.

I tapped my nails against my teeth. I could probably disguise myself well enough. I just needed to make sure my hair color wasn't obvious.

After a moment of hesitation, I headed down the hall to Skylar's bedroom to raid her closet for anything that would help to disguise me. None of her clothing would fit, of course. She was a lot shorter than me. But I was hopeful she had scarves and hats that would work in a pinch.

I opened the closet door and yanked the string to turn on the light. Her selection of clothes was fairly extensive and suited my style more than Cassidy's. I allowed myself a moment to lament our size difference before reaching for her limited collection of hats.

I tried on a few, ones that would shield my face and cover my hair. I chose a black military-style hat that touched the tips of my ears and pulled my red locks into a bun. Then I pushed aside some of her blouses, looking for scarves. Thankfully it was cool enough that a scarf wouldn't seem out of place. I grabbed a tan, knitted one that was thick and soft.

I wrapped it around my neck and yanked the string, plunging the closet into darkness before I shut the door. On my way out, I found a pair of bug-eye sunglasses sitting on her dresser. I swiped those and slid them on as I made my way to the front door. A prickle of fear sent a tingling sensation down my arms into my fingertips. After all, there was a murderer loose.

Leaving town would take me out of danger.

I stiffened as I reached for my jacket. I rocked back on my heels.

Just go. Do it.

There was no reason to suspect the killer knew I was here. But it was one more reason I needed to hit the road. Integrity be damned.

I snatched the jacket, ignoring the nerves twisting up my stomach. I yanked the front door open and stepped into the dim hallway, the echo reverberating in the cave-like space. I cringed as if it would alert someone to what I was doing.

I lifted my chin in false bravado as I walked out into the autumn breeze. The sun was warm, but the wind had a bite that made me grateful for the scarf, pulling it up to cover my chin and nose.

Still, the fresh air was crisp in my lungs, and it soothed the jitters.

The apartment complex sat on the edge of the Square. I hesitated on the corner. Walking through the Square meant more people and, thus, the possibility of being recognized, but it also was the quickest way to get to the bus station on the other side. I could figure my next move as I walked, decide if sneaking away with stolen funds was what I really wanted to do.

I squeezed my eyes shut for a moment before deciding I'd chance it and headed toward the first block of shops and boutiques that made up the Square. I cursed myself for not paying attention to the time.

People were sitting down for lunch next to restaurant windows and gathered outside under heat lamps on cafe patios. I had to shuffle around those coming and going and was rammed into once by a man with a take-out bag in his hand. He mumbled an apology and turned away from me quickly as he jogged across the street. I felt his eyes on me as I continued, but I was too distracted when the coffee shop on the corner came into view.

I froze, the man dropping out of my mind. Patrons had spilled out onto the sidewalk, sitting at the cheap, wire tables, sipping steaming cups of liquid out of bowl-sized mugs. It was the exact shop in which I had pickpocketed the knuckle cracker. But that wasn't the reason I'd stopped in my tracks.

My eyes were glued to the man sitting at a table alone, his face half in sunlight, half in shade. His broad, muscular shoulders were hunched as if he were trying to make himself smaller. His eyes stared, unseeing, at the large cup in front of him, the steam from his drink dancing sinuously upward, begging for his attention.

Hercules looked less heroic with the blank stare and the way his sadness seemed intent on pulling him toward the ground. I debated the wisdom of turning around or walking past him. He didn't seem to be very aware of his surroundings, so maybe it didn't matter much either way.

But it was as if I'd called his name. Evan's gaze drifted upward and locked on my face, even though the bottom half was burrowed in the chunky scarf, the upper half obscured by the large sunglasses and the hat. Recognition lit in his eyes immediately. He stood so quickly he knocked the table and whatever he was drinking listed in its cup, splashing over the side. He didn't even glance down.

Being on the receiving end of an emotional outburst wasn't on my list of priorities at the moment. Neither was explaining exactly what I was doing there and what my hand was fisted around inside my jacket pocket. My desire to run was almost overpowering.

He seemed to sense my impulse and stretched a hand toward me. "Wait."

I shifted my weight uneasily but did as he bid while he moved around the table to join me.

"Hey," he said as he stuffed his hands into his pockets. He was almost eye-level with me, only a couple inches taller.

I said nothing as his gaze searched my mostly-covered face. Could he tell what I was considering?

"What are you doing out here?"

I offered a tense shrug. "Just, uh, out for a walk. I was getting antsy stuck inside."

He nodded and looked down. "Do you mind if I join you?"

My first impulse was to say no. But I heard myself saying "all right" before I could stop. What difference did it make? I couldn't exactly skip town now, even if I made a final decision.

He stepped aside for me to lead the way. My movements were stiff as we began walking. He left his drink on the table and his eyes remained on me, making me more jumpy than I had been locked inside Skylar's apartment.

"Was this your attempt at a disguise?" he asked.

I concentrated on trying to relax, willing my muscles to loosen, so I could focus on the conversation. "I thought it was pretty good."

He grimaced. "It is. I mean, for the average person, probably. But I'd know your face no matter what."

"Isn't that romantic?" I quipped.

He finally looked away and squinted ahead of us, the pain a flicker in his eyes.

I almost apologized. Almost. But my nerves were shot, and

self-control was a little lacking at the moment.

"Listen," he started. "I'm sorry about the other day."

I blinked, not having expected that. "You don't have to apologize for anything," I said quickly.

"Yeah, I do." He frowned. "I haven't been the nicest guy lately, and I need to get myself out of that before it becomes who I am."

I narrowed my eyes, looking at him askance. "All right, Dr. Phil. Apology accepted."

A hint of a smile played at his lips. "You're kind of a smartass, aren't you?"

I gave one short bark of laughter. "I try."

"That's definitely different," he murmured.

"I take it your Cassidy was more smart than ass."

He shrugged.

Of course.

"Perfection," I muttered.

"What?"

I shook my head. "Not important."

He let it go, and we walked in silence. I glanced into storefront windows. If my plans were going to be thwarted, I might as well get some enjoyment out of the situation. I'd always liked window shopping.

The eclectic array of displays, from a pet food bakery to a hobby store, drew my focus. One boutique offered bejeweled women's clothing, the cheap rhinestones catching the sunlight and winking at me.

"Any news on the alternate universe thing?" Evan asked.

I cleared my throat and shrugged. "Nothing conclusive. We talked to a guy who might have a theory." I didn't want to add that I might have believed him.

"What guy?"

"Some professor. Drew thinks he's a crackpot."

"Who wouldn't?" Evan said. "Alternate universes?"

I huffed an awkward chuckle. "Right."

We rounded a corner, and the silence stretched tighter, threatening to snap.

"This must be hard," I said suddenly.

His eyes shifted to my face. "What?"

"Me being here. Complicating your life." It was hard enough for me, seeing how my life could have been, how much better she'd had it. . . I pressed my eyes shut for a second to fight a flash of animosity. Not the time or place.

He inhaled deeply and looked away. "It's not your fault."

"But you blame me."

He pulled his shoulders upward, wincing. "I'm trying not to. I get the sense you're not exactly happy about being here either."

I scoffed. "Yeah. Sucks, doesn't it?"

"Most things do these days," he agreed. He jerked to a stop.

"What?"

He reached into his pocket to pull out his vibrating cell phone. "It's Drew," he said, hitting answer and pressing the phone to his ear. "Hey."

I turned to the window of the store we'd stopped in front of. It was a photography studio. Glamor shots had me smirking—women with overly made-up faces, curls stacked high upon their heads, and the prototypical hazy filter haloing their faces. In the reflection of the window, I noticed the figure of a man across the street looking in our direction, hands in his coat pockets. I tilted my head slightly, feeling some sense of familiarity. Was that the guy who'd run into me?

"Dude, slow down," Evan said.

I turned to look at him, seeing the man move on in the corner of my eye. I pushed him from my mind so that I could zero in on Evan's conversation.

"She's with me." He paused, gaze flickering to me. "We're on the corner of Golden and Elm." He sighed and rubbed the back of his neck with a hand. "All right. Fine."

"What is it?" I asked as he hung up.

He frowned. "I guess Skylar came home for lunch, saw that you were gone and panicked."

I crossed my arms. So leaving today was not meant to be. It was just as well, given that I didn't have a plan anyway. "Lemme guess, Andy Griffith is on his way right now."

"Yeah, and he's pissed." He looked at the ground and kicked at a weed that had grown in the crack of the sidewalk.

"Sorry if I got you in trouble."

He shrugged. "It's not a big deal. Drew's just uptight because. . ."

I knew why he'd trailed off but decided to point out the other obvious thing. "His soldiers aren't following orders."

He shot me a surprised grin as the Charger I'd come to recognize whizzed around the corner and groaned to a halt at the curb beside us. Drew glanced out with a glare before getting out of his car.

He shifted his steely gaze from Evan to me, taking in my "disguise" with pursed lips.

He stood, a tower in front of us, and hooked his thumbs into his pockets. The stance was casual, but his eyes were tight with anger.

"I don't suppose you recall our conversation the other day about you being outside?" He asked.

I raised an eyebrow at Evan, who suppressed a smile. Apparently I could do the silent communication thing too.

"Why, Officer," I said in a feigned southern accent. "Have I done something wrong?" I pressed a hand daintily to my chest.

His expression darkened.

"What?" I dropped the accent. "I'm incognito." I pointed to the scarf.

"You're not a celebrity hiding from the paparazzi, Cassidy."

I held up my hands in surrender. "I wanted some fresh air." I worked to keep my eyes from sliding away from his face at the half-truth. "I was tired of being cooped up."

"You could've at least left a note," he suggested.

I balked. Fair point. If my intention had, indeed, been to come back. "Well, I'm not used to having anyone care where I am or what I'm doing. Sorry." I turned on my heel to head back to the apartment. I only made it two feet.

"Cass, wait." A hand slid around my arm and pulled me to a stop.

I twisted to look up at Drew and was glad that my face was almost completely covered. He was standing so close to me that my arm was pressed against him, and his breath dancing across the only exposed part of my face. Unexpected electricity rushed through me.

I could tell by the way his eyes narrowed on my face that he wasn't unaffected, which exponentially complicated the already confusing nature of my presence here.

Should've run when I'd had the chance.

We stared at each other for one long beat, and his hand tightened on my arm slightly.

"Sorry," he finally said, his voice almost a murmur. "I didn't think about how you might be feeling." His eyes traced over my face, lingering in a way that made the heat creep into my cheeks. "I want to keep you safe. Alive."

I peeked at Evan. The intensity of his gaze on us kicked my heartbeat up a notch. I pulled my arm from Drew's grasp. "It's fine. Maybe try not being a patronizing ass next time?"

He wasn't even offended, his eyes lighting with a hint of humor. "Sorry. I get that way sometimes."

"Well, sometimes I'm a smartass," I admitted. "It'd be pretty hypocritical of me to hold a grudge against fellow asses."

"How gracious of you." A wry smile tugged at his mouth. "Are you hungry? Skylar brought lunch over to her place."

"Yeah, I could eat."

He turned to Evan, who shoved his hands deep into his pockets. "You want to come?"

Evan looked across the street as if asking the realty office for permission. He looked way too uncomfortable to have missed what happened between Drew and me. "Nah," he said. "How about I swing by for dinner though?"

Drew nodded. "All right. Sounds good." He looked at me. "Come on, I'll take you back."

I folded my arms across my chest and raised a brow.

We had a stare down before I remembered seeing the guy I'd run into earlier across the street.

"Fine," I conceded, stomping my way to the cruiser's passenger side, casting my gaze up and down the road to check for him again. Just in case it wasn't random.

Drew tried to hide his satisfied grin as he buckled himself in.

13

Ambushed

The smell of dinner cooking permeated the room with a tangy warmth as I lounged across the couch. Images flashed on the TV screen as I flipped absently through channels.

"You've certainly made yourself at home," Skylar said, walking into the living room.

I sat up and gave her a sheepish grin. Because she was right, and I had almost left without a word of warning after her kindness to me.

I turned the TV off and grappled for the humor that would cover my guilt, grasped something trivial, and went with it."You're lucky I'm too long for this thing. Otherwise, I'd be here for life."

She put a hand on her hip, raising a dubious brow.

"Seriously. It's probably the cushiest thing I've slept on in months."

She straightened like she'd been poked in the back.

I laughed, my discomfort finally melting away. "Relax. You don't have to tiptoe around the nitty-gritty details of my colored life."

She sighed. "Can't help it. It's human nature to avoid awkward situations."

"I must not be human then because I have a tendency to barge right into them." I pushed myself to my feet.

The front door swung open. "I brought beer," Drew announced as he walked in.

"Speaking of barging in," I said.

Skylar shot Drew an exasperated look.

He looked from her to me. "Did I do something wrong?"

"Could be that walking into someone's apartment without knocking isn't really polite," I informed him.

"But. . . I brought beer."

"Then you're forgiven," Skylar said, walking forward to take the six-pack from him. "For now." She grinned and went into the kitchen.

He beamed at me and put his hands into his pockets, rocking back on his heels. It was the most laid-back I'd seen him since arriving. If I didn't know better, I would have thought this was the original Drew I'd met, and he'd somehow jumped to this universe with me.

But maybe it was something else entirely that made his mood so light.

He lifted his chin, sniffing the air. "What's cooking?"

"Uh, lasagna." I tossed the remote I was holding onto the couch to avoid continued eye contact.

"Sounds scary," he said in a stage whisper.

"Hey!" Skylar protested as she came into the living room with three open bottles of beer.

"It's store-bought," I assured him, taking one of the bottles from her.

"Snitch," she teased, offering the other to him.

I concentrated on the light-hearted banter, told myself to try to enjoy the moment. Not focus on Skylar's hospitality, Drew's efforts to protect me, and the attachment I could feel brewing. It meant nothing. None of this did.

Say it until you mean it.

I took a sip of my beer as a distraction then grimaced, looking at the offending drink. "Ugh, what is this?"

"Low-quality IPA," Drew announced proudly, raising his bottle in tribute.

I wrinkled my nose. "Hoppy."

"Just the way I like it." He winked.

"Gross. Lagers are where it's at."

Drew shrugged, his grin tipping one side of his mouth more than the other.

A warmth spread through my middle at that smile, and I told myself it was because they were so hard-won. Not because they transformed his handsome face into something almost otherworldly.

He sidled closer, a sly look in his eyes as if he sensed my response to him. "I'll keep your beer tastes in mind for future reference. Even if I disagree with what kind is *actually* the best."

I jabbed an elbow playfully into his side. "Well, then I guess I won't hold your preference against you. Even if it is absolutely terrible."

He laughed, and the sound sent a zing from my head to my toes. "At least I left room for opinion to be opinion. You can't objectively say my favorite is terrible."

"I think I can. Because it is," I insisted, not able to contain my smile.

Skylar cleared her throat forcefully.

I glanced over and caught the tightness of her expression before she turned back to the kitchen.

"Dinner's almost ready," she called over her shoulder.

Drew took a long pull from his beer and turned to stare out the window even though it was dark. He must have seen her look as well.

After a moment, Skylar came back out of the kitchen. She raised a brow at me, and I definitely wouldn't mistake what it meant. A warning. I gave a quick shrug of acknowledgment and took a sip of the beer, the bad taste to wash the worse one from my mouth.

"It's cooling, so we have about five minutes. Didn't you say Evan was coming?" she asked Drew.

He nodded, looking at the floor. "He said he would be here."

A sting of guilt flashed through me. I'd seen the look on his face earlier in the day. Would he skip dinner with his friends because the copy of his fiancée was throwing a wrench into a decades-old dynamic?

I swallowed against the lump in my throat, the guilt that locked my chest in a slowly tightening vice.

I excused myself for the bathroom to take a breather, to get my emotions and my mind under control before he arrived. I didn't want to make anything worse.

I made it to the mouth of the hallway when the knock sounded. I paused and pressed my hand against the wall as I turned to watch Skylar open her front door.

Evan's eyes locked on me immediately, as if he knew exactly where I'd be standing. I narrowed my eyes, confused by the look on his face. He almost seemed. . . guilty. Which was weird, considering I was the one who was in the wrong here.

He walked into the living room, nervous energy vibrating

off of him in waves. And I suddenly understood why.

Two people came into the apartment behind him. One face I'd known my whole life, the other I'd only seen in pictures. They were more heavily lined than in the photos, and I recognized the aging influence of grief on their faces.

My breathing picked up; the pain stabbed at my chest. How dare he? How could a man who was so hurt by my very presence bring that pain upon these people and add it to the struggle I already had knowing they existed?

I shot a searing glare at Evan, any sense of blame I'd felt earlier was set on fire by the fury that lit through me.

"Cassidy!" Cassidy's stepmother choked out the name. She stumbled toward me, her hands outstretched, tears glistening in her eyes.

I shrank away from her, and she froze, confusion distorting her delicate features. I looked at Cassidy's father, and it was difficult not to think of him as *my* father. The uncertainty wasn't obvious in his face, but it was obvious in the way he lingered near the door, the way he curled his hands into fists.

I chanted the truth in my head that he was someone else entirely even as the resentment flooded my blood, burned into me the betrayal I still felt all these years later.

Skylar stood with her hand still on the doorknob, panic frozen on her face.

Drew shot Evan a steely glare. "What is wrong with you?"

Evan's eyes flickered from me to him.

"What's going on?" the stepmother asked, not turning from me. There was hurt in her face. She reached for me again.

I held up a hand to stop her as I took a step back. "Please don't touch me." It came out a hoarse whisper. It was all I could manage.

She reacted like she'd been slapped.

The remorse flared but was eclipsed by the crushing sensation in my lungs. God, I was going to pass out. Air. Not enough air. My head spun.

Drew touched my arm, and I flinched, my gaze wheeling to his face. Recognition lit in his eyes.

"Why don't you guys have a seat?" he said over his shoulder. "Take a minute. Cass and I are going to go for a little walk."

Evan's chin jutted out in frustration as Drew led me toward the front door, and I stumbled along, barely breathing as he shut it behind us. He guided me out of the hall into the crisp fall night. Goosebumps immediately broke across my skin, but the shock of the chill air eased the pain in my chest. I sucked in oxygen greedily.

"You all right?" he asked, maneuvering to stand in front of me. He bent his knees to lower his gaze to mine.

I shut my eyes against his look and took another deep breath. "Just feeling a little ambushed," I managed after a moment.

"I don't know what the hell he was thinking," he said, frustration edging his words.

I opened my eyes. His face was turned toward the window into Skylar's living room. He wasn't exactly angry. I couldn't put my finger on it. His expressions were subtle, sometimes difficult to read. Betrayed, maybe? But for me, not himself. Which didn't make sense. Why would he be so upset for my sake?

"What am I going to do now?" I asked, with no real desire for a response. It was more for myself than anything. Because now that my father and his wife were here, I couldn't ignore them, couldn't avoid them. As much as I wanted to. As much as I wished I could pretend they didn't exist at all.

A quick getaway would have been nice right about now.

Drew's face softened as he looked at me. "You don't have to do anything."

I shook my head. "I don't really have much of a choice."

14

Proof of Poppies

I stood outside in my t-shirt for as long as I could handle, until my head cleared and my teeth started to chatter. Drew waited patiently and silently with me until I set my jaw and marched back toward the apartment.

The muffled sound of discussion inside made me hesitate with my hand on the door handle.

"You don't have to do anything." Drew's words played back in my mind.

I didn't have to. It's not like I owed them anything, even my presence. But I was resolute, so I turned the knob and went inside.

Skylar stood in front of Evan, my father, and his wife who were sitting on the couch in a line. All eyes shifted to me, and I swallowed.

"So," I said. "Who's hungry?"

My attempt at lightening the mood fell flat. I had no idea what they'd been talking about, what Skylar said that had Evan looking chastised and the others looking cautious.

Skylar cleared her throat and looked at everyone on the

couch. "Are you staying for dinner?"

My father looked at me as he answered, "I don't think that's the best idea."

His wife's face fell, but she said nothing.

I had no intention of dissuading him. I folded my arms across my chest and looked away.

He rose and, out of the corner of my eye, I caught him offering his hand to his wife. She took it, and they walked to the front door hand in hand. Drew stepped aside for them to pass and shut the door once they'd gone.

The flinty look in his eyes returned when he rounded on Evan, sulking silently on the couch. "What were you thinking?"

"I already lectured him," Skylar said on a sigh. "And I tried to explain the situation to Pat and Jane. I'm not sure how well they understood it, but I'm not sure any of us really understand it."

I said nothing, not trusting myself to speak. After a moment, I walked toward the window. The blinds were drawn, but there was a gap where one of the slats was missing. My father and his wife were standing outside, and he was holding her, comforting her. Her body shook with what I knew must be grieved sobs. I couldn't find it in myself to soften at the sight. If anything, I felt more rigid.

Evan's voice came from behind me. "I thought they had a right to know."

"Clearly you didn't think that one through." Drew's tone was cutting.

"Give me a break, Drew."

"No. You don't get a free pass on this one. You know what they must be feeling right now. Didn't you think it through before you brought them? And what about Cassidy? Did you think about her at all? Or was it only about you?"

There was a flurry of movement.

I turned in time to see Evan shoot up from the couch, trying to stand nose-to-nose with Drew, who held his ground. The difference between them became more pronounced. Light and dark.

Anxiety pulled my muscles taut, made my head ache. "Please," I said, "If you're going to fight, can you do it somewhere else?"

"She's right," Skylar said. "I think you guys should go. Maybe cool off at home before you do or say anything you'll regret."

Drew took a step back, more than willing to end it.

"Take your crappy beer," I suggested, always compelled to have the last word.

Evan looked at me, and there was a coldness there that chilled me. I couldn't say it wasn't entirely undeserved. How much damage was I going to do here? Inadvertently or not, I was a problem. As I watched the two shuffle out of the apartment, I thought back to Skylar asking me about second chances. I'd screwed up my life in my world, and here I was doing it with my second chance.

She shut the door and leaned back against it. "Are you hungry?"

I pulled a face. "Not anymore."

"Me neither. But we should probably eat something anyway."

I didn't respond, but she went into the kitchen.

I turned to the window again. Evan and Drew walked out of the hall nearly simultaneously but split at the courtyard path and went in opposite directions. Evan's spine was ramrod straight, his hands clenched into fists.

Skylar touched my arm and handed me a plate when I turned. Her large eyes searched my face. "That was rough."

I shrugged, following her to the table, and sat. But I chewed on the inside of my cheek instead of my dinner.

"They're really nice people, Pat and Jane," she said in a rush, stabbing into her lasagna with a fork.

"I'm sure they are," I murmured. The fist around my heart didn't loosen its grip with the admission. It only constricted at the realization that I wouldn't be able to avoid them now. Unless I left. Cassidy's ID and debit card were still tucked in the pocket of my jacket. By sheer force of will, I kept myself from looking at it hanging on a hook by the door.

"Jane meant well. But Evan didn't explain everything to them." Skylar shook her head.

I huffed. "I don't get what he was thinking in the first place."

She lifted a shoulder, let it drop. She wouldn't look at me.

"Apparently you do," I said, my tone flat.

She pressed her lips together, a war going on behind her eyes.

I took the moment to bite back my irritation. It would only attach barbs to any words I might choose to let loose, and I was knee-deep in apologies owed already.

"I don't think he should have done what he did," she said slowly. "But I understand why he did."

I stared at the untouched food on my plate and gripped my fork like it was a dagger.

"Cass, he didn't come with us to that meeting the other day. I don't think he can wrap his mind around the whole thing."

"Because we've certainly got it figured out," I countered.

She raised a brow. "He thought your parents—"

"*Her* parents," I corrected.

She glowered at me. "He thought they should know, that they should have a say in it."

"How nice of him to care about their feelings. I'm just the counterfeit version of his fiancée, who cares what *I* think?"

Her gaze softened, and I knew my snide tone didn't cover up the hurt like I'd intended. I looked down at my food, pushed it around with my fork as if it would make it look more appetizing. The sound of our forks scraping our plates filled the quiet.

Then: "So, what's going on between you and Drew?"

I gave her a sharp look. "What are you talking about?"

She scoffed. "You were flirting with each other as soon as he got here."

Dammit. Got me there. "*Nothing* is going on."

"An attraction is something." How did someone so much smaller than me make me feel two feet tall?

The defensive tone was hard to keep in check when I responded, "I don't control that. But I do control my actions. And nothing has happened."

"Okay. I believe you," she assured me. Heavy pause. "But that doesn't mean nothing will."

I sighed and looked away. After a moment, I set my chin in my hand and stuck my fork into the lasagna.

She reached across the table to place her hand on my wrist. "All I'm saying is be careful. Everyone is in a rough place right now."

"I get it," I said, determined to burn a hole in my food with my gaze. I took a bite, not tasting it.

We ate in silence for a few minutes. I chanced a look at Skylar. She was concentrating awfully hard on her food. A question nagged at me. I hoped for a more complete answer than when

I had asked Drew.

I tried to tread lightly. "Was there anything between Drew and the other Cassidy?"

There was a wry twist to her mouth, and she gave me a knowing look. She waited several seconds to answer. "Not really."

Getting a second cryptic response frustrated me enough to press. "What does that mean?"

She winced like answering the question caused her real pain. "There was always this back and forth thing with them. She liked him, but he was dating someone. He liked her, but she wasn't interested. Timing was always off. Then Evan came along, and it was the love of a lifetime. Like, *Bam*! *The One* kind of love. So Drew moved on. He even dated a girl seriously a while back."

"So whatever is between us now is because I look like her," I said, nodding. I was grateful that the disappointment wasn't obvious in my voice. "It has nothing to do with me."

She considered it. "I don't know if that's it. I mean, there's a reason she clicked immediately with Evan. And it's obvious that's not happening with you guys. And it's no wonder. Like we've said, you're not really her."

"I thought you were against anything happening. You sound like you're encouraging me."

"I'm not trying to do either. All I said was be careful."

"Right." I stabbed my fork into the lasagna again. "Well, since we're going to find a way to send me back, you don't have anything to worry about." Or I was going to hit the road. But I kept that addition to myself.

She looked skeptical but didn't say anything.

***

The drama from the night before was motivation enough to start actually planning my departure. No waffling, no *if it works out.*

I wouldn't allow myself to feel guilty, promising myself that a one-time withdrawal wouldn't hurt anyone. I would destroy the card right away and disappear. Leave these people to grieve in peace. Get on with my new life. I would do things differently this time. Not falling in with the wrong crowd. No more stealing.

Well, not including the money from Cassidy's account. . .

I winced at the thought, and that left room for the niggling doubt, that realization that if I did go now, I would never get the answer for how I'd gotten here. And while maybe I didn't want to go back to my world, it was certainly a crazy enough mystery to warrant a resolution.

Can't have both.

Not if I did it my way.

I stood by the window with a blanket wrapped around me, hair a tumbling mess down my back, and indecision a rock in my stomach. Sleep was elusive, emotions wound so tight inside me that it felt like something would snap.

I'd contemplated sneaking out during the night, decided against it. I felt vulnerable at night, especially low on sleep. Going while everyone was at work would probably give me a better head start anyway. Not to mention more people traveled during the day. It would be easier to disappear into a crowd.

Soon enough, the sky was saturated in heavy oranges, vibrant pinks, and hazy purples, and Skylar was up, banging around in the kitchen.

"I'll see you for dinner," she called, breathless as she rushed out the door.

I was too slow to respond, and she'd disappeared, leaving me in silence again. It was just as well since answering might have been a lie. I watched through the window as she turned right down the sidewalk, hurrying to get to work on time. Apparently, punctuality was not her strong suit.

A woman dressed in workout gear jogged past the window. I'd seen her the day before. I'd also seen a tall man who walked laps around the complex, hood pulled over his head, one hand in a pocket, walking his dog. Kids from the apartment complex walked in clusters to the school a couple of blocks over, youthful voices echoing against the buildings. Oh, the excitement of small-town living when on house arrest.

I bit my lip, in no rush to hit the road. Not with the fog over my brain from little sleep. I looked at the sofa with longing, considered settling back in to catch another hour or two of sleep. The delay would cost me. Probably too much.

But I could afford a shower. Something to wake me up, give me time to lay at least the foundation of a plan.

I turned the temperature in the shower high enough to be almost unbearable and rubbed the soreness in my back, and I mentally took back my estimation of the "cushy" couch the night before. I let the tingling heat of the water run over my head and down my face, and my mind emptied of any planning, any sense of urgency.

I stood under the pounding water until it grew tepid, and I got out to wrap myself in one of Skylar's thick towels.

A cloud of steam escaped the bathroom with me when I stepped into Skylar's bedroom. I'd only made it a foot when I heard frantic pounding on the front door. I glanced at the clothes laid out on the bed, and then the pounding rattled the door again. My name came right after, muffled, urgent.

I sighed and jogged down the hall, hand clutched around the towel to hold it in place. Through the peephole, I saw Drew's concerned face before his fist came crashing against it again and blocked my view. So my plans for hitting the road would be delayed. Again.

I unlocked the door and pulled it open, my sopping hair heavy and dripping against my shoulders. "What?" I demanded.

He pushed me aside, striding into the living room, scanning every inch as if someone would be hiding somewhere.

"Come on in," I muttered, shutting the door.

He craned his neck to check the kitchen, down the hall, and tossed a peek out to the patio for good measure.

"What's going on?"

He whirled to face me, a single red flower in his hand.

I offered him a sarcastically sweet smile. "Aww, is that for me?"

He curled his lip and flung it onto the table with disgust. Pacing, flexing his hands, he lasered his gaze on me. "Did you see anyone hanging around this morning?"

"Hanging around?"

Frustration twitched at his face. "Watching the place, spending an inordinate amount of time nearby, anything?"

"Nothing out of the ordinary," I said. "But, you know, I'm new in town. Haven't learned everyone's names yet."

He ran both hands through his hair, ignoring my sarcasm.

"Okay," I said slowly. "Well, do you mind if I get dressed while you calm down? Then you can explain yourself."

He stopped and looked at me, his eyes traveling over my towel-clad body as if noticing for the first time. He swallowed.

"Fine."

I pulled the towel tighter as the heat crept into my face. I walked past him and high-tailed it back into Skylar's bedroom. Her caution the night before no longer seemed silly. My assurance that nothing would happen did, however.

I dressed quickly and towel-dried my hair, letting it fall in a damp curtain down my back. I had a feeling if I took any longer, he would come stomping down the hall to check on me.

I padded out into the living room barefoot right as he was ending a phone call. "You want anything to drink? I can make coffee."

He shook his head. "Hold off on the coffee for a minute."

I tilted my head, taking in his controlled expression. He was in cop mode again. "All right. What's up?"

"I found the flower on the welcome mat outside."

I looked at the bloom, a deep, bloody red. "Okay."

"Red poppies are symbolic of death and sleep." His eyes were intense on my face.

I waited for the rest.

He huffed an exasperated breath. "It's his calling card, Cassidy."

15

Death and Dear Old Dad

That one slid home. Suddenly, his behavior made more sense. If the killer left the flower here, that meant he knew I was staying here. And he'd left it sometime between when Skylar left and Drew arrived, which meant he was watching the place. I flopped down onto the couch, the blood draining from my face.

Drew was eerily still. "He leaves them on the body after he's killed them."

I looked up. "But this is different."

He nodded, sighing a little. "He's never left the flower at the victim's house before."

"So why now? What does it mean?" I was grateful there was no tremor in my voice.

He shook his head and rubbed the back of his neck. "Besides that he knows you're here? I don't know. Maybe he wants *you* to know he knows. Scare you a little."

"Well, it worked."

He grimaced, ran his hands over his face.

I waited a beat to ask the question I wanted to. I knew what it might do, to ask him to remember. "What does he do to them?" My voice was quiet, but his head snapped up.

"You sure you want to know?"

I mulled it over. Yes, it was frightening to think that this man was fixated on me, that he knew where I was. But what if his method gave me a hint, helped me to know what could happen? Maybe I was just morbid. "I think I do."

Drew looked at me for a long time, his lips pressed together. Finally, he came and sat next to me on the couch. Still, he waited to start, either to gather the facts in his mind or to steel himself against remembering the details he'd probably rather forget.

"He stalks them for a while, learns their habits because he always takes them when they're alone, during routine activities. One girl was an avid runner. He snatched her from one of the trails she frequented."

I thought back to the woman I'd seen running earlier, the one I'd seen the day before at the same time. Lucky for her she was a brunette.

"He keeps them for a couple of days. Uses a knife to make superficial cuts all over them. We guess it's some sort of thrill he gets from that. Then he strangles them. Cuts them more. Deeper." He took a shaky breath. "There's never any evidence that he's. . . violated them or anything."

Small mercies, I thought. But that didn't matter. Not to Drew. Not when it had happened to someone he cared about.

He took a breath, more steady this time. "After that, he dumps them. Always within a block of the station. Like he's baiting us."

"Did Evan find her? Cassidy, I mean."

He sighed. "Not exactly. He was pretty distraught after she

was taken. He was always checking in with me, always coming around the station. So when we found her, he was not far behind. Saw her all. . ."

"Cut up," I supplied, remembering Evan's words.

He nodded and swallowed hard.

I couldn't even imagine, struggled with how to comfort him in this. "It must have been hard seeing her like that," I said softly.

His gaze remained fixed on the coffee table, and I wondered if that was the image he was seeing.

I touched his arm. "I'm really sorry."

He looked at me for a fraction of a second. "I almost got pulled off the case, even though I'd been working it up until then. Conflict of interest. But I have to see it through now. I have to get this guy."

No doubt, this meant that he would put more constraints on my movements, not that I'd had much freedom there anyway. But it was likely he'd have someone babysit me twenty-four-seven. Which meant leaving would be doubly hard.

I admitted some part of me was grateful that someone actually cared about my safety.

Something he said nagged at the back of my mind. "If he's dumping them so close to the station, is there not a way to keep track of likely places?"

"We've got our tech guy on security cameras from the local businesses, and we have someone patrolling regularly. But it's like he knows what we're up to. We're considering the possibility that he's got a line on the inside."

The idea made my stomach twist. "That's an unpleasant thought."

"No kidding." He looked grim. "It means I'm going to have

to keep a closer watch on you. I don't know who I can trust to keep things on the down-low."

"I was afraid of that."

"Is my presence that much of a burden?" There was a small smile playing about his lips, but the humor didn't reach his eyes.

"Only when it means I'm cooped up all the time," I said. "Or I'm stuck in the middle of a macho man showdown."

That wiped the smile from his face, and he looked down. "I'm sorry about that. A lot of emotions flying around."

"I'm not blaming anybody. I'm just saying."

He leaned back into the couch and scrubbed his hands over his face. "How did this get so messed up?"

I raised my hand. "Guilty as charged."

His hands plopped into his lap. "This isn't your fault."

"Maybe not directly. But it *is* because of me."

"That doesn't mean you deserve to be ambushed."

I shrugged and picked at the seam of my jeans. "To be fair, he didn't really know the extent of the situation."

"No, I guess not," he conceded. "And neither did your parents. Her parents," he corrected himself.

"What do you say to a woman you've never met and a man who left you all alone when you were eight years old?" I wondered aloud.

He waited a long beat. "I'd ask him why."

I looked at him. I'd forgotten he'd said his father left his family, too. The one person in the world who would actually know what it felt like. But I shook my head. "I don't care why."

"You're still angry."

It sounded like an accusation, and my temper snapped into my words. "Aren't you?"

He leaned forward to rest his elbows on his knees and clasped his hands. His dark gaze lingered there and mine followed. I noted the callouses, the hard lines of his long fingers. Working man hands.

"Sometimes," he answered finally. "More that he left my mom with the responsibility of raising me and my sister alone. She worked two jobs to keep the house so we wouldn't have to move."

I exhaled, trying to breathe out my frustration. I wasn't sure I would be as okay with it as he seemed to be. But there was something to be said about having at least one parent. I'd been left alone, to be raised by strangers. Some of them kind, some of them not.

"Plus, it kind of made me who I am today," he said, interrupting my thoughts.

"What do you mean?"

He lifted one shoulder. "For a long time, I was obsessed with finding him. I researched, dug deep, tracked his every move starting the day he left. I was a one-man missing persons unit. I learned I had a knack for detective work."

"Did you ever find him?"

"Yeah, I did." His words hung heavy in the air, incomplete, but he didn't seem keen to elaborate.

But I wanted to know. "Did you ask him why?"

He shook his head slowly, eyes still focused on his interlaced fingers like they were the most fascinating things in the world. "He was dead by then."

I sucked in a breath before I could stop myself.

"They labeled it suspicious, but there wasn't much of an investigation. He certainly didn't seem to be living life on the up and up, but who's to say for sure?"

I didn't know what to say. Maybe because the idea had never crossed my mind that something like that could have happened to my father. Or maybe because I still didn't understand Drew's desire. Here was the chance that he wished he had, but I couldn't bring myself to take it.

Still angry. Yeah, I was angry, all right.

"Honestly, it was your dad who stepped up to do some of the fatherly things mine wasn't around for." There was an imploring note in his voice.

I worked to keep myself neutral, could only manage a noncommittal sound.

He plowed on. "Since they lived a couple of houses down, he often checked to see if my mom needed help with projects around the house, coached my baseball team every year through high school, even taught me how to change the oil in my car."

"What a good Samaritan," I said in a flat voice. Every part of me clenched, reigning in the hostility at the thought that someone got even the dregs of my father's attention where I'd had nothing.

"He's a good guy," he insisted. "You could give him a chance," he added when I said nothing.

I stood up. It seemed like a good time to make coffee, maybe have some breakfast. Or throw some dishes at the wall.

He stood to follow me. "He might be able to help you understand why—"

I spun on my heel to glare at him. "He was grieving, and he couldn't handle it!" *Couldn't handle me*, I added silently. "What else is there to understand?"

Drew froze, staring at me in silence.

I turned back to the kitchen to start the process of making

the coffee, all while trying to regulate my breathing, to cool the heat that coursed through me. I slammed through cupboards, further incensed that I still couldn't remember how Skylar had everything organized.

A drop of wetness fell onto my hand, and I reached up to my cheek to find unexpected tears running down my face.

"Do you want some help?" Drew asked softly.

I swiped at my cheeks and cleared my throat. "No. I've got it."

He lurched forward at the sight of my tears, but I turned away, deciding to get myself some breakfast when I failed to find the supplies for making coffee. I pulled a bowl down.

"Do you want some cereal?" I asked without looking at him.

"No, I'm fine."

I spun to the fridge to pull a cereal box down, but he was there, grabbing it for me. I jerked my hand back as if I'd touched a hot stove. He held the box out to me, and I snatched it from him, spinning away. I willed the redness to recede from my cheeks, but the heat stubbornly burned on.

"I'm sorry I pushed," he said after a moment.

I concentrated harder on pouring the cereal.

"I think I'm just jealous that you get a second chance with your dad, and I don't."

I glanced at him as I turned to the fridge for milk. He was angled away from me, and I wondered if it was hard for him to admit that.

I poured the milk, fighting the monster of resentment back into chains. "What if I don't want a second chance? I mean, he might not even have the answers for something a different version of himself did, anyway."

His dark eyes flickered to my face. "Wouldn't it be worth a

try?"

I stuck out my chin and grabbed my cereal bowl, using the time it took to walk from the tiny kitchen to the dining room table to avoid answering. Could I move past more than a decade of bitterness to give this man a chance? *Was* it worth a try? Just because he yearned for a do-over didn't mean I did. I set my bowl down as the red poppy caught my eye, bringing my attention back to the whole reason Drew was even there.

Here we were, talking about damaged relationships with our fathers when there was a more pressing matter at hand: a murderer had me in his sights. We had thought I was safe, that he didn't know where I was. Or that I even existed. How confused would this guy be to see one of his victims up and walking around like it never happened? Or would it be like some sort of jackpot—to get to track and kill the same person twice, relive the sick obsession?

"Lose your appetite?" Drew asked.

I flinched. "Yeah, well. . ." I gestured to the flower.

I felt him come up behind me. He reached over to grab it and crush it in his hand.

I balked. "Isn't that, like, evidence?"

"Of what? It's a common poppy. No identifying markers, nothing unique to track." He stuffed the bruised bloom into his pocket. His tone hinted that they'd been through it all before.

"What about fingerprints?"

He shook his head. "It's nearly impossible to pull anything from an organic surface like a flower. Besides, it would take months to get it analyzed at a lab. It's not like on TV. The process is more hassle than it's worth."

"So, then, what's the next move?"

16

Candid Camera

"I still don't see why I had to come with you. Isn't there some drop-in daycare you could leave me at?" I folded my arms, my incognito hat resting in my lap.

Drew slid a glance in my direction. "Very funny. Put your feet down." He slapped at my boots which I'd placed on the dashboard. "And stop pouting."

I dropped my feet and straightened in my seat as we pulled to a stop at the station. "I'm not pouting," I muttered.

He squinted up the steps toward the station as I yanked the same scarf up higher around my neck and slid the hat on. He opened his door.

"I can stay in the car," I offered, tucking my red hair away.

He paused in the act and gave me an exasperated look. "Don't make me handcuff you."

"It's deja vu," I said under my breath as I sighed and opened my own door. I followed Drew up the stairs, wondering if this was a better option if what he suspected was true about the killer having an inside man at the station. It was yet another opportunity for people who knew the other Cassidy to see me.

But I supposed the killer already had a line on my whereabouts, and Drew was willing to chance it to keep an eye on me. The rest was just a nuisance.

Drew shoved open the door and scanned the lobby. People were bustling around. A woman in uniform sat at the front desk, her hair pulled back in an austere bun that added an extra edge to her already sharp features. Her eyes were lasered in on a handcuffed teenager sitting on a bench nearby.

Her tight gaze snapped up to me as I followed Drew. He stopped in at the lab where I'd been fingerprinted.

"Creedy," he said to the young guy, the same one with the flop of brown hair. "You're exactly the guy I want to talk to. Can you find any traffic cameras on the corner of 5th and Cherry, any others at Cherry Street Apartments we might have access to?"

"Something you're looking for?" Creedy asked, glancing at me standing behind Drew.

"I'm not sure yet," Drew answered. "Just a case I'm working."

Creedy lifted a shoulder. "I'll see what I can do."

Drew slapped Creedy's shoulder and continued to lead me into the chaos of the station. He stopped at a desk that was kept meticulously clean. He pawed through the drawers with the ease of intimate familiarity.

"Sit." He nodded to his desk chair without bringing his eyes to my face.

"I'm not a Labrador," I said, crossing my arms.

He gave me the squinty cowboy look as he rubbed an envelope he'd pulled out between his forefinger and thumb. "Sit. Stay."

I stuck out my chin in defiance, squared my stance.

The cowboy look turned into a cowboy grin, but instead of arguing, he headed to the back of the room, to an enclosed office. When he shut the door, the name on it told me it was the captain's office.

I rolled my eyes, incensed enough to spite him by staying where I was until another officer hollered "coming through!" and shoved by me. The handcuffed woman he brought with him glared at me as they passed, and I begrudgingly sat in the chair to avoid being in the way.

Because I was childish and because Drew took longer than I anticipated, I decided to rearrange the items on his desk. In one of his drawers, he had a small container of paper clips. I made it my mission to link every single one of them.

I finished linking the last one and stuffed the chain back into its container and then the drawer. I tapped my fingernails on the desk for all of thirty seconds and glanced toward the office Drew disappeared into, pursing my lips.

It was clear he wouldn't be coming back anytime soon. So I got up and wandered toward the break room on the other side of the room. A few people were scattered around, talking, getting coffee, eating breakfast.

There were bagels on a platter on the counter next to the coffee maker. I moved in that direction, boredom disguising itself as hunger. I examined my options as voices swelled around me.

"I took her to a movie," a man was saying.

I glanced over at him and his companion.

"A movie for a first date?" his friend asked, sliding in next to me to get to the coffee. I took a step back, and he raised a brow at me, smiled.

"What's wrong with that?" the other guy asked, defensive.

The friend made a face but schooled his features before he turned around. "Nothing. But it doesn't leave a lot of room for conversation. Isn't the point to get to know her?"

"Aw, Chelton's a romantic," someone from the other side of the room crowed.

His eyes darkened. "Actually, it's for *her* benefit. You know any woman who's willing to, uh, spend the night when you haven't heard all the adorable names for her cat?" When his gaze flickered to me, I knew he'd cleaned up the description.

I smirked and snatched a bagel from the platter, sliding into the nearest chair, out of the way.

Creedy came in after that, packed lunch in hand.

"Ask Creedy, here. He's got a way with women," Chelton said.

Creedy smiled at the praise, a humble-brag grin as he slid his lunch into the communal fridge.

"All right," the movie date guy said. "Creedy, how do you get a lady in an *agreeable* mood?"

Creedy shrugged. "I take them for a tour of the city."

"What?" Chelton asked as his companion barked out a laugh.

"No, seriously," Creedy insisted, not even offended. "Old Main is my favorite. My dad was an architect so I know all about the old buildings, history, all that. You do something like that, she thinks you're an intellectual powerhouse."

Chelton laughed. "That won't work for Wagner. There is no way anyone would believe he's an intellectual anything."

Wagner punched Chelton in the shoulder.

I smiled and tore a piece of bagel, looking around at the others in the room who laughed at the exchange. My gaze froze on a man in the corner, sitting alone. He was watching the group intently.

The hair on the back of my neck stood up. I'd swear I'd seen him before, but I wasn't sure where. That day in the street? When I'd encountered Evan? Same hooked nose, wavy, slicked-back hair.

I stood, moving toward the door, uncomfortable.

"Hey, you're a lady," Wagner said, stopping me.

I looked down at him. "Astute observation."

Chelton guffawed.

"You think a movie is a good first date?" Wagner continued.

"Sure, why not?" I responded, eager to get back to Drew's desk. I glanced back at the guy in the corner, a chill running through me. What was it Drew had said? They thought their killer had an inside man. Maybe the killer *was* the inside man.

I turned my attention forward just in time to run into someone. Strong hands gripped my arms to keep me from losing my balance. Drew stared down at me in surprise, then his gaze darkened.

"What are you doing?" he asked. He wasn't quite angry, but he had that authoritative tone that made me bristle.

Still, at this proximity, only inches apart, I could smell the soap on his skin, feel the heat of his hands on my arms. He dropped them quickly as if he could sense the direction my thoughts had gone.

"I was bored waiting for you," I said. "You're not supposed to keep a lady waiting."

"I'll make a note of it." He leaned around me to peek into the break room. "Creedy, you get that footage for me?"

Creedy's gaze snapped to Drew. "Give me a minute."

Drew nodded and led me back to his desk and bent forward to wiggle the mouse and wake the computer up. "Good bagel?" he asked.

"Kind of stale." I dropped it into his trash can.

"Hmm," he said absently, logging in to get to his desktop.

I looked toward the break room as Creedy walked out. The man from the corner came out right behind him. He cast a look at me before heading in a different direction.

"Who's that?" I asked.

"Who?" Drew glanced up, catching sight of the man's retreating back. "Oh, Russo? He's on vice."

I kept my eyes on Russo until he disappeared into the lobby and out the front doors.

Creedy joined us, offering me a smile. "You want me to pull it up here?" he asked Drew.

"If you can. I want my friend here to take a look at it."

"Sure."

Drew stepped aside so that Creedy could sit in his chair to work his magic, then shifted to stand behind him. His eyes sharpened in that cop way that always made criminals squirm. I had to fight the urge to shift my feet. I wasn't under that scrutiny. This time.

"Check between 7 am and 9 am this morning," Drew instructed.

Creedy nodded, his fingers flying over the keys, his hand twitching at the mouse.

"Stop there," Drew said. "You see that?"

Creedy leaned forward and squinted at the screen.

Drew put his palms down on the desk to look closer. "Yeah, that might be him." He looked at me, nodding for me to come check it out.

I moved closer, also looking over Creedy's shoulder. The view was from a camera set at the entrance to the hall in Skylar's building. A man walked into the hallway, wearing a bulky coat and a black cap. He was in and out within a minute, but his face wasn't visible from any angle.

"You see this guy wandering around the complex before?" Drew asked me, straightening.

I squinted. Maybe the guy who walked his dog every day. But he always wore a hoodie, no cap. I shrugged. "I couldn't say for sure."

"What about traffic cams nearby?" he asked Creedy. "Catch the guy driving away? Walking somewhere? Anything?"

Creedy typed some more, flipped through screens from various angles, and stopped. "Maybe this one?"

We both leaned in. It was definitely the same guy, and his face was tilted up a little bit.

"Can you zoom in?" Drew asked.

Creedy typed again, and the picture was enlarged, pixelated and choppy. Still, his features were obscured except for his mouth, which was curved into a wicked grin, face lifted at exact the right angle to catch the smile and nothing else. It was not the sort of smile you ever wanted to be close enough to witness in person. It made my stomach turn.

17

Victimized

"That son of a bitch knew exactly where the camera would be," Drew growled. "Can you print this out? Even if we don't have a clear image, it could help us."

Creedy nodded right as his watch beeped out an alert. He checked it, the glowing face illuminating his speculative expression, then focused back on the computer. "I'll see if I can clean the picture up and print it for you guys." He stood and headed back for his office.

"Thanks." Drew slid into his own chair and brooded at the image on the screen. He must have been livid, recognizing that smile as a taunt. He would take it personally, more so than anyone else because he'd lost a friend to this man.

The longer I gazed at the picture, the more my skin began to crawl, sweat slicking my palms. Not only did this guy know where I was staying, but he knew we'd see this picture. Planned for us to find it. He was playing with me. With us.

I was desperate to distract myself, slow my accelerating heart rate. I glanced around the room, looking for anything in the frenzied activity that might catch my attention. "Is it always this busy?" I asked lamely.

He frowned, taking a moment to think through the question. He looked up. "Um, no. Not always. It's been a hectic week."

Yes. Conversation. Keep it going. I grasped at my first thought. "Mr. McGregor escape the nursing home again?"

He blinked. "What?"

"Oh, sorry," I said, remembering. "That was a conversation I had with the *other* you."

His gaze slid around the room, but no one was looking at us.

"Relax," I said. "It's not like I shouted it. Besides, you're the one who brought me in here. Didn't it occur to you that some of them might recognize me?"

He squinted at me, still brooding. "It's a risk I was willing to take. I don't like that this guy knows where you are. I don't want you alone anymore."

I crossed my arms, a heated retort on my tongue.

He spoke before I could. "Don't argue with me." I read the cop's warning in his eyes.

I ground my teeth, not really keen on making a scene in the middle of a police station anyway.

He stood and nodded for me to follow him back through the crowd of the station toward the door. He didn't even check to make sure I did, and a tingle of irritation ran through me. He was way too used to having authority over people.

It was a concerted effort not to make a face at his retreating back, noting once again how childishly I was acting. I could be grumpy about it all I wanted in the presence of twenty cops. But when it came down to it, I was grateful to have someone looking out for me.

The laser-eyed receptionist stared me down as I passed, but I ignored her as I made my way to the door, held open by Drew.

I walked out into the bright sunshine, which was at odds with the winter chill on the wind. Goosebumps broke across my skin at the temperature change, cold air biting at my cheeks and nose.

We walked down the steps to his car in silence. He was shrouded in a melancholy that pulled him deep within his own thoughts. I struggled to find words to break through.

As soon as we got into his car, his phone beeped out a short rhythm. He pulled it out to check the readout.

"Skylar heard back from our sci-fi professor," he said. "She set up a meeting for tomorrow."

"Thank God," I said. "It would be nice to finally get some traction on something. I don't like being at the mercy of someone else."

"I noticed." He started the car and pulled away from the curb.

I jerked my seat belt a little too hard. "There's nothing wrong with wanting to be in control of my own life."

"Yeah, seems like you're really in control. Is that why you're living in your car?"

The question hit me hard, a low blow that nearly knocked the wind out of me. I grabbed onto anger to give me fire.

"You have no idea what you're talking about," I spat. "You're just mad that this guy is playing with you, and you're taking it out on me."

His tone sharpened in response to mine. "No, I really want to know exactly how running is being in control. Because that's what you're doing, isn't it? Running?"

"I am not going to talk to you about this," I said, folding my arms across my chest.

"Fine."

We fell silent, but the frustration crackled on the air, hot and stinging. I stewed in it, getting angrier the longer we stayed silent. How dare he bring that up, criticize *my* life choices? He had no idea why I did what I did, and this was not the way to find out.

I shifted in my seat, wanting to move, to hit something, scream, run, anything; my anger was always an energizer. I glanced at him out of the corner of my eye. He was the opposite, still and focused as he drove, eyes narrowed.

I reminded myself of what I'd witnessed at the station, that he'd just seen the man who'd brutally murdered his friend taunting him, barely out of reach. It didn't make what he said right, but I could at least understand the desire to direct that anger.

Hell, I was being anything but pliable about the whole situation. But, man, anger was easier than fear. Sadness. Loneliness.

The car slowed, and I focused on where we were. A townhouse I didn't recognize sat nestled between a row of copies of itself.

"Your place?" I guessed.

He glanced out the windshield. "Yeah."

He unbuckled and got out of the car, and I frowned, doing the same. The large window in the front was covered by blinds, but the long, vertical slats moved at the edge as a nose nudged them aside and pressed a wet print against the glass. Immediately, my heart fluttered.

"You have a dog." I smiled, grateful for the distraction.

"I do." He pulled out his key and unlocked the door.

I was expecting to be bombarded by an exuberant furball, but Drew led me into his house with no impediments. It took my eyes a moment to adjust to the dim light of his living room, but I still spotted the German Shepherd sitting at the base of the stairs patiently; the only movement was his tail whacking the carpeted floor.

With a hand gesture, Drew signaled the dog, who calmly walked forward to investigate me. I waited while his nose traveled over each of my legs, my hands.

"He's well-trained," I commented, sensing that I would need approval before I could pet him.

Drew tossed his keys into a bowl on a table beside the door. "Retired police dog."

"Ah."

"Wil, sit."

The dog obeyed without hesitation and gazed up at me with lazy curiosity.

"Wil?" I repeated, watching his head tilt at his name.

"Short for Wilhelm."

"Cute."

"You can pet him now."

I reached out to stroke the top of his head, and he lifted it in eager anticipation, giving my palm slow, happy licks. I smiled, letting the dog melt my dark mood.

"You want something to drink?" He was being polite, detached. I couldn't tell if it was because he was still mad or because he was calling a truce.

"What do you have?" I asked, matching his tone.

"Water, tea, beer."

"Water's fine."

He stalked off, past the stairs, to the kitchen I could see around the corner.

I knelt to give the dog a solid scratching behind both ears and let my gaze wander the room. It was sparsely decorated—not surprising given his profession and his bachelorhood. The furniture looked well-loved, to put it nicely. Probably leftovers from college days.

Out of my periphery, I saw Drew walk back in with two glasses in hand then stop, gazing down at me.

"I'm spoiling him."

"He's definitely not starved for attention."

I didn't look at him, didn't stand to take my water. Instead, I took in the pleased furry face before me, rubbing my fingers through the dog's thick coat. It was soothing.

"I'm sorry I was a jerk," Drew said after a moment.

I raised my eyes.

"You were right. I was worked up over the case, and I was picking a fight." He tapped a finger against one of the glasses then set them both on the coffee table. "But I wasn't lying. I really want to know."

I turned back to Wil, concentrating on his beatific face, tongue lolling out of his mouth.

"You *are* on the run, aren't you?"

"Not at the moment," I answered.

He sighed. "Cassidy—"

I stood. "Fine, yes. Does that make you feel better? To have me admit it?"

His eyes softened. "No. It doesn't."

The silence stretched, and I wrapped my arms around myself as if I could deflect the question I knew he would ask next.

"Who are you running from?"

Who, not what. Like he knew. Like he could see right through to that exposed vein. I shut my eyes, tried to gather the broken parts of myself, hide them from view. It didn't matter who did the breaking or why. There was shame all over those jagged edges and a kind of pride, and he'd seen it the whole time.

I chewed my lip, and the dog shifted restlessly behind me, probably affected by the tension in the room. Light peeked through the blinds in thin lines like claw marks on the floor. I watched the slats swing slightly as the air blew up from the heating vent in the floor.

"His name is Callum Gallagher," I finally said. The rest of the explanation caught in my throat like it was coated in glue. Flashbacks assaulted me. Words hurled like weapons, angry fists, ripped clothing.

"Cassidy?" Drew's voice had gentled.

I reminded myself that he was a cop who dealt with victims all the time. *Victim.* The word almost made me gag. More than feeling helpless and weak under that label, I was humiliated. I had promised myself that I would never go back to that place, never be powerless again. I was no longer going to give someone else the control.

To salvage my pride, I turned, my steady gaze meeting his. I would tell him. I would do this without flinching because that's what a strong person did. "He's an ex-boyfriend. A criminal, though I didn't know it when I started seeing him. He's charming, clever. Took him years to get caught, and it was only a minor charge." I paused, and that harsh promise whispered through my memory.

Drew waited patiently.

"I tried to break free of him so many times. He always dragged me back." I had to break eye contact this time. The admission sent another stab of shame through me. I hated to even think about it, let alone talk about it. To admit it now cost me the steadiness I'd started with. I dropped into a soft, well-worn recliner, and Wil shuffled up to lay his face in my lap.

To give me something to do, I looked down at his sweet face and stroked the soft fur of his ears. "When they arrested him, he just grinned at me. Before they took him away, he whispered in my ear. He said he would always find me."

Drew softened, his eyes cautious. "Was it verbal? Controlling behavior?" he asked, but he sounded dubious enough that I could tell he knew there was more.

God, why did I have to admit it all, show how weak I had been, how someone had actually controlled me like that? I shut my eyes, my chest aching. I pressed my hand against my ribs where they'd been broken once, remembering the excruciating pain.

"There was more," he guessed.

I opened my eyes and caught his gaze locked on the hand at my rib cage. I dropped it.

He sank into the couch, careful, calm.

Wil whined slightly, shifting his feet.

I scrubbed under his chin to reassure him. "He was a pretty scary guy when he wanted to be. Looked and acted like the nicest person in public. Very. . . affectionate." I said the word with disgust, hating how I'd always felt. The way he'd pet, hold my hand. But it was torture acting like it was all fine.

Drew's nostrils flared, a reaction to the look on my face as much as what I'd said.

I focused on petting the dog, whose eyes, liquid chocolate, silently communicated his support.

"Why didn't you go to the police?" His words were low, still careful. "I know it doesn't seem like they can do much, but there's a protocol we could follow, a—"

"I had no real proof," I interrupted, my voice rising a notch. "And a restraining order is only a piece of paper. I figured I'd have better luck on my own."

He shook his head. "There may have been more they could've done. If he's a criminal, your information may have tipped the hand in an investigation you don't know about."

I stared at him. "And if they couldn't nail him, he'd come after me for revenge."

"They could've put you in protective custody."

I shook my head. "You're an idealist."

He crossed his arms over his chest to deflect my accusation. "I am not. I know the system is broken, but that doesn't mean it never works. Just give it a chance to."

"If you say so," I answered, still entrenched in my skepticism. I had no doubt he was part of that minority with the purest of motives that believed he could enact justice in spite of the obstacles. And he would do as much as he could to accomplish that. But it changed nothing for me.

He shook his head, but he was careful about what emotions he showed me, and I hated that he was walking on eggshells.

"It doesn't matter anyway. He can't hurt me here. This only bothers you because you can't separate her and me. Before I got here, you didn't even know I existed."

Pain flashed into his eyes. "If he hurt you there, he may be hurting someone else here."

I scoffed. "So what are you going to do?"

"I can make some calls to other precincts. If you know about his activities—"

"You expect me to help?" I surged to my feet, and Wil stumbled backward with a grumble.

"Easy, Wil," Drew said, taking his eyes from me to lock them with his dog. Wil sat, intently focused on us. Drew turned to me again. "I won't make you do anything you don't want to."

I swallowed. Why wouldn't I want to help someone else escape from a man like Callum? Why wouldn't I want him to be locked away, in any universe, for however long we could nail him for?

I dug my thumb against the side of my ribs where they ached. Why was I resisting so much? Selfish girl.

Scared girl.

"Just give it some thought," Drew said, breaking into my inner monologue.

I looked at him but struggled to find an argument, to find a cutting word to wipe the kindness off of his face, to take the pity out of his gaze. Because I was no longer only the counterfeit version of his childhood friend. I was now a victim to help.

18

Wil Gets All the Ladies

I watched the weatherman, in his pressed black suit, gesture vaguely as he described the snowstorm that was headed our way. It's what they'd been talking about for twenty minutes as I'd avoided eye contact with Drew and gave all of my focus to petting his dog, who sat at my feet with a blissful look on his face.

I could tell Drew wanted to say something to me, but my continued silence seemed enough of an indication of my mood and my willingness to talk. He gave up and retreated to his office up the stairs, muttered something about checking in at work.

Wil stayed with me. But after a while, it was too quiet, even with the drone of the weather report in the background. I made my way up the stairs, pausing on the first landing to look at the pictures set in a large frame. There were several of Drew and his family. One was old, wrinkled. It wasn't surprising since it was a picture of the whole family. I imagined motherly hands shaking as they crumpled the picture that represented a promise broken. It was surprising it was even still intact.

I touched the glass covering the photo, seeing the clear resemblance between Drew and his father.

"I had to fish it out of the trashcan."

I turned to see Drew standing at the top of the stairs, hands in his pockets.

"My mom said she didn't have the heart to rip it up or burn it. I wouldn't have blamed her if she had."

"Weren't you angry?" I asked.

He frowned and came down the few steps to the landing. "Not at first. I think I was mostly confused and hurt. I was really close to him, and it didn't seem real."

I turned back to look at the picture. If I thought hard enough about it, I supposed the anger came later, after I'd been in that first foster home for a bit, realizing that he wasn't coming back to get me.

"I remember watching her." His voice was soft, his focus on the picture. "She was standing in the living room, crying. Della was in bed, and I'd gotten up to get a drink of water. I stopped right at the end of the hallway because I saw her standing there. She grabbed the picture frame like she was going to hurl it across the room. But she just ripped the back out and crushed the picture and threw it in the trash."

"Then you saved it."

He nodded. "I put it in a book he'd given me, trying to flatten it out. But I forgot about it. Or maybe I chose to." He shrugged one shoulder. "I don't know. I didn't touch the book again until I moved out for college."

"Are you glad you did?"

"It's in the frame, isn't it?" He gave me a sad half-smile.

I chewed on my lip for a moment, puzzling over his ability to forgive the man who walked out on his family.

"Were you coming upstairs for a reason?"

I brought my eyes up to meet his. For someone who was a pro at pushing people away, it seemed ridiculous for me to admit I'd felt lonely.

"I guess I decided to help," I said after a moment. "I'll help you find Callum."

"You don't have to," he said softly.

I shook my head. "But I should."

"Take some more time to think about it."

I nodded.

He seemed like he wanted to say something else, pausing beside me instead of brushing past to head the rest of the way down the stairs. Warmth buzzed between us, and I fought a weird urge to touch him. But he pressed his lips together and continued walking down the steps. Wil was sitting at the base and stood as Drew approached, his tail swaying lazily back and forth.

"Oh, you're my buddy now, are you?" Drew said, casting a glance my way as I started down after him.

I gave him a small grin. "You're still the one who feeds him. I'm sure that counts for something."

"Only at dinner time," he said, squinting as Wil wagged his tail harder and walked up to me. He tucked his head eagerly under my hand.

I obliged, offering a shrug to Drew.

"Thought so." He turned to head into his kitchen and muttered, "Traitor."

I knelt and gave Wil a good scrub all over his body, and his tongue flopped out while he grinned.

"If you keep spoiling him, he'll walk right out that door with you. I don't even think he'll care if you feed him or not." Drew leaned against the wall, a beer in hand.

I looked up. "I don't mind letting you come over to feed him."

"Gee, thanks."

Wil suddenly closed his mouth, pointed ears perking up.

"Wilhelm, here." Drew straightened, patting his leg once. The dog immediately obeyed, his eyes locked on the front door.

The knob turned, and the door swung open to reveal Skylar bundled in a puffy winter coat that seemed to swallow her up. Her nose and cheeks were a wind-bitten pink.

"It's cold out there!" she said as she spun to shut the front door. "I think they said it's going to snow tonight. I'm not surprised; it smells like cow crap. You know, like it always does right before the first snow." She unwrapped the scarf from her neck. "I read somewhere that it's because of the wind blowing from the north, you know, where all the farms are."

"Are you going to get a breath in there somewhere?" I asked, standing.

She glanced at me as she unzipped her coat, but there was a smile on her face. "Sorry. I talk when I'm cold. I think there's a fact somewhere in my head that any kind of movement keeps me warm, even if it's just my lips. It's a killer on a first date."

I had no response, not sure if I even understood her logic, but I was distracted by the soft whine that came from Wil.

Skylar hung up her coat in the closet, grinning. She knelt and opened her arms.

Wil looked up at Drew, who raised a brow. "All right. Fine."

The dog bulleted into Skylar's arms.

"Apparently he likes all women more than he likes me." Drew folded his arms across his chest.

"Maybe you need to get him a girlfriend," I suggested.

"Then he might care a lot less about us."

Skylar stood. "He still listens when you give him commands."

"I'm not convinced he wouldn't listen to either of you out of sheer devotion."

"Love is greater than fear," I said as the dog made his way back to me to lean his weight against my leg.

"Apparently." Drew narrowed his eyes on the dog.

"So, you have news," I said, turning to Skylar, who was watching the exchange with a smirk.

The smirk brightened. "Oh, yeah. I made an appointment with Dr. Thibald again for tomorrow morning."

"The question is whether he's got any more of an idea of what to do from here. I'm not even sure I understand anything he's said so far." I stroked the dog's thick coat as I spoke.

"There's so much more than on theories involved in this. I'm not sure we'll ever fully understand what happened," Drew said. "Who knows if we can even make it happen again?"

"Well, I don't think it matters much either way. I'm not staying regardless."

Skylar's bright expression dimmed as she looked at Drew. He took a breath like he was going to say something, to agree or to protest I wasn't sure. But he snapped his mouth shut. Instead, he rubbed the back of his neck and locked at the floor.

Their trepidation frustrated me. "We don't have to tip-toe around it. That was the whole point, wasn't it? To send me back? And if we can't, the only other option is for me to leave, let you all get back to your lives."

"It doesn't have to be," Skylar said. Her face was too earnest, and I knew I wouldn't be able to trust their judgment on this topic. Because even though I was not really their friend, I was close enough to make them forget their aching grief, and that might seem worth it to them. For now. Someday, the differences would be too much, too disparate to protect them from the eventual disappointment I would be.

Drew spoke up as I remained silent. "Let's wait and see what the professor says. That isn't our only option."

I kept my mouth shut. Let them have their delusion. That way I wouldn't have to deal with the drama of the aftermath. It didn't matter what he said, I wasn't going to stick around for the day they realized I couldn't be what they wanted. I stuffed my hands into my pockets and maintained my silence.

The two exchanged another look but let it go.

"So. . . how about dinner?" Skylar said, stumbling over changing the subject.

Wil's ears perked up from beside me.

Drew eyed the dog. "Not for you, dummy."

"Sorry, buddy," I said, giving the top of his head a scratch. "I could eat," I responded, looking up.

"My eyes are open, aren't they?" Drew said, the seriousness sliding away.

"Out somewhere?" Skylar asked.

Drew winced, tilting his head. "Ahhh. . ."

Skylar raised an eyebrow. "C'mon. We can't keep her locked in the basement like some sort of prisoner."

"I'm not sure I want to expose her like that. I already brought her to the station after the situation this morning."

"What situation?" Skylar demanded.

The color drained from my face, and she looked at me like I had kept something from her.

"What happened?" She turned to Drew.

"When I got to your place this morning, I found a flower on

the doorstep. The same kind as the ones he left on the bodies."

Skylar balked. "He knows where she is."

They shared a silent communication, all in the eyes, and I stood like an outsider not understanding the deep connection that came from years of friendship. Again.

"I bet he's just as confused about me being here as we are," I quipped, trying to cover the anxiety I felt.

Skylar stared at me, incredulous.

"Actually," Drew said slowly, rubbing a finger over his bottom lip. "That might work to our advantage."

Skylar's brows shot up. "What do you mean?"

"Her presence here is a distraction. If he's fixated on her, he's not stalking anyone else. And it might cause him to slip up, make a mistake."

I tilted my head slightly, considering. Of course, I didn't know nearly as much as Drew did about murderers and how they worked, but the situation was enough to throw anyone off. Could it be the key to nailing the killer?

"But how do we catch him in his mistake?" I wondered aloud.

Drew's pensive expression sharpened, and he raised a brow. "There's no 'we' here, Cass."

The trickle of anger started at the back of my throat. "I don't get a say in this now?"

"*I'm* the cop." He jabbed his hands into his chest. "It's *my* job to catch the bad guys. You have no role."

"The very fact that I'm here means I have a role. The flower on Skylar's doorstep this morning has dragged me into this, and I don't know if I can just sit back. At least let me be part of the offense."

"No." He seemed to grow taller as he stared me down.

It only served to fuel my growing anger. "You think you're in charge because you wear the badge, so you have the final say in all of it. But this affects me too. I'm the one who dies if he gets his hands on me."

Drew's face hardened at my words, but I didn't regret them yet.

I stomped toward the closet to grab my borrowed coat, threw Skylar hers.

"Should we really be going back to my house?" Skylar asked. "If the killer knows you've been staying there?"

"Skylar's right," Drew said. "We have to find you somewhere else to stay."

I froze, every muscle in my body seizing. Anger and fear wrestled for dominance inside me, but I shoved my arms into my coat. "We have no guarantee he wouldn't find me somewhere else even if I could find another place to stay."

"That may be true," Drew said grudgingly. "And I don't trust anyone else with this." His eyes were still alight with his own frustration as he looked at me. "Until we can find you another place, I'll post a couple of guys to watch the place."

"Oh yeah, to babysit your resurrected friend?" I snarled. "Good luck explaining that one."

"I'll tell them something else. They don't need to know the real reason."

"Fine." I yanked the door open, cringing as it slammed against the wall inside, but I was making a statement. Apologizing would come later.

Skylar skipped down the front steps after me, her short legs pumping double-time to catch up with me.

"Slow down, Cass," she panted.

I halted for a moment and glanced back at her.

She was shaking her head.

"What?"

She lifted her shoulders, let them drop. "This is like watching a soap opera."

"Yeah, it really is. And I'm the evil twin ruining everybody's carefully planned lives." It was hard to maintain a bitter tone, though the idea had a ring of truth. "Maybe I can capitalize on this freak phenomenon and write a story arc for *Days of Our Lives* or something."

Skylar pressed the fob on her key ring. "You'd probably make a lot of money."

"Which would not go unappreciated."

She smirked and got into her sporty car.

I followed suit, sliding the passenger seat as far back as it would go to allow for my long legs. My knees still bumped the dash.

"Just when I almost feel like you're *our* Cassidy, you go and remind me that you're someone completely different."

Even though that was probably a good thing that she was able to make the distinction, it stung like a rejection. Like I couldn't live up to the shining example the other Cassidy had set.

"I bet she didn't fight with Drew like that," I said, successfully keeping the bitterness from my tone.

"True, but they also didn't spend nearly this much time together the last few years. She was almost always with Evan."

"Right. Epic love and whatnot. Let me guess, they spent every waking hour together." I chewed on the inside of my cheek.

"Basically," Skylar agreed, glancing in my direction. She sucked in a breath and opened her mouth to say something but shut it again, tilting her head.

"What?" I heard the irritation in my own voice and had to remind myself that I'd left the argument back with Drew.

She shrugged one shoulder, reluctant. "It's just. . . your tone."

I made an effort not to release the long-suffering sigh that built up in the back of my throat. "Sorry. I'm still worked up."

She grimaced. "That's not actually what I mean."

I fisted my hands, edgy about what I knew must be coming.

She pursed her lips as if mulling it over before she said anything. "The way you said 'epic love' makes it sound like you think it's stupid."

I exhaled in a huff. "I don't think it's stupid." The phrase hung in the air, sounding half-finished, while I tried to find what I thought would convey how I really felt. But I wasn't quite sure what I thought.

"It does seem pretty stupid when you've never experienced it," Skylar said as she merged into traffic on the highway. "I haven't. But when you witness it, it kind of gives you some hope for yourself."

I didn't say anything. What I wanted to say stuck in my throat, mired in the acrid knowledge that what I'd experienced would ruin her fantasy. Because I knew better than anyone that something that looked perfect on the outside never meant it actually was behind closed doors.

"Just because you're not *my* Cassidy doesn't mean I don't understand your silence means you're upset."

"It's nothing," I replied, forcing a brief smile.

She glanced at me with a raised brow but let it go.

We sat in silence as I mulled her comment over. No, I didn't think it was stupid. It was just foreign. A tantalizing image of something I'd never had. Epic love. Love at all, I countered. Parents who cared what I did, who pushed me to do better. And a man to adore me, friends to support me.

Bitterness was a solid thing, a heavy stone in my chest. I tried swallowing against it, pressing my knuckles into my sternum.

"Sometimes I think it was too much," Skylar said, her voice careful.

I looked at her. "What was?"

"Evan and Cassidy. It's like the universe thought it was too perfect and had to tear it apart somehow to make the rest of us feel better about our lives." Her cheeks reddened, shame written all over her face.

"And I'm the bitter one?" I asked.

She frowned. "Not bitter, per se. Cynical, maybe. I think that's kind of a given when your parents get divorced when you're 10."

"That probably sucked."

She shrugged. "It was better that way. All they ever did was scream at each other. And my step-parents are pretty great. But still. It kind of makes me feel like nothing can last, you know?"

"Yeah. I do."

"But my parents have been happily remarried for well over a decade each." She looked at me, and there was a speculative look in her eyes. "That makes me believe in second chances."

I gave her a dark look. "Is that what this is about?"

She lifted her shoulders, not taking her eyes from the road. "I was just making conversation."

"I don't know what you're trying to convince me of." My tone was harsher than I meant, but the anger was too close to the surface. "You said yourself that things don't seem to last, that the universe took Cassidy away. I'm not a second chance. I'm a cruel joke sent here to taunt us all about what we can't have."

"That's not what I meant—"

"It doesn't matter," I interrupted, bringing my volume down, but not softening the edge in my voice.

She pressed her lips together, and I could see the tears glistening in her eyes. Still, I offered no apology. Because I was tired. Tired of talking about this, feeling the weight of their grief. Sick of being convinced of this or that, or denied the right to make my own decisions.

It was my turn to decide.

19

Of Dreams and Indecisions

The business district was empty as I walked. The coat I wore was not my own, the snow boots foreign to me. But they kept me warm, so I couldn't complain. Snow swirled around me like I was caught in a snow globe. I had to admit the town was pretty picturesque, so it wouldn't have been a stretch.

The wind picked up, and I started at the sound of a hanging sign banging against the wall of the building it represented.

I pressed a gloved hand to my chest, laughing at myself for being scared.

"Cassidy."

The voice seemed to come on the wind, dancing around me, mocking. My laughter died in my throat as the fear crawled across my skin. I spun to find no one behind me. All I heard was the banging of that damned sign.

The window beside me afforded a clear view into the deli restaurant the sign advertised. It was empty. Lights were on, meats and cheeses on display in an immaculate glass case. No one stood behind the counter.

The voice spoke again: "I will find you."

I whirled again at the sound, but I was alone as before. Still, the fear chased me across the deserted street to the music shop, and I burst through the door. My heart hammered a syncopated beat to the Led Zeppelin song that played softly through their PA system.

"Hello?" I called.

Guitars hung in every color along the wall. Brilliant red electrics to deep chocolate acoustics. They shone proudly in the recessed lighting, waiting for adoption, for fingers to lovingly make their strings sing.

When no one answered me, I went toward the back to the door marked "Employees Only." I opened the door, surprised to find it unlocked and the room empty.

I went back to the front door and out into the cold. Someone had to be here. Someone had said my name.

I looked down the street in either direction. No one walked the sidewalks, which I could attribute to the temperature, but no cars came from either direction. In fact, it seemed too quiet; the distant sound of the freeway should have been a soft whisper in the background, but I heard nothing but my own breathing, too close. Any window that offered a view inside the shops showed that no one was inside.

I spun again and froze. Across the street stood a man. He was tall, thick, clad in a black wool coat, black beanie pulled over his ears. He stared at me, made no effort to move.

"Cassidy."

His lips didn't move, but my name was a rough caress against my cheek. It had to come from somewhere.

I turned away from him, ready to run. The shops in front of me became a hallway, its darkness familiar and oppressive. I walked slowly, counting on my socked feet to be quiet on the hardwood floor.

If I could just make it past the bedroom, the front door would be within reach. I could be free. The light from the TV splashed flickering blue light on the wall opposite the door. The volume was turned low, which meant he was using it to lull himself to sleep.

One step at a time, one cautious breath to keep me going. I was bathed in the light, and I glanced in, seeing the screen change to a commercial. The blankets were rumpled down around his feet as they always were when he'd fallen asleep, and I sensed the closeness of my victory, freedom a delicious scent on the air.

There was the front door, that innocuous piece of wood between me and my freedom, my escape. It gave me too much hope, and the anticipation distracted me. I forgot to step over that one spot in the floor where the board was loose, where it groaned under the slightest weight.

I winced, listening for the sound of him getting up from the bed, angry at being disturbed, angry that I was sneaking around the house like some kind of criminal.

But I heard nothing, and I kept going, faster now that I was scared.

I reached, one hand stretching before me. If I could reach the knob, get out the door, run, run, *run*.

A hand, rough and calloused, gripped the back of my neck, its expanse more than enough to almost wrap completely around it. He squeezed, and the pain made me weak in the knees, but he held me upright.

"Going somewhere, Cass?" he growled in my ear.

Of course not, I wanted to say. *No, never*. But the pain.

"It doesn't matter if you go. I will find you." He ground

the words through his teeth, the gravel in his voice like rocks against rocks.

I will find you.

I jerked awake with a gasp. But it was never like in the movies. There was no thrashing, no sitting bolt upright in bed, no scream on my lips. Only inner turmoil, a stormy sea inside. Cold fear settled like a ship, sunk to the bottom, everyone drowned.

The heater kicked on, and I glanced toward the vent across the room where it groaned and hissed the warm air out through metal teeth.

My heart stopped, squeezed in a vise at the sight of the figure in the chair across the room from me, head propped in one hand, long legs stretched in front of him, waiting or sleeping. It didn't matter which.

He lifted his head to look at me—could he see me awake in the darkness? That didn't matter either. The panic crashed over me in a wave from that turbulent sea. I would be forced to bend to his whim. I would never really escape. He was always right.

"Are you awake?" he asked.

I sucked in a breath. That wasn't his voice. No, it was too tender, too kind. And I remembered that I was in Skylar's apartment, sleeping on her couch, and Callum didn't even know I existed.

I pressed my palms against my eyes as the sea poured from them. The sob crested and escaped, lashing angrily up my throat. I was too relieved to be embarrassed when I felt the weight of Drew sitting next to me on the couch, his hands tentatively rubbing against my arms.

"Cassidy?" he asked, worried.

But I couldn't make myself stop, couldn't alleviate his concern by explaining myself. The shaking sobs almost hurt as they bubbled up and out of me. And I cried not only for the relief of being here, safe, but for the time I'd wasted with a man who hurt me, who liked to see me cry, and all the time and energy I'd spent hiding from him. I cried for my spent life, the people who hadn't loved me at all and made me think that what Callum had offered me was all I'd deserved.

Drew sat quietly while the storm slowly burned itself out, the seas calming. He kept rubbing up and down my arms, his palms against my skin a comfort.

I took a long, shuddering breath and swiped my palms across my eyes. The embarrassment came back, the pressure of it adding to the headache my crying jag had created.

I looked at Drew. The light, always sneaking through that tiny gap in the blinds, cast a glow over his face. All of the angles and lines were more prominent, his eyes darker.

"I'm sorry," I said. "Bad dream. Stupid, I know."

He shook his head. "It's not stupid." He waited a beat. "Are you going to be okay?"

I nodded, wishing there had been no truth to it at all, that I hadn't been reliving a real-life event. I almost started to cry again and took a shaky breath.

"What was it about?"

Would it be cathartic to tell him? To talk about the fear that had been my life for too long?

"Callum," I said after a moment. "It was one of the times I'd tried to leave him, when he fell asleep watching TV."

Silence hung heavy in the air, a living thing demanding to be noticed. But he let it be, and just his presence, the strong assuredness in that, was a balm to my exposed nerves.

After a moment, I realized that he was in Skylar's apartment in the middle of the night. "What are you doing here?"

He focused on me, a frown slowly pulling at his mouth. "Skylar's mom called a couple of hours ago. Her grandmother had a stroke and is in the hospital. She drove down to be with her."

"Will she be all right?"

"They're not sure. It sounded pretty serious. Skylar was crying." He paused, looking toward the window as if debating with himself. "She's very close with her grandma. She used to go to her house every day after school after her parents got divorced."

"Is there anything we should do?" I asked, sitting up. He had to pull back to give me the space, though it was only enough to leave a few inches between us.

"Not at the moment," he said softly. "It's three in the morning."

I could suddenly hear my pulse in my ears, and the implication of how late it was, and the fact that we were alone suddenly became very clear to me. Skylar *had* warned me. Even with her words running through my mind, I felt the pull, like gravity was somehow centered inside of him, tugging me closer.

In that moment, there was an entirely different look in his eyes than I had seen before. Careful restraint pulled his muscles taut, but the heat in his gaze was unmistakable.

Some part of my brain must have been attached. Even as I inched forward, my right hand, almost of its own volition, pressed against his chest to stop me from drawing closer.

He sucked in a breath at my touch but didn't move away. His heart beat a mad rhythm under my palm, telling me this was affecting him as much as it was me, and it was almost enough to make me drop my hand. Let the chips fall where they may. This was my life, not hers. I betrayed no one if I did what I wanted. If I gave myself to the darkness and the look that burned in his eyes.

I toyed with the top button of his shirt, fighting with myself. Because this moment could dictate my steps from here on out, could change everything that came next.

He scrutinized my face, looking for a clear answer to his unspoken question. The one that I was trying to figure out for myself. How badly I wanted to say yes. But I was afraid to.

"I'm sorry about the argument. Before," I said, desperate for a distraction.

His smile was slow, igniting a fire deep within me. "If we went a day without arguing, I'd think there was something wrong."

I laughed, breathless. "I guess it's the one constant in everything that's happened."

"Things *have* been a little chaotic," he conceded.

We stared at each other across the yawning gap of hesitation. But the heat of him was a breath away, and that knowledge was agony. I ached to pull closer, just two inches. Eliminate the cold air between us, the reluctance, the questions.

He brushed a lock of hair out of my face, and his finger lightly grazed my cheek, lingering.

Then, with great effort, he pulled back and stood. He scrubbed a hand over his face as I grappled with my disappointment and relief.

"I should let you get back to sleep," he said, looking down at me. His face was now shrouded in shadow, and I couldn't make out his expression. "No more bad dreams, all right?"

"Yes, sir," I replied, unable to inject my words with the sarcasm I usually kept close at hand. My voice was too breathy, and I felt doubly stupid after crying. I decided not to push my luck with another attempt at humor.

I watched Drew move slowly back to his chair and lower himself into it with a grunt. He leaned his head back, letting out a sigh that dropped into the air like a weight. I wanted to address what almost happened, this thing that made me wired and seemed to have drained him of any energy he may have had. But I was afraid, remembering that old adage that nothing good ever happens after midnight.

I settled back into the couch, turning away from him and tucking my blanket under my chin, the mixture of emotions swirling inside me. The fear and anger earlier. The dream. And Drew, calming me in the dark. A day of emotions, and on top of it all, a sense of rejection that I tried to talk myself out of feeling.

But a lifetime of being unwanted was hard to combat.

20

Professor Disappointment

At least I didn't dream. Sunlight crept in around the edges of the blinds and through that one slat that never seemed to take its job seriously. I stirred at the change in light, feeling like I had never really fallen asleep.

I turned over slowly, freezing at the sight of Drew. His head was propped against his hand again but had fallen back against the chair. His brows were furrowed, knit together by whatever he may have been dreaming about. Why was I not surprised that even in sleep, he never quite relaxed? He played it cool, but I was sure that he carried around his stress somewhere inside, hung up neat and tidy, to be brooded over when he was alone.

I snuck out of the room. I doubted he slept well in that chair, so I figured I'd let him rest as long as possible.

He was up, drinking coffee when I came back down the hall, freshly showered and dressed. His back was to me as he stared out the window, one hand in his jeans pocket. His shirt was already straightened and tucked back in, and the gun was clipped at his hip. I wasn't sure it had ever left its home.

He turned when I got my usual bowl for cereal out. He walked over and leaned against the archway, bringing the mug to his lips as he gazed at me over the rim. For having an almost-moment, he seemed pretty unabashed.

Good for him, I thought acerbically. That made one of us. My stomach twisted in nervous, uncertain knots, and as much as I fought it, the heat crept into my cheeks from my embarrassment.

"Morning," he said, his voice gravelly from sleep.

A new kind of knot twisted in my stomach, and I had to concentrate on not licking my lips and giving away exactly what was running through my head. Apparently I wasn't embarrassed enough.

"Morning," I replied a little belatedly, before turning to snatch the cereal box from on top of the fridge. I chanced a glance at him as I poured it into my bowl, and there was laughter in his eyes. I pretended not to see it, not wanting to let him goad me into a reaction.

"Skylar's driving up for the meeting at the college," he said after a moment. "I'm dropping you off at ten."

"You're not coming with us?" I asked.

He raised a brow. "I think it's pretty obvious I don't put much stock in his theories. Besides, I have to work."

I nodded, pretending not to be disappointed. I brushed past him and walked to the table to eat my cereal, fighting the unease that coiled in my stomach. Because today, I might be getting my answers, the instructions for how to get myself back to where I belonged. But as much as I'd fought to convince both Drew and Skylar that this was for the best, I'd gotten a taste of what enduring friendships looked like. I was already hooked on the leftovers of it that leaving would prove difficult.

And now this thing with Drew. . . I glanced over at him, standing by the window again, a picture of ease, whether he actually felt that way or not. My mind drifted to our near-moment the night before, the control he'd had despite the pull. My own lack of it had the heat burning in my cheeks again.

I forced my mind away from that path and focused on finishing my breakfast. I needed to have my focus back for the meeting.

Again, I dressed the part Skylar wanted us to play, examining myself in the mirror. I tilted my head, tugging on the hem of the button-down shirt I wore. This was the other Cassidy. The one who had a career, a fiancé, a family.

"Cass, you ready?" Drew called from the living room.

His voice snapped me out of the trance, and I hurried to the closet and pulled on the wool coat from last time. I headed down the hall. He was standing by the door, his own coat already on, his hands in his pockets.

Silently, we left the warmth of the apartment into the frigid air. The sleek, heeled boots I wore were not the best for traction in the wet snow that had fallen overnight and continued accumulating into the brisk morning.

Drew was chewing absently on his bottom lip. Even though he maintained that he didn't believe any of what the professor said, I wondered if he was thinking that this could be the key to sending me back, ending this whole fiasco.

We pulled into the parking lot in front of the science building at the college right as Skylar was getting out of her car. We parked next to her.

I looked at Drew before getting out. He offered me a small smile, and it was stupid how that flustered me just enough to fumble with the door handle. Which made his smile grow wider.

I finally managed to join Skylar on the sidewalk, tugging on the hem of my coat to avoid looking at Drew as he pulled away.

"How's your grandma?" I asked.

She grimaced. "Touch and go right now. I'm driving back down as soon as we're done here."

I nodded.

"Ready?" she asked.

"I guess so."

Skylar navigated the snow in her own impractical-looking heels and looked up at me. She hesitated then asked quietly, "Are we sure this is really what we want to do?"

"Skylar. . ."

"I want to make absolutely certain this is really what we should be doing." That same earnestness from the night before was all over her face.

"Should and want are two very different things," I said, reminding myself as much as her.

"When did you become the reasonable one?" she asked, smiling. But it shook and her voice was coated in the emotion she tried to suppress.

"I've been spending too much time with you. I'm supposed to be the comic relief around here."

She laughed nervously, and I led the way inside the building. Students trickled into classrooms, sneakers and boots squeaking on the linoleum floor from the melting snow they tracked inside.

She pulled the gloves from her hands and stuffed them into her pockets as we walked down the quickly emptying hall. My heels clicked loudly, echoing around the space. I was self-conscious of the sound.

Skylar blew out a breath as we approached the office's closed door. She rapped her knuckles against it, meeting my gaze with uncertainty.

A gruff "come in!" sounded from inside.

She turned the handle and opened the door, easily playing at confident. I followed her with more trepidation.

I almost ran into her when she stopped abruptly. A man stood behind the desk, but it was not Professor Thibald as we were expecting. An older man, bowed slightly with age and responsibility, squinted at us over his reading glasses

"I'm sorry. Are we in the right office?" Skylar asked, looking behind her as if the answer would be there.

I took in the details of the room. The same framed pictures of fractals and the hand-woven lotus flower boldly proclaimed that this was the same office we'd been in only a week prior.

"If you were expecting Professor Thibald, then yes, this is the right office. I'm Dr. Gary Steele, head of the physics department," the man said. He pulled the glasses from his face and tossed them onto the messy desk. Papers littered its surface, and it was clear he'd been searching through every file Thibald owned. Half the books from the shelves against the wall had been put in the boxes that sat on the floor.

Skylar noticed as well and gestured to the disarray. "Are we missing something?"

Dr. Steele raised his eyebrows and looked around him as if for the first time. He turned back to us, an apology in his eyes. "I'm afraid that Professor Thibald was fired and escorted off the campus this morning."

Skylar shook her head. "I don't understand."

Dr. Steele's face reddened slightly. "Some pretty damning evidence has come to light about his behavior. I'm afraid that's as much as I can share at the moment."

She looked to me for help, but I just stared back at her, at a loss. Something twisted in my gut, a strange mingling of relief and dread.

"I know you came to meet him. But is there something that I can help you with?" he asked, sensing the tension that vibrated between Skylar and me.

"Well, we're writing a novel," Skylar began, still struggling to wrap her mind around the news. "It's science fiction, and we were meeting with Professor Thibald about parallel dimensions."

He placed a large hand over his chest. "A lady after my own heart."

She was actually able to smile. "Well, unfortunately, not quite. We're not exactly experts on the topic. Hence the meeting."

He chuckled, a rumbly sound in his chest that didn't quite escape the cage of his body. All the same, it rolled over us in a pleasant wave. It helped ease the strain. "No one can really be an expert on it, to be honest. There are a number of theories, none of which can be proven in the slightest."

"Thibald seemed to think otherwise," she said.

He sobered a bit, wincing slightly. "Yes, he did. But I don't see why that would matter much. It's fiction, after all."

Skylar laughed nervously. "Yes. Right." She shifted the notebook to her other hand. "We were hoping to be as realistic as possible."

He acknowledged that with a nod, resting his fingertips on the surface of the cluttered desk. "Well, I guess the theory and its facets really depend on what sort of story you're trying to tell."

Skylar glanced at me and licked her lips.

"Our main character," I said, taking over, "is transported to an alternate universe. In it, her life is completely different. And in this universe, her alternate self has died."

He pursed his lips, thoughtful. "Very interesting concept," he said after a moment.

"Interesting, yes. But is it plausible?" Skylar asked, her confidence bolstered by his interest.

He gestured with his hands, his gaze shifting upward. "Well, they are theories but based on scientifically proven concepts. Wormholes, for instance, might exist in the center of a black hole. That's a common explanation for travel between parallel universes in fiction." He smiled. "But we have no proof wormholes are real. Einstein's theory of relativity basically uncovered the theoretical existence of black holes, and the first one was discovered in the '70s. But they are far enough away that we can really only speculate about what happens inside of them."

"But that's out in space," I said.

"Correct."

"Thibald seemed to think alternate dimensions were accessible here on earth."

Dr. Steele nodded. "That's right, he did."

I didn't miss the implication of his tone. "But you don't?"

He grimaced and lifted a shoulder. "I wouldn't necessarily *discount* his theories. It's just that the energy needed would be exponential. Far beyond our capability to produce."

"But some force can bridge the gap between dimensions, couldn't it?" Skylar's voice was barely a hint below desperate.

"You mean in the way Thibald thought?" He raised a brow.

She tensed, worked to keep it from showing. "Something

like that."

"I'm not sure what he proposed would really be as plausible as he seems to think. The only thing I can think would cause it is maybe you have wormholes in your story that exist all around, which no one can see. And somehow, your character comes across one."

"But how would the wormholes get there?" Skylar asked, almost pleading.

"The aforementioned energy fields, I suppose. It's fiction, is it not?" He smiled.

Her returning smile was just a fraction too slow. "Yes, of course."

I couldn't even bring myself to react. Disappointment was cold in my veins.

"I'm sure you could say it happened however you'd like to," he suggested unhelpfully. "Unfortunately, parallel universes are purely theoretical, and your guess is as good as mine."

Skylar's expression fell, but she tried to rally. "Thank you for your time, Dr. Steele. I don't suppose you have a way for us to contact Professor Thibald?"

Dr. Steele winced. "Ah, I'm afraid not."

"I'm sorry," she said quickly, trying not to seem as pushy as she sounded. "We were counting on the specific information he had for what we were going to incorporate into our novel."

"I understand, but I'm not at liberty to give out that information, especially while he's under investigation."

She nodded, shoulders slumping. "Well, thank you for your time."

"If you have other questions, feel free to let me know. I'm sorry I'm a poor substitute for Professor Thibald."

"Oh, no. You were very helpful," she lied. "Thank you

again."

He nodded his acceptance and watched us leave the office.

21

Grave Walkers

We made our way back down the hall, and the clicking of my heels was like a nail driving home in my skull. Neither of us spoke as we digested the hopelessness of our situation.

I could admit that I had hoped for at least an inkling of how something so impossible could have happened to me. Because understanding was, at some level, a form of control. Everything about my situation had felt so far beyond my grasp, I'd wanted something, anything to give me some sense of authority. And now all of that was gone.

Skylar led the way through the front doors into the softly falling snow. Even with the busy street only a few yards away, the world had a sort of muted quality about it thanks to the blanket of white. I wished I could feel as peaceful as it looked.

Skylar and I got into her car, and she blew out a breath. "That wasn't helpful."

"If only we were really writing a book," I added.

She pulled out her phone. "Maybe Thibald will respond to his email, and we can set something else up."

I watched as she speed-typed into the phone, brows pulled

low over her eyes. Each tap of her finger was a stab at my heart. The dread in my bones made me certain we would be out of luck.

She lowered the phone and sent me an anxious look. The phone pinged back almost immediately. She looked at it, and her lips disappeared into a tight line. "It bounced back. Deactivated."

"We don't have a plan B?"

She shut her eyes briefly. "Not really. Our only expert is unreachable, and his boss couldn't help us. I wonder if we should research the police station."

I furrowed my brow. "What do you mean?"

She started the car. "We could research it to see if there's something weird about it. Magnetic fields, urban legends, anything."

I raised a brow. "You mean, like if it was built on an Indigenous burial ground or something?"

My derisive tone irked her and she jabbed the button for the heater. "We're talking about a parallel universe here. Theoretical physics and the supernatural are like kissing cousins."

I surrendered, leaning my head back against the seat. "If you think it would help." She backed out of the parking spot. "What else are we going to do?"

It was true, and the molten heat of desperation sat deep in my gut. There were so many events in my life that I'd had no control over that I needed to grip this one with my own two hands. There was a desperation to understand.

As we rode back to her place, I obsessed over all the theories we'd learned about. Some of them postulated that there were millions upon millions of alternates. Every choice a person made created another timeline to account for the various paths available.

How many other mes were there? How many other universes were ones in which my father had never left, and my life had ended up perfect or at least better?

Was there one in which my mom had never gotten sick at all?

I glanced at Skylar, heat creeping into my cheeks as if she could hear my thoughts and would judge me for sounding like a hopeful child. She was worrying at her bottom lip as she drove, lost in thought. I turned back to my window, watching the dull, white-washed town flutter by.

I chewed on my thumb as my memory lingered on my mother's face. The images were faded, cracked at the edges from time and overuse like an old picture. I'd always feared I would forget her if I didn't routinely go over them. I had been so young, but hers was the last loving face I could really remember.

I thought back to her funeral, that cold day in November. My father hadn't even held my hand as we'd walked to the plot where she was buried, so fresh that there wasn't even a tombstone yet. Just like Cassidy's.

"Have they put in the tombstone?" I asked suddenly, though my words were soft, tempered by the memory of that day. I remembered how any word spoken had seemed like a serrated edge.

Skylar swallowed but didn't take her eyes from the road. She knew what I was talking about and nodded. "Yesterday."

What did it say, I wondered. The temporary one had been simple, not a true representation of everything the people in her life wanted to remember about her. What would mine say if it had been me? The ache at the thought was not one I wanted to explore.

Skylar's hesitation hung heavy in the air, a weight I could almost touch.

"What?" I asked.

"Do you want to see it?"

It was my turn to swallow. Now that I had seen it once already, it seemed less daunting. And some morbid part of me wanted to see it again, this time to feel those words carved into stone with my own fingers, most likely etched by a machine, but meaningful nonetheless.

"I do," Skylar said, breaking into my thoughts. "But I can go some other time. Alone."

"No. I'll go." It was not a place anyone should go alone, not when it was still this fresh.

She nodded, still not looking at me, and flipped on her turn signal. We traveled through the same fancy neighborhood, and they looked so idyllic surrounded by the snow.

The road curved and crested the hill. Before heading down into the valley below, we turned into the small cemetery. With the sweeping white that covered everything, the wrought-iron fence looked less severe.

Skylar pulled into a parking spot, her tires crunching in the snow as she slid to a stop. We both sat, hesitating after she turned off the engine. Our trepidation came from different places, but it mingled together like one giant anchor.

Finally, she broke the trance and opened her door. It groaned in protest against the cold. I followed suit, glad I was wearing boots but wishing they had more traction as my toe slid in the slush.

Skylar moved slowly through the entrance and I kept my eyes on her. She licked her lips, clenched her fists.

I knew what she was feeling. As she faltered, I pressed forward, leading the way through the rows of tombstones and plaques half-obscured by the snow. Fake and fresh flowers bowed in the chill wind, snuggled into the blanket.

We stopped in front of the shiny gray stone, a stark contrast against the white.

"How did you know where it was?" she asked.

"Drew brought me here that first day." I stuffed my hands into my pockets, afraid they'd start shaking. "Looks the same. Except for the tombstone."

She let out a breath and stepped forward, placing one of her small hands on the top.

"It's still hard to believe she's gone." The tears brimmed, crystalline reminders of the relationship she'd had with the girl who wasn't me.

I wanted to argue that it was harder thanks to me, but I realized this moment shouldn't be tainted by my bitterness. Skylar needed to mourn her friend.

My eyes traced the inscription below the name. *Beloved.* Simple, short. It encompassed all the things Cassidy Marchand was in this world. Daughter, friend, fiancée. It was amazing how strong a weapon one word could be, the sharp pain it could cause. I covered the stutter in my breathing with a cough and turned away in time to see Hercules making his way toward us.

Evan was bundled in a puffy coat, dark against the gray day, his golden hair covered by a bulky knitted hat. His expression was hard to read, a stony facade almost as cold and unfeeling as the stones that surrounded us.

Skylar sniffed and noticed my preoccupation behind us.

"Evan," she breathed, his name caught in the cloud of her

breath.

She and I shuffled to the side, huddling closer together. She slid her arm in mine. I stiffened at the touch, but I kept my eyes on Evan. He didn't look at us as he approached.

He stopped almost ten feet from the stone. There was no recognition in his eyes as they traced the shape, the engraved words. He merely stood, hands in pockets. There were still dark circles under his eyes, and a gaunt look to his face I knew was not natural. We all stood still as the world ticked on the indifferent minutes, stopping for no one.

"It's unfair," he said after a while. There was no sting in it, but still, it snapped in my ears.

He didn't look at us, but his gaze darkened as he squinted at the tombstone like it was a mortal enemy, the representation of all that was wrong in his life, in the world.

"This is not what was supposed to happen," he continued.

His words made me suddenly more aware of the snowy air biting at my face, the wind cutting through the thin material of my slacks. But I was afraid to move, afraid to draw his attention to me. He had every right to loose the venom of his hostility on me, but it didn't make me want to bring it on myself.

Evan's face softened slightly. "We didn't ask for this." His eyes swept over us, and I could see that he included me in that. Some part of him excused me from whatever had happened to bring me here.

I exhaled slowly.

He finally walked forward, close enough to touch the stone as Skylar had done. But his hands remained in his pockets, and I imagined him curling them into fists, hiding his anger. And I thought, *no, this really isn't fair at all.*

I clenched my jaw to keep my teeth from chattering because

I still felt our situation was tenuous, that his calm was a wire held too tightly. Like it would snap at the slightest weight. Skylar was tense beside me, and I knew she sensed it too.

Still, it was frigid. My fingers and toes and heart ached, and his back was turned. I gathered my courage and tugged Skylar toward the parking lot. It was probably better that Evan spent this time at his fiancée's gravesite alone.

Skylar glanced at me but complied and moved with me toward the car. I looked backward. Evan still stood where we'd left him, and I noted the way his back was hunched. Not only from the cold, I thought. Because he'd been battered by life as much as the winter wind. I hoped that he wouldn't close himself inside the metal shell he was building around himself.

Skylar held tight to my arm until we got back to her car, our steps careful in the slushy snow. She released me as we went to our respective doors. The engine grunted and groaned when she started it, and I understood the protest completely.

Skylar frowned as she glanced up at Evan, still as a statue. Maybe metal had been the wrong material. It was stone he was building himself out of. Equally cold and hard, but heavy too.

"I think he'll be okay." I put as much confidence in it as I could muster. I willed it to be true, hoped that I hadn't caused irreparable damage. Grieving was difficult enough, a long and arduous journey that never really ended.

Skylar pursed her lips, a lopsided move that conveyed her skepticism. "I hope so."

We fell into silence. I was sure her mind had gone to the place only those who were mourning went. Mine went to planning mode. Because my only option for finding a way home was now unreachable.

Skylar's continued insistence that I didn't have to leave was a sure sign that I needed to. And that meant I had to get money and get out of dodge.

When we reached her apartment complex, I had a plan in place. We got out of the car and trudged through the snow to her building. She stopped at the bank of mailboxes just inside the entrance, and I continued to the door, wanting protection from the sting of the wind.

It took me a moment to register the image as I approached her door, but the spike of panic it inspired made me grateful Skylar wasn't looking. I snatched the flower and photo from the welcome mat and stuffed them into my pocket before she joined me.

I wasn't even sure why I was hiding them, why I didn't want her to see. But it slowly dawned on me that if I told her about it, she would call Drew, who would be there in a matter of minutes. And I would never be alone long enough to make my escape.

She unlocked the door, a bundle of mail in her free hand. She tossed it onto the table as we entered, but she was already distracted. She'd gotten a few texts in the last ten minutes. "Will you be okay here alone until Drew gets off work?"

It was almost too perfect. "Of course," I answered, giving her what I hoped was a reassuring smile.

"I hate leaving you," she said. She was too preoccupied to even realize how mad Drew would be that she left me alone at all. But I wasn't going to remind her of that.

"It's fine. Go be with your grandma."

"Thanks." She turned as she opened the door. "I'm sorry we didn't get the answers you wanted. But I'm sure we'll figure it out."

I forced another smile. "Sure."

22

To Steal and Start Again

Stealing came too naturally to me. I told myself I only resorted to it when desperate, but that was starting to become a habitual state of being.

Last time, I promise.

I worked to convince myself that I wasn't stealing this time, not really. Because I *was* Cassidy Marchand. And this was her money. So, in a way, it was mine too.

I stood in the lobby of the bank, the snowflakes melting in my hair, chewing my bottom lip. This all seemed too easy, like everything was being handed to me. And I rarely trusted anything so simple.

I joined the line behind the lunchtime errand-runners, hoping I didn't look as nervous as I felt. I ran over the account number in my head to make sure I had it down. It was a stroke of luck that Skylar had been asked to shut down Cassidy's accounts, that she'd had all the information right there on her desk. And another stroke of luck that she hadn't gotten to it yet.

The woman in front of me inched forward, and I used the

standing desk amid the lines to fill out the withdrawal slip. I was afraid that if I didn't write down the number, it would slide right out of my head. I paused on the amount. I only needed a few hundred dollars to get out of town, but she had a few thousand in the account. It had been a long time since I'd seen that much.

"Line's moving," a man said from behind me.

I glanced up and moved forward, the slip half-filled out. My palms were sweaty despite the chill that crept into my bones, my fingers nearly numb. I held the slip by the edge between my thumb and forefinger.

It was so stupid how my heart pounded. *This isn't really stealing*, I reassured myself. *I am Cassidy Marchand.*

"Next person over here," a teller said, waving her hand impatiently.

I stepped up and slid the deposit slip onto the counter. She looked at it, looked at me.

"I need your ID, please."

My heart stuttered for a second. But there was no suspicion on her face. Still, I fumbled with the wallet as I pulled Cassidy's license out.

She paused to glance at the picture, and I swallowed hard. Her eyes came back up to my face, lingered for what felt like a second too long. Then she handed it back.

"How much are you withdrawing?"

I expelled a breath. "Um, five hundred?"

She raised a brow at my uncertainty. "You sure?"

I nodded. "Five hundred."

The woman filled it in and ran it through the computer.

I wiped my hands on my jeans as she counted it out in twenties.

I took the cash and folded it.

"Anything else?" she asked.

"That's it. Thank you," I replied, slipping the cash into my pocket.

She was already looking at the next customer in line, and I made my way toward the door, relief and guilt at war within me. I could buy a bus ticket out of here, and no one would know where I was. I would be free.

But it would be a lie.

The words jabbed at me just like the chill wind. No, no. I was in control. I was living my *own* life, free from Callum, free from the expectations of the people here who wanted me to be someone I wasn't.

But I still couldn't be Cassidy Marchand. I would have to change my name to stay hidden, to make a life. Because Cassidy Marchand was dead.

I cut through the parking lot and pulled my hood up. The bus station was four blocks east, and at this temperature and through the snowdrifts, it would be a trek.

Running.

I shook my head, hating that I heard the word in Drew's voice. I was *not* running. Not this time. Fear wasn't controlling me. *I* was making this decision.

I hunched my shoulders as if the mental argument was a physical onslaught. Each step was a rebuttal, and it was a struggle to keep moving at all.

I stuffed my hands into my jacket pockets and felt the flower and photo I'd stuck in there earlier. In my rush to get out of the apartment, my hurried search through Skylar's papers on her desk, I'd completely forgotten about the surprise left on her doorstep.

I pulled out the flower, the bloom a violent red against the snow that surrounded me. I flung it aside. It would tell me nothing. But the picture afforded me some insight into a moment the killer had seen.

It was of Skylar and me walking out of Drew's house, zoomed-in tightly. She was a blur, but my face was in sharp focus. I read the frustration in my expression from my argument with Drew.

I wasn't sure how long I stood there in the snow, staring at the picture, but my fingers had grown numb. I stuck the picture back into my pocket and continued. It was not the time or place to analyze a murderer's intentions.

By the time I reached the station, my teeth were chattering so hard I thought they would break. I shuffled up to the booth to buy my ticket, shifting back and forth in an attempt to warm up.

"Where to?" The ticket seller barked.

I stared at the boards, trying to decide where I wanted to go. My recent foray in the snow had me considering San Diego or Miami. Warm and sunny, by the ocean, which I had never seen in person.

"Lady, you gonna buy a ticket or what?" the ticket seller asked.

"Uh, I need a minute," I managed, offering an apologetic smile. I rushed to sit on a nearby bench, uncertainty a heavy stone in my stomach.

Why was I second-guessing myself? I rubbed my hands together to warm them up, trying to convince myself the cold was the only thing making them shake. This was what I wanted. To start over, be someone new without fear. No one would be looking over my shoulder.

I pulled the picture out again. I thought that it would give me courage, a reason to make this leap. Because if I stayed I'd still be in a serial killer's crosshairs, still fearful for my life.

But it had the opposite effect. Staring at the image, this breach of privacy, made my resolve waver. I looked up at the ticket booth and the ticket seller who was using his downtime to peruse the internet on his phone. My moral dilemma shouldn't have any bearing on his day, but my whole world was tilting, and I wondered why he wasn't thrown as badly as I was.

I stared down at the picture again, and a shiver ran down my spine. The realization slowly formed in my mind. I *was* still running. It wasn't just me; I wasn't in control of this. And that was supposed to be the whole point. This guy was taking that choice from me.

Besides, he was focused on me, and that meant he wasn't paying attention to anyone else. The police had no way of knowing who he'd go after next. If I left, he might shift his focus. By staying, I was protecting someone else from becoming a victim. Drew had managed to keep me safe thus far. Maybe I could stay only until this was over. If we could somehow lure the killer out. . .

But if yesterday was any indication, Drew wouldn't be willing to let me help out in any way. I understood why, but I would have to make him see my side. I could use the extra time to convince everyone that my leaving was right, not sneak away when they weren't looking. Because I didn't need guilt chasing me either.

As soon as the guy was caught, I could hit the road with no qualms. No one could accuse me of running. I would be starting my own life for my own reasons.

I stood and headed straight for the door, determined. I hunched my shoulders against the frigid air, making the two-block trek to the police station. I knew I wouldn't be able to handle the cold for the six blocks back to Skylar's apartment. Besides, I needed to hash this out with Drew now.

By the time I arrived, my face, fingers, and toes were numb. I couldn't feel the handle as I pulled the door open, couldn't tell if I actually smiled when I walked past the woman at the front desk. I headed straight back to Drew, who was sitting at his desk, intently staring at his computer screen.

He didn't look up until I was two feet from him, and it took him a moment to even register that it was me.

"Cassidy?" He shot up. "What are you doing here? Is something wrong?"

I shook my head. "Not exactly. I need to talk to you about something."

"Okay," he said slowly, nodding toward an empty conference room.

He shut the door as soon as we were inside, and the sudden quiet enveloped us. It was a wonder he'd been able to concentrate in the chaos of the station.

I pulled my hood off.

"Why is your face so pink?" he asked, reaching up to touch my cheek. "You're freezing!" He took my hands in his own. "Did you walk here?"

As heavenly as the warmth of his hands was, I couldn't let myself be distracted. I pulled my hands from his grasp and took the picture out of my pocket, holding it out to him.

Every plane of his face hardened as he took it. "Where did you get this?"

"I found it on Skylar's doorstep with a flower."

His expression tightened ever so slightly. “This was taken at my place.”

I took the money out next and tossed it onto the table.

He looked down at it, back up at me, confused.

“I stole this.” I gestured to the wad.

“What do you mean?”

“I withdrew it from Cassidy’s account.”

I expected him to be mad, to yell at me, but he simply lowered himself into a chair at the table. “You were going to leave.”

His expression, the disappointment in his voice, made me instantly defensive. “The professor thing fell through. And I was desperate. I thought leaving was the only option.”

“So why didn’t you?” His voice was tempered with anger, and I thought maybe it was to cover the hurt I saw in his eyes.

“Because I didn’t want to run. Again.” I paused, forced myself not to turn away. “I realized that I could do this a better way.”

He looked away, down at his hands clasped before him. “You mean, you’re still going to leave.”

“Yes.” It was almost a whisper.

He raised his eyes to me. “Is this you saying goodbye first? So you won’t feel guilty for sneaking away?” His words stabbed at me, and I worked hard not to flinch.

“That’s not the only reason.”

He gave a short, mirthless laugh. “Of course it isn’t.” He looked away, jaw clenching against his anger. “I don’t get it. You know this guy is playing with us, can get to you, basically anywhere. Doesn’t that scare you?”

I threw my hands into the air, looking heavenward. “What difference does it make? I live my life scared, since the first time Callum hit me and the first time he dragged me back after

I ran. Hell, I've been scared since the day my dad never came back for me."

He grew still, was practically a statue.

"Don't you get why I'm always so angry? It's *easier* to be mad. Otherwise the fear takes over." I swiped at my eyes where tears had formed.

"And running?" So quiet, I almost didn't hear him.

"At least running feels like I'm *doing* something. It's better than cowering in the dark." I turned away, taking a deep breath to calm myself.

When I looked at him again, I felt steadier, bolstered by the new goal before me. "But right now, I can actually do something *better*. The killer knows where I am, is toying with us, with me. But he hasn't taken anyone else. I need to be the distraction, to make him slip up."

He stared at me. "You want to be bait."

"He's clearly obsessed with me right now. He's stalking me, not some other woman you don't know about. It's an advantage—"

He stood abruptly and turned away from me, running his hands through his hair.

"How often do you get a chance like this?"

He spun to face me. "How exactly do you propose we go about dangling you in front of a serial killer? This guy is smart. Do you really think he'll fall for some ploy?"

I shrugged. "I haven't worked it out yet—"

"Haven't worked it out yet." He shook his head and gave a dark, almost painful laugh. "If we do this—and that is a big *if*—you don't run the show. I have to be the one in charge."

"Drew—"

He held up a hand. "I know you have this control thing, and

I get it. But, Cassidy, I can't handle losing you again if things go wrong. Please," he said, his voice almost breaking. "Please, work with me on this."

I fought to swallow the lump in my own throat. What he was proposing was fair, and at least I got a say. "Okay. We'll do this your way."

He sighed his relief and rubbed the back of his neck. "I'll need to get a team of guys together."

I thought about Russo, Drew's words a few days earlier. "You said there's a possibility that the killer has a guy on the inside," I reminded.

He looked at me, nodding. "I'll be careful about who I choose. Which means it will take me a little time to weed through. I also have to get this photo analyzed."

"Okay," I answered slowly.

"And I can work faster if I'm not distracted."

"So you want me to leave."

He grimaced. "I don't like the idea of leaving you alone. Not until we have an actual plan in place for how we want to work this. And we know he's found you at Skylar's, and now my place." He gestured to the picture.

I put a hand on my hip, fairly certain I wasn't going to like whatever he was dancing around. "So, what then?"

He looked up at me like a little boy trying to get away with something he knew was a long shot. "I think you should go to your dad's."

Was that my stomach that just dropped to the floor? I was too surprised to be angry. "You can't find a better babysitter? Like a dentist or something? I'll sign up for a root canal."

He raised a brow. "You said I get to call the shots."

"Isn't there some basement you can lock me in?" I implored.

He sighed. "Stop being melodramatic."

"Fine." I rubbed my fist against my chest, admitting to myself that I did give him permission to run this thing. I'd opened myself up for this one, let him walk right in with the left hook. It wasn't fair for me to be upset. I'd done my own hurting only moments before.

"I have to call and let them know we're coming."

I didn't trust myself to respond, and he left the room to give me a moment.

23

Second Chance Serenade

I'd have to be in the same house as my father. No, not my father. *Her* father and his wife. Literal strangers. How could this be the only solution? Wouldn't I just cause them heartbreak? Cause myself stress, bring up my bitterness and anger? I'd get to see everything I'd missed out on. I imagined her room was kept the same even after she'd moved out, bought her own place. Yes, there would be frilly curtains over the windows, stupid figurines on shelves, items redolent of indulgent parents, spoiled child. A room that she'd called her own, everything in it *belonging*. Would there be relics I recognized? Things I'd lost in the transition to foster care and group homes?

It was wrong to hate her, this other me I'd never met, but I couldn't stop it. She had all the things I'd always wished for. And now I would have my nose rubbed in more of her perfection.

Drew came back in a matter of minutes, sensing the tenuous state of my mood, and said nothing as we walked to the door. I tried not to hate him for putting me through this, reminding myself that it was a means to an end.

The silence continued on the drive. I stared out the window, seeing nothing we passed. Maybe I should have been paying attention so I'd know where I was going if I couldn't handle it and had to escape. The longer we drove, the tighter I gripped my own hands, wringing them together like a rag full of water. Squeeze out every last drop.

Drew reached over and grabbed my hand, startling me. Despite how I'd hurt him earlier, his expression was sympathetic, and I hated myself for everything I'd done. I reminded myself that he had some knowledge of what I might be going through. He was on the other side of the bitterness. He lived in a land called regret.

But this is different, I argued.

We pulled up to the house, and I recognized it as the one he'd driven me to that first day. The other Cassidy would know the house she'd spent a majority of her life in. It was foreign to me, and it represented everything I'd been denied, pain around every corner.

Drew squeezed my hand then released it so he could put his car in park. He turned off the engine and got out. I wavered, simply staring at the cheerful yellow house.

He opened my door and looked down at me as I unbuckled. "Maybe this will do you some good."

I stood and gave him a dark look.

"Get to know them," he insisted. "Pat might actually have answers. It wouldn't hurt to try and understand him."

"I don't need to understand him."

He growled in frustration, slamming the door. "Forget it then. You said you didn't want to run anymore, but you're still playing the victim." He held up his hands. "But I get it, you want to stay that way."

Too much abrasion against my already raw nerves. "Go to hell," I spat, marching past him.

He grabbed my arm, and I jerked to look at him. The apology was in his eyes, but it didn't pass through his lips. "Go ahead and be mad at me. But please don't take any risks. Don't leave this house alone. Not until we're ready."

The door opened, and I yanked my arm from his grasp without saying anything. My father's wife, Jane, stood in the doorway, her demeanor cautious. But there was no mistaking her expectation.

She stepped back to let me in. I caught sight of Drew walking back to his car, worry etched into his face, and he cast one glance back at me before the door closed.

I shed my jacket, and she took it. I couldn't bring myself to let my anger spill all over her, innocent in the whole situation. I couldn't guarantee anything if my father were to join us.

She turned from hanging my jacket on the coat rack and smiled at me uncertainly. I had no idea what to say. *Sorry I'm here. I had no choice in the matter?*

"Are you hungry?" she asked. "I can make you some lunch."

"I'm fine, thanks." I rubbed my frozen hands together to keep them busy.

"Please, come in and sit."

She led the way into the living room, decorated in classic, clean lines. Modern style mixed with lovingly restored antiques. The walls remained white, interrupted only by picture frames set up in a collage with framed hand-lettered quotes and sayings interspersed. A wide, arched doorway led into a breakfast nook and kitchen to my right.

A battered upright piano sat in one corner, its keys yellowed with age and overuse. I had always wanted to learn how to play, and I brushed my fingertips over the keys.

"Do you play?" Jane asked. Too careful, too polite. I didn't deserve it.

I shook my head. "I never had the opportunity."

"Cassidy hated practicing. She quit as soon as we allowed," she said.

The caustic taste crawled up my throat. I disdained her squandering the opportunity. Like a rich girl disparaging the innumerable open doors money offered her. But I clenched my teeth against the vitriol I wanted to let loose. Jane didn't know what her words would mean to someone like me.

She watched me as I stared determinedly at the piano.

When I could trust the neutrality of my expression, I met her eyes.

She smiled a little, tears shining in her eyes. She pressed an elegant hand to her mouth. "I'm sorry." She turned away to gather herself. "I didn't realize how difficult this really could be."

"I knew this was probably a bad idea." I pulled my hand from the keys as if they had stung me.

"No," she said, turning back to me, her hand cold against my arm. "I want to help. Your safety is at stake. I would hate it if something happened, and we could have prevented it."

Her words echoed with something else I couldn't place at first. Then it registered. Guilt. Some part of her must blame herself for not preventing Cassidy's death. This was her way of making it up, as if she owed her stepdaughter that. Like with everyone else, the line was blurred between me and their Cassidy. Second chance, just like Skylar had said.

It was at that moment that my father came into the room. He was rigid with anticipation, as if braced for hurricane winds.

His expression was stony for protection not to be cold, but it struck me that way regardless.

All I could think was I shouldn't be here. I belonged in a world where I didn't hurt people, where they didn't hurt me by simply existing. This felt like an ambush. I'd dealt with physical abuse, but at least I could see that coming, throw up my hands to protect myself. There was no defense for this, even with all my anger and resentment. They were poorly constructed walls.

"I need water," I whispered, the battering ram knocking the air from my lungs. I made my way toward the kitchen to get the space and the oxygen my lungs were suddenly begging for.

I gulped the air to calm my heartbeat as soon as I was alone in the kitchen. I was overheated, claustrophobic. The marble counter was cold against my palms, jolting clarity into my mind. Snowflakes swirled around in front of the window as I stared out into the backyard. Huge trees lined the fence, offering privacy. One large cottonwood had a wooden swing attached, snow gathered on the seat. I imagined Cassidy pushing herself back and forth under the shade during the summer growing up.

"Cassidy."

I stiffened. "I should call Drew to pick me up."

"I don't think that's necessary."

I turned to look at my father standing in the doorway. "It might be. This is hard for you."

"I imagine this is just as difficult for you." He didn't move closer.

"How much did Skylar tell you?"

He swallowed, his gaze going everywhere but my face. "Just that in your world, I wasn't there for you."

I laughed mirthlessly and it almost became a sob. I looked down at my feet, clenching my teeth against the emotion.

"It's still quite a lot to wrap my head around," he said, moving slowly into the kitchen, approaching with caution. "It's easy to forget that my little girl is gone, to imagine her driving up every Sunday as usual for family dinner."

I chewed on my lip. It was hard not to pity him, in spite of all the rest.

"It's harder knowing you're here, knowing you wouldn't want to see me. Because you're her. Not entirely, but you are still my daughter; we share DNA and at least some memories."

I swallowed and refused to meet his eye.

"But I know there's some anger and hurt here. I wonder what it is that I did to you in that other world."

The lump in my throat was sudden and insistent. I blinked the tears away. I would not cry in front of this man.

He got a glass from the cupboard and set it on the counter, clearly meant for me. "I'd appreciate it if you wouldn't take out any of your feelings on Jane. She's got a soft heart."

"I wouldn't," I said, stung because I projected an accusation that wasn't there.

He nodded once. "If you want to discuss anything, I'll be in my office. You probably would do better without me around."

I didn't move as he walked out of the kitchen. But the tears wouldn't be stopped once he was gone, running hot down my cheeks. This pain in my chest, like someone stabbing one spot over and over, was almost unbearable. I hated Drew for this, hated my father for being here, hated Jane for not being someone I could blame, for being soft and kind. I wished she was cruel, that she and my father were the evil villains in all of it. It would make it easier; it would make it fair that I hated them.

But how could you erase over 15 years of what I'd endured, pretend it was okay, and believe these people had nothing to do with it?

"Some tea might make you feel better," Jane said softly from the kitchen door.

I wiped the tears with my palms and cleared my throat. "Water is fine," I managed to say.

She walked forward, a motherly tenderness in her face. She took the glass my father had gotten out and filled it with the water. She handed it to me, watching my face very carefully.

I took it but merely held it in my hand.

She rubbed my arm, an intimate gesture I couldn't quite bring myself to flinch from. How long had it been since a maternal figure had comforted me this way? I would never say I was an easy foster child, but I was far from troublesome the way a lot of kids could be. Most of them were pulled from abusive homes, where unimaginable horrors had tainted their perception of the world. I had abandonment issues and poor taste in men.

"Do you want to be alone?" she asked. Soft hearted, indeed.

"I honestly don't know," I said, laughing a little.

She smiled. "That's understandable. Well, feel free to wander around the house. Maybe it will distract you a little."

I nodded, finally taking a sip of the water she'd given me.

"I'll be around if you need me."

I nodded again and watched her walk back to the living room. I could see why my father was protective of her. I wondered how well the other Cassidy had gotten along with her. Was she like a lot of kids who struggled to accept a replacement for a parent they'd lost? Or had she bonded with Jane easily? It was hard to imagine anyone not getting along with such a sweet person.

From what Skylar had told me, not long after my father had married Jane, the family had moved to this small Colorado town. That was a lot of change for an 11 year-old.

After a moment, I set my glass on the counter and wandered through the living room, which was empty, back into the entryway. I could see the french doors down the hall where my father's office must have been. There was a den to my right where Jane was rifling through some scrapbooking materials laid out on a craft table tucked in the corner.

I made my way to the staircase directly in front of me. Pictures lined the wall as I walked, images of various stages of life, the vibrant red hair I recognized. One of the framed pictures was of my family as I knew it, my mother smiling through the illness that had begun to be obvious. The bones of her face had become more prominent, the dark circles under her eyes impossible to conceal.

I continued up the stairs, not wanting to linger there. The memory was enough. My father helping her walk from the car into the photographer's studio, how she could hardly spend any time on her feet.

I focused my attention on the bedroom doors that stood open in greeting. One was obviously the master, its ceiling high, the king-size bed immaculately made, and the wide opening into the bathroom giving it away.

There were two other rooms. One was decorated in neutral tones, a queen-sized bed in the center. It looked comfortable and welcoming, especially in comparison to the couch I'd been sleeping on for the better part of two weeks now.

I hesitated outside the other room, which had obviously been mine in this other life. The brightness of the teal walls was a giveaway. It was still a favorite color of mine.

I lingered for a few seconds more. Would I feel the loss everyone else felt for her if I saw more of what made her real, instead of just some phantom version of myself they all talked about? Or was it that I didn't want to ruin the illusion of perfection she seemed to represent? After all, some part of me acknowledged Drew's words as being true. I liked playing the victim.

I walked in slowly, as if the room were a sanctuary, too precious to be tainted by my tarnish. I was relieved to see that most of the room was Spartan. She'd probably taken all of her most cherished items to her own house. I had no idea how long she'd lived in this room, but obviously until an age that disdained girlish frivolities and remnants of childhood. It breathed sophistication and maturity.

It was also obvious that the room was slowly being converted into a second guest room. But there were still flavors of Cassidy. Pictures she hadn't taken with her, a bulletin board and calendar that still had events written on it from five or six years earlier.

A boxy computer sat on the desk, a film of dust on the screen and keyboard. I wondered if it still worked and was connected to the internet. I thought about the research we could still be doing. Since Skylar was preoccupied with her grandmother, I might as well be useful.

I checked all the wires to make sure they were plugged in and held my breath when I pushed the on button. When nothing happened, I frowned and double checked the plugs.

"Oh, we've been meaning to get that old thing out of here for years," Jane said from the doorway.

I jerked my head to look at her.

"Sorry to scare you. I was bringing up the laundry." She bumped the basket she carried with her hip. "Do you need a computer for something?"

"I was going to do a little research," I said, shrugging.

"My laptop is downstairs in the den. Feel free."

"Thanks," I said. My knees popped and protested as I got to my feet.

She smiled and headed into their bedroom.

I made my way back downstairs and into the den, appreciating the warm colors and the oversize couch that faced the fireplace, a pleasant blaze flickering in its depths. I found the laptop and booted it up, settling into the couch, tucking my feet up under me.

While it brought itself to life, I stared into the dancing flames in front of me, imagining cozy afternoons, reading books or sipping hot cocoa. It was a pretty picture. I even pictured Cassidy, myself, feet tucked under her, studying for finals. Peaceful.

The computer flashed onto its home screen, and I clicked on the internet icon, waiting for Google to pop up.

I started with some basic history of the town to get a bearing on time periods, populations, growth, and so on. I wasn't exactly sure where to start as far as the other stuff was concerned. Supernatural? How did one search for that? Old ghost stories?

I tried it all. There was the usual mish-mash of ghost sightings in various cemeteries in town. Most notably—or most humorously—was the one about a man from Transylvania buried under a crudely made tombstone. Supposedly, a tree had grown right through the center of where the body would be. Wild speculation and fanciful stories surrounded it. As interesting as it was, that was not the sort of thing that would give me any idea what had brought me here.

I looked into old legends and myths, checking for Indigenous burial grounds, sacred sites. If I could admit I came from another world, maybe it wasn't scientific at all. Maybe it *was* supernatural. I was desperate for something, anything, to make sense.

The best I could come up with was speculation about a naturally occurring magnetic field spanning most of the four block square that made up the business district. That led me to long discussions about the old mines underneath the town, the tunnels dug during prohibition and the ghost stories attached.

By the time I emerged from the time-suck, my stomach was growling. Jane was sitting in the corner, crafting. I hadn't even noticed her coming in or sitting down.

She seemed to sense my gaze and straightened to look at me. "Find some good info?"

I shrugged. "Nothing overly helpful."

"What exactly are you researching?"

I sighed and shut her laptop, stretching my back. "Basically, Skylar and I have been trying to figure out how I got here. So far, we haven't had much luck."

The interested look on Jane's face slowly retreated. No doubt she understood that if we were figuring out how it happened, we were going to find a way to send me back. "Oh. Well, I can't imagine it's easy to figure out something so. . . implausible."

"Right." I chewed on my lip. Again, I was reminded that I shouldn't be here. This woman was already attached to the idea of me being around, even if it had only been a few hours.

"Are you hungry?" she asked, the smile too bright.

"I'm getting there," I answered, playing it down. The guilt flared at the idea that she would be serving me at all, doing things for me.

She stood, glancing out the window. "It's really been coming down. I'll have to go out and shovel soon. Patrick can't do it because he threw out his back the other day." She smiled at me again. "Old age."

"Why don't I do it?" I offered, standing. Maybe it could serve as penance.

"Oh, you don't need to do that!" She waved her hands.

"No, I don't mind. I could use the workout."

She couldn't seem to come up with any further argument. "Well, if you really want to. . ." Her tone was uncertain.

"I do," I insisted.

She nodded. "The shovel's in the garage. I'll open it for you. If you want some gloves and a hat, there are some in the mudroom on your way."

24

Thunder

The snow continued its lazy descent, but it would be easier for whoever shoveled later if I removed the build-up of the previous three inches. Keeping up with it was the biggest hurdle.

The snow was light and fluffy, not the heavy, wet stuff that was more of a workout to scrape to the side. Still, I was already heating up after shoveling half of the long, sweeping driveway, and the cold air felt good against my flushed cheeks.

I was glad I'd insisted on doing the chore. After being cooped up, being useful again was satisfying; to get to flex my muscles, to have my heart pumping was soothing. Plus, it made me feel like a normal person doing an everyday activity. This was one place where I wasn't reminded of how out of place I was.

The scrape of the plastic bowl of the shovel against the concrete was oddly soothing as I pushed it across the surface and dumped the gathered snow onto the pile on the lawn.

"Cassidy?"

I jerked my head up, freezing in the act, fear skittering through me that someone would recognize me. How many neighbors would notice me and know that there was no way I should be here?

The fear abated at the sight of the man at the end of the driveway. The slightly nerdy computer guy from the police station.

I straightened and pushed the beanie I wore up on my forehead a little to let the air cool it.

He was dressed in a navy-colored puffy jacket, hands in pockets, beanie over his own head. His jeans were tucked into some pretty heavy-duty snow boots. A dog snuffled around the snow at his feet.

He smiled. "It's Creedy," he reminded me.

"Right, sorry," I said, waving my hand as if I could wipe away the awkwardness in the air. "Out of context."

"Oh, I understand. I realize I never actually introduced myself. You only heard Seward say my name a few times."

"Sure." I leaned against the shovel. "What are you up to today?"

"Oh, I was just out walking." He gestured to the dog. "Just because it's cold, doesn't mean my dog doesn't need exercise."

"You'd think he'd make an exception." I looked down at the wiry, black canine that was now sniffing at my boots.

He laughed. "You'd think. We're pretty religious about our walks, though. Plus, I grew up in North Dakota, so this isn't bad to me." He looked at the shovel. "I like the way it's quiet and soft out here when it snows. Helping out around the house?"

"Well," I said, surprised at the sudden change of subject. "Yeah. Figured I'd pitch in since I'm here visiting."

"Oh, you don't live here?" he asked, his green eyes lighting on the house.

"Um, no. I'm not actually from this area. You live nearby?"

He took my change in topic much easier than I had his. "Yeah, I live a couple of blocks over."

"It's a nice neighborhood," I said, not knowing what else to say.

"Hey Cass, lunch is ready," Jane said, emerging from the open garage. She smiled at Creedy as she joined us. "Hello."

"Uh, Jane, this is Creedy. He works with Drew."

"It's actually Gavin," he said smiling. "They refer to me by my last name at the station."

"Oh, like on television."

"Pretty much," he agreed. "Well, I don't want to hold you up. Gotta get Archie here home." He tugged the dog, who happily continued on in the snow.

She waved, and the two of us headed into the house through the garage. I leaned the shovel against the wall.

"So you met him before?" she asked, watching me knock the snow from my booted feet against the step before going inside.

"Yeah. Drew brought me into the station a few days ago. He was the one who ran my fingerprints that first day I, uh, got here."

"Seems friendly. I think I've seen him out before," she added thoughtfully.

"He said he walks his dog pretty regularly."

"That must be it." She shut the door behind me while I pulled my boots off then brushed past me to get to the kitchen. I hung up my coat and followed her, pulled by the spicy scent of chili mingling with the sweet warmth of cornbread, a perfect combination for a snowy day.

Jane handed me a bowl once I got into the kitchen, and I muttered my thanks. My father joined us, stiffening as soon as he saw me. I wasn't sure exactly what it was that made him react like that—was it my own animosity that always flared at the sight of him? Or maybe it was like Evan—the pain of seeing someone you loved die and then come back as a lesser version, a bad copy when all you wanted was the real thing.

Jane was sensitive to the change in atmosphere, keeping quiet and stealing glances between us as we all got our share of food and sat at the table. I wondered at her ability to take it in stride more smoothly. I certainly held less bitterness toward her. It may have made it easier. Or she was a better actor than everyone else.

I picked up my spoon, ready to dig in when both my father and his wife joined hands and bowed their heads. I tensed, clenching the spoon in my hand. It had never been a common practice growing up, but this seemed routine, lived-in.

He spoke the prayer quietly, mostly for the two of them. I felt like an intruder, violating something sacred. Had this become a regular part of life for them? Had Cassidy been a willing participant?

My father cleared his throat, the two of them lifted their heads, though not their eyes, and dug into their food as if I weren't there. Or maybe it was that my father was determined to pretend I wasn't. Jane lifted her face every once in a while to give me an encouraging smile.

If that was her way of trying to get me to talk to him, she was mistaken about my willingness. I tucked my chin down and ate in silence. The only sound between the three of us was our spoons hitting our bowls.

Even with the awkwardness, it was one of the best meals I'd had in a while, and certainly the first homemade one I'd been given in years. There was something about the warmth of a homemade meal that softened me a little.

"So, Cassidy, what do you do. . . back home?" Jane said, grappling for something to fill the silence.

I stiffened, pausing in the act of scooping more chili. It only lasted a moment, my stillness, and I swirled the spoon around, watching the chunks make room for the utensil as it forced its way through.

I waffled between telling the truth and fudging a little. I didn't want to invite more questions, but I didn't want to be deceptive either. I settled on ambiguity.

"I'm between jobs at the moment. I move around a lot."

She tilted her head. "Why do you move so much?"

"Jane, don't press," my father said.

I glanced at him. He wouldn't meet my gaze. Avoiding me. Just like he'd done the days leading up to his disappearance.

"I was in a bad situation," I said, answering Jane but watching him. "I felt like I had to cut and run. It's a family trait, I think." I didn't miss the stricken expression on Jane's face even though I was watching my father. He stiffened at my words.

Jane had the good grace to force a smile but turned her attention to her food. I pushed the shame down, lifting my chin a centimeter.

"What is that supposed to mean?" my father asked, voice low.

I shrugged, pushing my food around. It was childish of me to want to push him. But my bitterness was hard to contain. I'd let it make a home in my life, fed it, never anticipating the chance to let it loose. And it was sickeningly satisfying to see his reaction to my words.

When I had nothing else to add, he practically stabbed into

his own food. Even though it had been almost two decades since I'd seen him, I knew the look of something brewing from experience.

Some part of me acknowledged that what I was doing was unfair, but I couldn't seem to stop myself. "I've heard," I said, wanting to see that storm come to a head, "kids often follow in their parents' footsteps. We only copy what we see."

He set his spoon down with a clatter, and Jane startled at the sound. "That's enough."

"I'm just making conversation here, *Dad.* Don't you want to know how my life turned out? Because you certainly didn't before."

He stood up, heading for the door, leaving little room for argument.

But I always had a knack for squeezing into tight places. "What? Not the reunion you had in mind? Go ahead and leave when things get tough. It's what you're good at."

He spun to look at me, face reddened by anger. "You have no right to put that on me!"

Ooh, here comes the thunder.

"You have no idea what you're talking about," he continued, low and dangerous now. And that bolt had more punch.

"Patrick," Jane said softly.

The flinch was only visible in his eyes.

I had such skill for ruining a good meal. I stood as well and snatched my bowl from the table. "Thank you for lunch, Jane. I'll go finish the driveway."

My father watched me as I made my way to the mudroom, slamming the door behind me. It didn't drown out their voices as I'd hoped.

"How dare she—" he began.

"Patrick," she interrupted. "Can't you see that poor girl is hurting?"

"That is no excuse," he continued.

"She was perfectly polite before you came in. This is a problem for you and her to work out. And I think you need to be the one to—"

I banged out into the garage before I could hear more and snatched the shovel from against the wall where I'd left it. As if he could fix anything. Oh, I could admit this was not the man who'd left me to the mercy of the state. But just as they all struggled with that line, here I was blurring it too, willing to blame him anyway.

His anger surprised me. He'd always been slow to it, rarely exploding, but there was a fierce protectiveness there that I vaguely remembered from my mother's days in the hospital. And here he guarded his wife and his deceased daughter's name from my hostility.

I chewed on that, on the life he'd built here with Jane, and wondered exactly what it had been to make him stay. What had this Cassidy done differently to earn his devotion the way I had not?

Why had she deserved this, and why hadn't I?

The sound of the shovel against the concrete was violent, echoing across the snowy silence around me. The vibration jarred my body like someone was shaking me. I shoveled like it was a madness, grunting with the effort several more inches of snow, wet now, had added. Rhythmic, toiling. It's what I was used to. Pointless effort and rough resistance.

Once I finished the driveway, I shoveled in either direction on the sidewalk. When I finally stopped, I turned to find Jane standing in the glow of the porch light she'd turned on in the growing dark.

I didn't acknowledge her as I walked up the sloping drive to put the shovel away, setting it back on its hook.

"Thank you for your hard work," she said from behind me.

I grunted a reply, tired from my efforts, but also afraid of what I might say to her. I knew she didn't deserve my surly attitude.

Innocent bystander, I reminded myself.

She followed me dutifully into the mudroom, pressing the button to close the garage door, the rumbling sound loud enough to, thankfully, discourage any talking. I didn't look at her, hoping that she'd move on through to the main part of the house, but she waited while I removed my boots and coat.

As soon as the garage door was silent, she spoke. "Would you like some hot chocolate to warm up?"

Unavoidable. I sighed, resigned. "I'm pretty warm actually. A glass of water will be fine, and I can get that myself. Uh, but thank you."

She clasped her hands in front of her. "All right," she said softly.

Still, she followed me into the kitchen where I picked up my glass from earlier. I did my best to ignore her presence as I filled it and drank deeply, wishing I'd taken more time to hydrate. But I couldn't find myself regretting my decision to spend the last couple of hours outside.

Finally, I looked over at her waiting patiently near the table. I had a sneaking suspicion that my father underestimated her hardiness. She may have been soft and gentle, but something spoke of quiet strength. And she had *mom face* on.

"Are you going to scold me now?" I asked flatly.

She gave me a wry smile. "Should I?"

I set my glass down and sighed. "Probably."

"Honey, I don't really know if that's what you need right now."

My head snapped up sharply. "Don't call me that. I'm not your daughter, and you're definitely not my mother."

I stalked out into the living room, wondering in my hastiness where I could shut myself in when Drew stepped out of the shadow of the entryway. Judging by his pursed lips and the way he seemed to look down his nose at me, he'd heard my outburst.

I licked my finger and held it up like I was testing the wind. "I feel a lecture coming on."

He rolled his eyes. "Just grab your stuff, and we can talk about it later."

"Yes, *Officer*," I spat as I shoved past him to get my recently removed boots and jacket. I opted to leave the jacket unzipped, still warm from shoveling and the flush of anger.

"Thank you, Jane," Drew said hastily as I made my way to the door.

He caught my arm before I went down the porch steps. "What is wrong with you?" he asked.

"A lot, actually," I threw back.

"They have been through so much, and this was a tremendous effort on their part to take you in today. And all you did was be antagonistic."

"Yes, what a *sacrifice* they made to take care of a burden like me. I'm so grateful they deigned to even *look* at me." The traitorous tears were hot in my eyes. "*You* were the one who brought me here. What did you think was going to happen?"

He sucked in a breath. "Cassidy."

"No." I brushed away the hand he lifted to comfort me. "I

know I don't deserve it." I turned away and walked the length of the porch since he seemed inclined to hash this out right here, right now. "You're right. I've been mean. I can't. . ." I gripped the edge of the porch railing, an anchor in my spinning equilibrium.

He moved toward me and brushed his hand over my hair very gently, almost not even touching it.

"I can't stop myself. There's too much that hurts. Just looking at him rips at me," I said, my throat closing. I swallowed hard. "Because he didn't want me. I wasn't good enough for him to stay in my world. There's something wrong with *me*." I pressed my hands to my chest. "If you listened to my heartbeat, it would probably just sound like a bunch of pieces rattling around."

"Quite the image," he murmured.

I looked at him, and he was smiling sadly. He touched my face, wiping uselessly at the tears with his thumb.

"It wasn't you, Cass," he whispered. "That is on him, that other version of your father. *He* made that choice."

I was shaking my head as he spoke, but he brought his other hand to my face, holding it still.

"There's no reason a person wouldn't want you."

He was so close that I could feel his breath fan across my face. It was distracting enough to make me forget what my argument had been. I could forget a lot of things if someone spent their time looking at me like that.

His lips connected with mine so suddenly, I hadn't even seen it coming, barely had time to suck in a breath before the glorious heat of his mouth was begging for a response from mine. It was too easy to give in to the demand.

My hands fisted in his jacket, a flood of heat surging through me, starting at my core and spreading. But my self-control regained its footing, and I pulled back.

"What are you doing?" I whispered, my eyes still shut.

He leaned his forehead against mine. "I've been wanting to do that for a long time."

Meaning her, not me.

My eyes flew open, and I jerked out of his arms. Pain lanced through me, and the lump immediately formed in my throat.

His brows drew together in confusion. "What's wrong?"

I clenched my hands into fists and fought the tears that threatened again. "I think we should go." I left off the word "home," not really knowing where he might take me for the night, and because I knew I needed to start making the distinction clearer to everyone that this was not where I was supposed to be.

His eyes shifted away, the rejection subtle but recognizable, even on such a stony face as the one he turned to face me again. "All right." He stepped back to let me walk down the stairs in front of him.

25

Cassidy Vs. Cassidy

Rigid silence made the car ride almost unbearable. But I refused to break it. How many times had I pointed out that I was not their Cassidy? I should have known better. I'd been feeling it all day. It had been more obvious at my—*her*—parents' house. It wasn't so clear with her friends because it was not as difficult separating it out for myself. I had not known them in my other life.

Still.

I should've left when I'd had the chance.

We pulled into the parking space in front of Drew's town-house. Even the sight of Wilhelm in the window didn't bring my mood up. It didn't seem to help much for Drew either.

He got out of the car without even looking at me. The cold shoulder was hard to handle. I was used to anger, outbursts. It was obvious how much my rejection had hurt him. Twice in one day.

I walked up to the door behind him, admittedly dragging my feet even though goosebumps broke out across my skin. I almost felt the physical freeze-out was preferable to the emotional one.

Still, I trudged into the house as he held the door open. Wil sat at the base of the stairs as he had the last time, whining in anticipation of greeting us.

Drew shut the door and took my coat, hanging it up with his in the coat closet. Finally, he turned to look at his dog.

"All right," he said, giving him the release gesture.

The dog ran up to me first but touched his nose to Drew's hand. It was obvious he sensed the tension between us, like he had during our argument the day before.

I sat on the couch, only to have him practically climbing into my lap to comfort me.

Drew shook his head and headed for his kitchen. "Hungry? I have some homemade enchiladas. My mom dropped them off yesterday."

"Sure," I replied, trying not to let his flat tone bother me. It's what I wanted. I needed to distance myself from everyone here. I needed to leave as soon as we had this thing figured out. He knew that was the plan.

And he'd kissed me anyway.

Wil whined as if he could hear my thoughts and scooted closer to me, sitting on my feet and warming them. I scrubbed his head reassuringly as the lump built in my throat again. My only consolation in leaving was that it was by my own choice, and I wouldn't be running from anyone. Just saving others the heartache of my presence.

After a while, I leaned my head back and stared at the ceiling. Its texture reminded me of fireworks, and I found myself wondering what kind of tool would create the starburst shape. Still, my hands worked a calming pattern over Wil's fur, and I could admit, if only to myself, that it was as much to soothe me as him.

"He knows you're upset."

I lifted my head to look at Drew as he came back into the room. He wasn't looking at me as he crossed to the chair and sat, sighing heavily as the worn cushions enveloped his body. He was probably exhausted after the night he'd had.

Wil turned to look at him but stuck with me.

"They're perceptive animals," I said. "He can tell you are, too."

His gaze flickered to mine then away. "But we can see where his priorities are."

I couldn't detect any bitterness in his tone but I still wondered if it was there. I'd rejected him, and now his dog seemed to prefer me over him.

As if he understood, Wil got up and ambled over to lick his hand.

"Too little too late, buddy," he said, scratching the thick fur along his spine. "But I appreciate the thought."

I looked away. It's better this way, I reminded myself again. *I'm leaving.*

I repeated it over and over like a mantra until the bell on the microwave indicated the enchiladas were reheated, and Drew stood to get them.

Wil followed him back to the kitchen, and I was grateful the dog showed where his loyalty really lay.

I went to sit at the small dining room table, tucked back by the kitchen, and silently let Drew bring me my plate and a glass of water. He joined me, but I kept my attention on my food.

Finally, I worked up the courage. "What did you figure out for the team you were going to put together?"

He maintained the aloofness, but the disappointment was

there in his eyes. "I pulled in a couple of guys I knew I could trust. I laid out some of the details, and we're working through a plan. We can probably get the ball rolling tomorrow."

"Tomorrow," I repeated, nodding. It's what I wanted. A quick solution to be able to get on my way. So why was part of me disappointed as well? I had proof that the line had been blurred too many times.

I looked over to see him determinedly cutting his food into bites.

He lifted his gaze. "You're sure you want to do this? Leave?"

"Don't you realize it's better this way?" I demanded.

He sighed, and the heat I'd seen in previous disagreements flashed into his eyes momentarily. "You don't have to—"

"Yes, I do. The fact you're arguing against it proves that I do. Kissing me on the porch—" I hated that even mentioning it made me breathless. "None of you see me as I really am."

"Cassidy," he started, his tone already a rebuttal.

"Exactly," I interrupted. "You can't separate me from her. Jane calls me 'honey,' Skylar treats me like we've been friends for years, and you kiss me because you never got to have *her*."

"Is that what this is about?" He shook his head, smiling a little as if it were a simple explanation. "It has nothing to do—"

"It does!" The table rattled with the force of my fist against it. "You can't deny that. I look *exactly* like her, I sound like her. I probably *smell* like her. And what about Evan? What would it do to him to know that you—that we—"

"Cassidy, I care about *you*." He was determined to ignore that last part. "I know you're a different person. I understand that probably better than any of them."

I shut my eyes briefly. "It doesn't matter," I insisted, taking a different tack. "We can't be together. Even if we made it work now, it wouldn't last."

"Why not?" The question was so innocent, his expression open, eager. A child wanting the one thing he hoped for most.

"Because it would fall apart. It always does." When had I started crying? The tears again, how I hated them. "I can't make things work. I'm broken, and that always makes them leave." The last word was almost a whisper.

The pain in my chest was sharp, the ribs constricting, the goal to crush my heart, my lungs. To make it all stop. Everything would be made right. Cassidy was meant to stay dead.

He was out of his chair, kneeling next to me. Another moment, so many in such a short time, where he was comforting me through my tears. His hands were warm against my arms, brushing my hair, caressing my cheeks.

"You don't make people leave. That's a choice *they* make."

I shook my head.

"Trust me," he insisted. "I went to therapy once. I'm an expert now."

I laughed, a shaky sound.

"Please," he said, his eyes imploring. "Don't write this off yet."

I nodded, but only to end the conversation, the torture it was to fight the part of me that wanted this so badly. It would be easier to concede. But easy didn't mean right.

He wiped at the tears with his thumbs, then hesitated a fraction of a second before pressing his lips where they'd been, on each side of my face. Tender, comforting. I shut my eyes.

Yes, it would be very easy to give in.

My resolve wavered as his lips continued a lazy trail down

my face to my mouth, which seemed to have a life of its own. It cared nothing for logic, only craved the feel of him. After being denied its wish more than once, it took its prize with a vengeance. Even my hands, co-conspirators, plunged into the softness of his dark hair, gripped like it was a lifeline. A growl rumbled deep in his chest in response, causing a sinful coil of warmth low in my stomach. He pulled me from the chair, pressed me against his body, heat connecting with heat.

I suddenly felt myself lifted up as he stood, carrying me toward the kitchen, sliding me onto the counter so that we were eye to eye. His hands slid up my arms, brushing my hair from my face, and I yanked him closer by the belt loops, feverish to erase any space between us. His mouth plundered mine, and his hands were everywhere, fiery through my clothes.

He broke away only to blaze a trail of kisses down to my throat, along my collarbone, back up to just beneath my ear, sending chills cascading over me. I wrapped my legs around his waist, hooking them at the ankles, locking him in. God, his hair was so soft.

Hot hands snuck very slowly from my hips, up under my shirt, to the bare skin above my jeans, lighting a fire as they moved up and up. I tilted my head back with a sigh as my fingers dug into his back.

I heard movement, and with my eyes half-closed, I barely made out the shape of the dog walking into the room. I opened them fully to really look at him, trying to focus, because. . . there was a reason we weren't supposed to be doing this, wasn't there? I had a reason. A shiver crested over me caused by warm breath against my throat, lips driving me crazy as they danced over my skin.

His fingers brushed my rib cage, and I stiffened. He froze,

pulling his head back to look at me, panting. "What's wrong?"

"We can't. . ." I swallowed, tried again. "We shouldn't be doing this." I put my hands on each side of his face, breathed out the agony of making him stop, and it was almost a groan.

His hands tightened, and I shut my eyes to keep him from seeing the want there. They would beg him to keep going because every second his hands remained on me, I lost my nerve.

Wil whined as if on cue, frighteningly in tune with me.

We both looked at him, our breathing the only answer in the quiet house. Drew looked at me; his hands, slow and reluctant, slid down my sides, my hips, and stopped to rest on my thighs.

I let my own hands land on his shoulders, and I concentrated on the top button of his shirt where it was undone, fiddling with it. "I'm not sure this is the right time," I said, my voice more even now that he wasn't touching me like a starving man getting his first meal.

"You're right," he murmured. His voice still had the husky sound of desire in it, and something clenched low, low in my stomach.

I fixated on that button, knowing that if I looked him in the eye, I would absolutely lose this battle with my self-control.

"Cassidy." It was almost a moan the way he said it.

My gaze flickered up to his.

"I can't concentrate when you have me locked in like this." His hands slid smoothly over the backs of my thighs, my knees, stopping to rest on my calves. Even that caress almost undid me, but I focused on what he was drawing my attention to.

"Oh." I unhooked my ankles to release him. "Sorry."

"Not as sorry as I am," he said, backing up. He ran his hands through his tousled hair and blew out a labored breath.

The loss of his body heat was almost like a physical ache, and a war raged on inside of me. I almost reached out to him, pulled him back. Logic be damned, that ache must be assuaged.

He ran his hands through his hair again. "I need something to do with my hands, something between us—I don't know. But I can't just stand here."

I licked my lips, struggling to keep myself from giving in. "How about dinner?" I suggested.

"You first. I need, uh, I need a drink."

I slid slowly off the counter, afraid any sudden movement would undo us both because that ache still clawed at me, and I was close, so close to surrendering.

"A strong drink," he muttered, his eyes tracing the shape of my body. Abruptly, he turned away to rummage in a cupboard.

"Is alcohol really the best idea?" I asked, sitting down at the table. I ran my hands over my hair to smooth it back into place, giving myself a moment to settle my heartbeat.

He slammed the cupboard shut. "Good point."

I forced myself to pick up my fork and take a bite, the food barely warm after all this time, but I didn't dare move to warm it up.

"Here, Wil," he said, slapping his thigh. "Want to go outside, buddy?"

Wil stood and bounced a little, tongue lolling out.

Drew went to the sliding door with the dog in tow. I watched his lean body and struggled to swallow a rise of desire. He went straight out with the dog, no jacket, and shut the door. Smart man.

* * *

As hard as it had been to drift off, I was deeply entrenched in a dream when Drew came into his room where he'd insisted I sleep. It was while he was rooting around in his dresser that I surfaced, light spilling in from a hall light.

I narrowed my eyes against it and groaned, throwing an arm over my face. "What are you doing?" I croaked.

I felt his weight settle on the edge of the bed "Sorry to wake you," he whispered.

I pulled my arm away to squint up at him. "You didn't answer my question."

He touched my hair, brushing it away from my face. "I got a call from the station. Another girl has disappeared."

As I had the night before, I sat up so quickly, he had to pull back to avoid a collision. "A redhead?"

He nodded.

"But our plan. . ."

He was grim, worry etching lines into his handsome face. "Serial killers don't exactly follow the rules."

"So you have to go in?"

He sighed and looked over toward the dresser he'd been rummaging in a moment before. "Yeah. I was about to grab a quick shower." He brought his gaze back to me. "Wakes me up better than coffee."

I tossed my blankets off of me.

"What are you doing?"

"I'm coming with you."

He raised his eyebrows.

I gave him a dark look. "Not for the shower."

"That's not what I was thinking," he said. "But now that you mention it. . ."

I punched him in the arm.

"Kidding." He sobered, rubbing where I'd hit him. "What makes you think you're coming with me?"

"We had an agreement. I still get a say in this. Besides, who are you going to call to babysit at this hour?" I gestured to the bedside clock, the glowing red numbers telling us it was 3:47 am.

"Fine." He stood, towering over me. "Be ready in ten minutes."

I pounded down the stairs, pulling a sweater over my head as I went. Wil met me on the first floor, his tail wagging excitedly. I ran my hand over his thick fur absently before heading to the first floor half-bath to splash cold water on my face. My eyes were puffy with sleep, but there wasn't much I could do about it. I ran my fingers through my unruly hair and pulled it up into a ponytail. It was the best I could do. Drew came down while I was pulling on my socks and boots. Wil sniffed around my face and hair, impeding the process.

"Wil, come."

The dog immediately obeyed and sat at the base of the stairs.

Drew's hair was damp, and he held a pair of clean socks in his hand. Apparently, middle of the night calls meant he could wear jeans and a sweatshirt into the office.

He sat next to me to put on the socks and a pair of beat up sneakers. "Listen. When we get there, you can't ask questions or get in the way. Stay at my desk."

"Do I need to ask permission to go to the bathroom?" I asked.

He shot me an exasperated look before standing and holding out his hand to pull me to my feet. He didn't step back, and we were a mere two inches from each other. Regret flashed across his face, and he sighed. But I didn't get any further response as we donned our coats and headed out the door.

The darkness always seemed heavier in the middle of the night. Sound was muted, echoey. I shivered against the eerie feeling I got, pulling my coat tighter around me as we got into the car.

I fell asleep on the ride over, lightly enough to sense when we'd parked at the station. I lifted my head in time to see Drew turn off the car, the heat that was blowing full blast suddenly ceasing.

We remained silent as we got out and walked up the steps, but he grabbed my hand and squeezed before releasing it to pull open the door for me. The sound of frenzied voices carried to us. Based on the size of the town, the night shift was probably not typically eventful. And as we entered the bullpen, I considered my hunch verified when seeing that most everyone was dressed as casually as Drew was.

A woman in her early fifties sat at one of the desks, gray streaks in her auburn hair. An officer crouched in front of her, another perched on the desk facing her as she dabbed her eyes with a tissue.

It wasn't hard to figure out she was the missing girl's mother.

Drew nodded to his desk, and I obediently cut through the crowd to get there. He was focused on the woman, and I knew already that this was going to be a long and boring few hours until we could work out a new plan. If there would even be one.

It had to be that somehow the killer got wind of a brewing offensive. Nothing had changed up until this point. Just yesterday, he'd left a gift for me. So he was either flying by the seat of his pants, or he'd had this up his sleeve the whole time.

My stomach twisted and roiled. If we'd gotten moving

sooner, this could have been prevented.

I thought I'd be able to glean some information by listening, but there was too much activity, a gentle hum buzzing around the room so that nothing was distinguishable. Even with the merry-go-round thought process and the noise level, I grew drowsy. I laid my head back and shut my eyes to relax and floated in and out of full consciousness.

A couple of times, I jerked awake at the sound of raised voices or a half-dream.

"You can go into one of the cells and lie down if you want," Drew suggested, leaning against the edge of his desk.

I looked at the clock. Almost 5 a.m. I sighed and stretched. "How about some breakfast?"

"There's bagels in the break room." He nodded in that direction.

"I actually would like to keep my teeth," I said.

"Coffee, then."

I stood, noticing that the frenzy seemed to have slowed down, and the mother was gone. A couple of cops were chatting softly in the break room when I came in, but they ignored me as I found the bagels, perusing despite my comment. I had no qualms about poking each one until I found one that was reasonably edible and slathered cream cheese over it.

I wasn't sure if it was the lack of sleep, but I felt the oppressive weight of desperation that blanketed the station. Things had been going on too long, and everyone was discouraged.

Drew came in after a minute, pouring himself a cup of coffee and joined me where I stood, leaning against a wall.

"There doesn't seem to be a lot of hope," I commented.

He grimaced as he took a sip of his drink. "He's taken things to the next level."

Fear's cold fingers tickled at the back of my neck. "So how do we catch him now?"

He shook his head, frowning. "I don't know. But these kinds of guys tend to think so highly of themselves that they almost want to get caught, just to be recognized for their genius."

"They mess up on purpose?"

"Exactly."

"So that's why he was playing with us. He was escalating."

Drew met my gaze. "Or distracting us so that he could take this girl. This is the youngest girl he's taken. She was in high school."

I swallowed, thinking about the poor kid's mother. "What happens if the town runs out of redheads?"

"Well, we know there's at least one more."

26

A Picture Worth a Thousand Kisses

We waited until sunrise before he called Jane and my father. Despite my behavior the day before, they were willing to take me back. I suspected it was Jane more than my father who'd made that decision.

I had no good ideas for luring the killer out. The team Drew had assembled more or less dispersed to find this girl. Something nagged at me. I had very little evidence, which was why I hadn't said anything before.

"You said that the killer had a line on the inside," I said.

Drew took his eyes from the road for only a split second. "And?"

"What if it's not just a line? What if he *is* the inside man?"

He wasn't shocked by my suggestion. Not even mad. "You have someone in mind?"

I hesitated. Despite his calm, I was afraid of how my accusation would be received. "Russo."

He raised a brow. "You have some sort of evidence?"

"No. I mean, the other day, when I was in the break-room, he was staring at me."

Drew actually laughed. "He was staring at you?" he asked. "You do realize that you're a pretty woman, right? Men stare at you all the time."

I folded my arms over my chest, ignoring his compliment. "He wasn't looking at me like that. It was kind of creepy. And I'm pretty sure he ran into me the other day at the cafe. He looked at me weird then, too."

He tilted his head, considering. "I don't think it's him, but I promise to look into it. It doesn't hurt to check."

"That's all I'm asking."

I leaned my head back against the headrest. We passed through the neighborhoods that I now vaguely recognized and I tried to calm my breathing, working through the emotions that waged a war inside me. Drew ran a finger absently over his lips. I could tell that his mind was back on the investigation. They had limited time to find the girl alive. She'd been taken the afternoon before. And the killer only ever kept them a couple of days before dumping them, strangled and carved up.

I craned my neck when I spotted the figure sitting on the steps of the front porch at my father's house. Drew dropped his hand and squinted, speeding up.

We slid a little when he braked at the curb.

He released a breath. "It's only Evan."

He may have been relieved, but I wasn't convinced it was a good thing. Evan's emotions were too volatile to trust an innocent motive.

Evan lifted his head as I got out of the car, his eyes narrowing on my face. His attention shifted to Drew as he rounded the front of the car. Drew was relaxed, casual, but Evan's expression tightened, his mouth disappearing into a thin line.

"Hey, Ev," Drew said amicably.

"Drew—" I reached out to warn him as Evan surged to his feet, meeting Drew halfway down the sidewalk before I could get another word out. His hands fisted around Drew's jacket, and he backed him all the way to the car with a shove. I sucked in a breath, bringing my hands up to my face as if I were on the receiving end of the violence.

"What the hell?" Drew spat.

Evan shoved him again, forcing his head to snap back against the hood.

"Evan—" I started, fear clutching at my throat.

"What is this?" Evan snarled, ignoring me.

I noticed belatedly that he held something in his hand. A picture.

He shoved it into Drew's face. "What is this?!"

"Evan!" I tried again, louder, panic clenching in my gut.

I heard the door behind me open.

"What is going on?" My father's demanding voice snapped against the tension in the air.

"You think you can do whatever you want with her because she's not the real Cassidy?" Evan continued through his teeth.

My father charged past me and yanked Evan away from Drew in one impressively fluid motion. "What is wrong with you, boy?" He wasn't yelling, but there was a ripple of authority.

Drew straightened his jacket and touched the back of his head with his left hand.

"You have no *right*!" Evan shouted, stabbing a finger at Drew as my father dragged him toward the house.

Jane stood in the open doorway with a hand pressed to her mouth.

"What is he talking about?" I asked, my voice shaking.

Drew's gaze flickered to me before he stalked up the walk

toward the house.

I glanced around the neighborhood. There were a few curious faces in windows and a couple of front doors gaping open, berobed people standing on porches craning necks to see what the commotion was about.

I turned and jogged up the walkway into the house and shut the door against the gawkers.

My father forced Evan to sit on the couch and stood above him like a sentinel, arms crossed.

"Just what the hell is going on?" he demanded.

Drew maintained his distance across the room, still as a statue, shame pulling his focus to his shoes.

Evan's glare was venomous as he trained it on his cousin. He tossed the picture onto the coffee table. Drew waited a moment before walking over to pick it up. The change in his expression was instant. I watched the brick wall slam into place.

"Where did you get this?" Drew asked. Quiet but sharp, a knife cutting the skin.

Evan ignored his question and the tone. "What made you think you had the *right* to—"

"*Where* did you get this?"

I started at the sudden spike in volume.

"It was left on my doorstep this morning," Evan said through clenched teeth.

I touched Drew's arm, and he flinched. He handed the picture to me.

I sucked in a breath. No wonder Evan was so angry. A stab of shame and guilt lanced through me.

It was a picture of Drew and me on the front porch of this very house. It had been taken right as he'd leaned forward to kiss me. And there was no mistaking it, even though it was taken at night. Someone had a very good camera. The picture must have been taken somewhere across the street. The killer had been a busy man. He'd already kidnapped the girl by that point.

Jane touched my shoulder.

"It's him," I answered her silent question. "He killed Cassidy, and now he wants me."

* * *

I sat at the table, staring out the sliding glass door at the blanket of white in the backyard. The brightness hurt my eyes, but I couldn't make myself look away.

"Would you like some tea?" Jane asked from the doorway.

"Uh, sure." I finally pulled my gaze away.

Drew left as soon as a squad car was stationed on the street. He'd taken the photo to be analyzed at the station. Evan left not long after when my father told him he needed to go cool off.

And here I sat, realizing that the killer had been here, had been so close to me that he could take a picture, steal a moment from me. And on top of everything else, I felt like the biggest jerk on the planet, as if I'd deceived everyone. Why couldn't I stop hurting people?

Jane filled a tea kettle and set it on the burner then joined me at the table. She touched my arm. "You have nothing to be ashamed of."

I winced. At least we were avoiding the *other* topic. "Don't I? My very presence here has hurt everyone, him most of all. He doesn't deserve this."

She smiled at me. "No, he doesn't. But he has no claim over

you. You are not his Cassidy. You deserve some happiness too."

I looked at her, really took in her kind face. How I had underestimated this woman. I wished I could have benefited from her motherly wisdom growing up like Cassidy had. I hoped to God she'd appreciated it, fostered the relationship. What I wouldn't give.

"I'm so sorry, Jane. I'm sorry for the way I spoke to you yesterday."

"Oh, honey. I helped raise a teenage girl. If I was so easily bothered by some silly words. . ." She patted my arm and stood when the kettle started to whistle.

She poured the tea into two mugs and brought them over to the table, but she only set one down. "I think the person you really need to talk to, though, is Patrick."

I opened my mouth to protest.

"Now, don't get argumentative. You don't have anything to apologize for. I just think you two should talk." She looked over to the doorway where he'd suddenly materialized.

I sat up straighter and bit back a retort, an excuse, anything. My desire to throw up a protective wall was almost uncontrollable. My best protection had always been my words.

Jane smiled again and left us alone.

He walked over slowly, debating which chair to take, then settled across from me. "Jane and I had a long discussion yesterday," he said.

I didn't respond and looked down into my cup, tendrils of tea swirling like smoke out of the bag.

"And she set me straight on the subject. As with most things, she was right."

"About what?" My tone was flat. *I don't care, I don't care, I don't care.*

"You're in pain, and it has to do with me."

I looked up at him.

"I know it's not *really* me, but I don't think it matters." He clasped his hands and set them on the table in front of him. I remembered those hands, square, strong, the fingers linked with my mothers, caressing her sallow skin as she wasted away in the hospital. I also remembered his tears.

"You should talk to me," he continued. "Tell me what hurt you so badly. Say what you would say to him, that other me."

I was startled. It would be painful, for both of us. I had words laced with acid, a caustic weapon that might permanently burn. And I knew that I wouldn't be able to keep protecting myself. Anger was a wall that I reinforced daily. This would tear it down and leave me vulnerable to attack. I already felt exposed.

I looked down. "I don't think—"

He put his hand on my arm. "Say your piece. In so many ways, you are my little girl, and I would want someone to do this for her. You have to get it out because it will drag you down."

"What, are you a therapist now?" I didn't bother trying to soften the bite in my tone.

He took it without reacting. "No, I'm not. But I have life experience you don't." He paused, looked out the backdoor. "Did you know that my dad was verbally abusive?"

His willing acceptance of my sting deflated my attitude, and I didn't answer.

"I grew up believing I was worthless. All I heard was that I was stupid and I'd never amount to anything. They told me to blame the disease, the alcoholism. But it wasn't always when he was drunk."

The drunkenness was vaguely familiar. My mother had told me his father died in a car accident that claimed his mother's life as well. Drunk driving, she'd said.

He dragged his eyes back to me. "Bitterness is a slow poison, Cassidy. It won't kill you, but it will suck you dry until you're toxic and hollow. And that's worse than death."

He was leaning forward, such earnestness in his expression. I looked down, stared at my hands, wringing my fingers together, around and around. Could I do this? What would happen if I said it all?

I opened my mouth, shut it. Tried again. "You abandoned me." I hurled the words, unable to stop myself.

He didn't quite succeed at keeping his reaction in check; his sharp intake of breath felt loud.

The sound spurred me on. "You dropped me off at school that morning and never came back." I looked at him then. Tears shone in his eyes, but he kept them at bay, didn't say anything, didn't try to defend himself.

"When they called social services, no one could even trace you. You'd withdrawn a few thousand dollars, whatever was left after the medical bills—not much—and disappeared.

"I always wondered what I did, why I wasn't enough for you." The sob fighting to get out shook my voice; the threatening tears made my chin tremble. "They sent me to foster care. At first, I tried to be good. I expected that you'd come back. But after a while, it was obvious you weren't going to." The anger lashed into my eyes. "You just left me. Ran out, like a coward."

He flinched.

"I started to hate you, to hate everyone. I threw temper tantrums, stole things, called people names, refused to eat. Some of the foster parents were nice. They took me to counseling, tried to be compassionate. But they'd always give up. Send me to someone else, make me their problem. And some of them weren't so nice. One woman would lock me in the bathroom for hours at a time just for crying."

He sucked in a breath and rubbed his hand over his chin, the sound of his palm against the stubble like he was rubbing sandpaper. His tears poured out silently, and he took it, absorbed those words like he deserved them.

And as much as it bothered me to see him do that, I couldn't make myself stop. That pain, almost constant in my chest, begged to be released, avenged. "So I learned to take what I was given and shut up. Because if I could be good enough, then maybe someone would want me. But no one ever did. Because there's something wrong with me. Something that makes people cringe and pull away. Because you left me, Daddy. You left me all alone when I was eight years old and my mother had just died."

He exhaled, shaky, bit his lip, tried to hold in the emotion.

"Then I got here, and she had all the things I never had." I curled my hands into fists. "And it was so unfair, you know? That she had you. What did she do that I didn't? What about her made you stay?"

I watched him fight for control of his emotions.

"Why didn't you stay?" The anger wasn't enough to hold back the sobs any longer; they were violent in their escape, ravaging.

He grabbed my hand, and I surprised myself by not pulling away. "I'm so sorry, Cassidy." He pressed my hand to his cheek, wet from the tears. "You have every right to hate me. I was selfish about my own pain. There is no excuse. Please, forgive me."

He whispered it, over and over. "Forgive me. Forgive me."

And that pain, the constant digging in my chest loosened just enough that I could breathe again. It was never about him, I realized. It was about me. About forgiveness. No amount of words on his part could wipe the damage away. *I* had the power to rebuild myself because I decided to.

27

Killer, Who? Call Drew

So many things swirled in my mind. My tea had long since grown cold, and I dumped it into the sink. Cassidy's father had excused himself to leave me alone with my thoughts. There were a lot of things to shuffle through.

Still, my lungs worked a little easier than they had before; the vise that always held me in its grip loosened. I had never realized I could get oxygen without so much effort until the impediment was gone.

But something else plagued me, something itching at my mind. I kept circling back to the situation with Drew and Evan. The twisted look of betrayal on Evan's face, the hurt there. Drew's shame. I tried to convince myself it had nothing to do with me. His greedy lips on mine the night before submitted as evidence.

No, it wasn't all of those things that really nagged at me. It was that picture, that moment captured in time from the cover of a hiding place. Someone had taken a private memory from me, corrupted it.

I knew Drew was having it analyzed, checked for anything

that could be a helpful clue. A reflection or angle to give them an exact location. But real police work wasn't like TV. It didn't just happen. Zoom in, bam, there it is.

But that picture still bothered me. More than knowing someone had been watching me.

There was a knock on the front door, and I turned at the sound of Jane's slippers on the hardwood of the entryway.

"Oh, Skylar!" she said.

I made my way through the living room to the front door as Jane released Skylar from a hug, her bulky coat obscuring her tiny body. The exhaustion was evident in her face as she looked at me, eyes softening.

I embraced her next. "How's your grandma?"

She frowned, unzipping her coat to hang it up. "She's doing a little better."

"I'm so glad," Jane said.

Skylar shrugged. "It's still hard to tell if she'll make it. I can't take that much time off work. But I'm going to have to go back and forth for a while, at least until I know she's getting better."

Jane nodded. "Well, I'll keep praying she gets well soon. Come in and have some tea. Let me make you lunch or something," she insisted, herding us into the living room before bustling into the kitchen.

Skylar sat on the couch with a heavy sigh, tilting her head back against the cushion. If I had to guess, she'd probably had less sleep than I had. A nap seemed to be calling her name.

"You look like you had a rough morning," I commented.

She smiled wryly. "Thanks. You don't look so hot yourself. I'd say it's been an emotional day for you too."

I sat next to her and looked at my feet. "I had a drag-out

with my—with Cassidy's father."

Her face instantly softened. "Serious? And?"

"It helped. A lot, actually."

"Good." She touched my arm.

"That was after Evan nearly punched Drew this morning."

"What?" She sat up straighter.

The heat crept into my face. "And Drew kissed me."

"You've been busy! Well, we know it was bound to happen," she said, shrugging.

"The kiss or the punch?"

She laughed. "Both, I guess. You kissed in front of Evan?"

I shook my head. "He wasn't here."

Her mouth dropped open. "You kissed *here*?"

"On the front porch," I said, sheepish.

"Then how did he find out?"

"Someone was watching us. They took a picture and left it on Evan's doorstep."

The color drained from her face. "Was it. . ?"

I nodded before she could finish.

She leaned back again, stunned. "That's creepy as hell."

"No kidding." I linked my fingers and stared at them. What a day it had been. "How did you know I was here?" I asked suddenly.

"I called Drew on my way back into town. He told me about the missing girl."

We were quiet for a moment.

"So. . . Drew kissed you?"

I laughed. "It's not a big deal."

She shook her head. "Actually, it kind of is."

"Well, it's been sort of ruined by the stalker picture." I didn't mention the fact that I was still considering leaving. It would probably just start another argument.

"Well, that's understandable."

I shook my head, trying to put my feelings into words. "I mean, something about it is bothering me."

She raised a brow. "You mean, aside from the fact that a serial killer may have taken it?"

"I know. It sounds stupid, right?"

She touched my arm. "Try not to worry about it. The police know what they're doing."

I nodded. Of course she was right. I couldn't do anything about it, not when we had no plan moving forward. But I couldn't shake the feeling that something was glaringly obvious, right in front of me. Taunting, just out of reach. *Think, think.*

"Skylar, how long are you staying? I was going to make some tuna casserole for lunch." Jane came back into the living room.

Skylar pulled her sleeve back to check her watch.

Time seemed to move in slow motion for a minute, and there was a ringing in my ears. It was there the whole time.

I gripped Skylar's wrist. "The watch."

Jane and Skylar stared at me, mirror images of confusion.

"Skylar, you need to call Drew right now."

"What? Why?"

"Please, just call him."

She pulled out her cell phone. "Okay. But he said he was going to be in a meeting."

I got up and paced. I would have to make sure my suspicions were true, that my memory wasn't playing tricks. It was probably better that we go to the station so I could look at the photo again.

Skylar shook her head and hung up. "He's not answering."

"I need you to take me down to the station, then. It's important."

Skylar looked at Jane then back at me. "Okay. . . Right this minute?"

"I'm so sorry. If you want to stay here, maybe Jane or my, uh, Pat could take me. But I need to get to the station right now."

"It's fine. I'll do it," Skylar said, standing.

"Are you all right, Cassidy?" Jane asked.

I gave her a reassuring smile. "I'm fine. But I think I know who the killer is."

28

To Catch a Watch

"You're sure?" Skylar asked, her hands white on the steering wheel.

"No." I couldn't ruin a man's reputation on some random connection I made unless I was certain. "But that's why I want to go down there. I have to see that picture again."

"All because of my watch?"

"Yes."

"Okay. . ."

My legs bounced as we drove. I knew we were making record time, but it wasn't fast enough for me, even after urging Skylar to punch it past the speed limit. If what I suspected was true, then we might save a teenage girl's life.

Finally, we pulled into the visitor's lot at the station, and I leaped from the car and sprinted for the door.

"Hey! Little legs here," Skylar called from behind me.

I held the door open for her, waving an impatient hand for her to kick it into high gear. As soon as she was in, I took off again without her, breezing past the front desk.

It was quieter than I'd ever seen, few people sitting at their desks. It looked like there was a pow-wow happening in one of the conference rooms. I didn't bother trying to get Drew's attention and went straight to his desk to see if he'd left the picture there.

As usual, it was immaculate, only a half-full coffee cup sitting beside the keyboard. I pulled the drawers open, shuffling through papers as Skylar finally caught up with me.

"It's not here," I huffed. I spun to look around the room, tapping my fingers against my leg as I flipped through possibilities. Was it possible he'd given it to someone else?

"He probably has it with him in the meeting."

I grunted. Then got an idea. "Where's Creedy?"

"Who?"

I rushed across the open space to the small room Drew had taken me that first day to be fingerprinted. I opened the door to see one person, a middle-aged man, working alone. He looked up in surprise as Skylar came up behind me.

"Is Creedy here?" I asked.

"No, he's not. He took a couple of personal days. His grandma died or something."

The first tendrils of fear seized me. "Did Seward give you the picture?"

The man raised a brow. "I scanned it into the system, but he has the original."

"I need to see it."

He hesitated. "I'd need to clear it with someone."

I exhaled through my nose. "Never mind." I let the door shut and thanked my lucky stars that Drew and some of the other officers were coming out of their meeting at the same time that Skylar and I walked back into the main area.

He furrowed his brow when he saw us and met us halfway.

"What are you doing here?"

"I need to see the photo again."

He looked at Skylar, who shrugged. He led me back toward the conference room. People were filtering out, deep in conversation.

"Creedy is gone," I said.

He glanced behind him, unconcerned. "Yeah. Personal days or something. It's actually a bummer because he's the best at the cyber stuff."

The more I heard, the more my anxiety grew. Of course he was the best. That meant it was easy for him to find out where the cameras were and track his victims.

Drew stopped in front of the info board and yanked the picture from the clip that held it and handed it to me. "What exactly is this about?"

I scanned the picture and nodded. "See this?" I pointed to a faint glow in the right-hand corner.

Skylar and Drew leaned over to look.

"What is it?" he said.

"It's a watch. It's the glow of its face reflecting on the window."

Drew snatched it from my hands and held it close, squinting. "He's sitting in a car."

"I think so."

"How did you know it was a watch?" He turned the squint on me.

"Because I've seen it."

"What?" The volume level with Skylar and Drew saying it simultaneously brought the attention of the others in the room.

"This whole time, I thought it was Russo because he'd given

me that weird look, but I remembered what they say about serial killers being right under your nose because they can seem normal, innocuous."

"Who are you talking about?" Drew asked, impatient.

"Creedy. When he was helping us pull up the footage from Skylar's apartment, I saw his watch." I'd been so locked onto Drew because he'd been angry, but in memory, I recalled the brief smile on Creedy's face at Drew's outburst.

"That doesn't mean anything." His skepticism was clear, but underneath, I could tell he was considering it.

"And he happened to walk by yesterday when I was shoveling. It could be a coincidence. But with how close this creep has been following me, it seems too convenient that he was on *that* street right when I was outside and supposedly lived nearby." I searched my memory for hints, clues. Anything. There wasn't much to go on, but it was the little things. His smile that day with Jane too. It was hardly damning evidence, but my gut feeling was too strong.

Drew's expression tightened almost imperceptibly, and he crossed his arms over his chest.

"Where's his desk?" I asked.

"Cass—"

I took off out of the meeting room before he could stop me. He caught up to me at the door to the fingerprinting room and blocked it, staring down at me.

"I have no problem going through his things if you won't," I said. "There's enough here to at least warrant a search. If I'm wrong, we move on. But we are running out of time, and there's no space for doubt here."

He sighed, chewing his lip as he debated, then he stepped aside.

I opened the door, and the middle-aged man snapped to attention again.

"Which one is Creedy's desk?" I asked.

The man's mouth dropped open. "Seward, what is this?" he demanded.

Drew held up a hand and led me to one of the three desks in the room. Skylar stood in the doorway, arms wrapped around herself.

I yanked the top drawer open and shuffled through the lab reports, the worksheets, the nonsense. The edge of a photo envelope was visible underneath it all. "Bingo," I breathed.

Drew yanked it out before I could and opened the envelope. His expression tightened as he looked through the images, a flash of anger lighting in his eyes.

"Jensen," he barked, looking at the middle-aged man. "Check the search history for anything Creedy had his hands on. I want some more to go on before we move on this."

Drew spun on his heel and headed back to the conference room, lips pressed into a thin line. Skylar and I followed.

"What are the pictures of?" I asked when we were away from the noise of the main area.

His nostrils flared, but he handed me the photos. He turned to their information board, brooding.

I shuffled through the pictures slowly. Skylar pressed a hand to her mouth. They were all images of me. Going to the college that first time, the one from Drew's house, Skylar and me at the cemetery.

And one that didn't belong. It took me a moment to realize why. Me in scrubs, a jacket I had never worn.

"This one isn't me," I said.

Drew turned so quickly, as if yanked by a string. He moved

closer again and looked over my shoulder. His breath was warm against my exposed neck, and I was momentarily distracted, memories from last night making the heat rise in my cheeks.

He took the picture from my hands, clearly not on the same wavelength.

Skylar and I followed him back out of the room.

"I want all the background we have on Gavin Creedy. I need addresses, vehicles, history, family, anything we can find."

Several people murmured at the barked order but set off to find the information anyway.

He stalked to his desk, the two of us still in tow. He sat down and wiggled the mouse to bring up his own search program.

"Do you remember anything else that might be helpful?" Drew didn't pull his eyes from his screen as he typed.

I shook my head and glanced upward, trying to remember details, things he said or mentioned in passing. I kept picturing the smile, the contempt that wasn't noticeable the first time. He'd been pleased with himself. That day in the break room, talking about how to impress a woman.

My eyes widened. "Oh, my God."

Drew stopped typing and turned to me.

"Old Main. He said he liked the old buildings on Old Main."

Drew practically leaped from his chair. "That must be where he's holding her." He jogged to an office at the back of the room.

I shivered, thinking about how close I'd been to the man who'd murdered at least three women. He could have grabbed me right from the driveway. Drew had said they suspected the killer had a line inside the police department. And he had a good line, all right. In the cyber department where he could easily doctor surveillance, photos. He could manipulate the footage, know exactly where the cameras were. No wonder he could dump the bodies so close to the station without getting caught.

* * *

It was nearly silent. Drew and several of the others had sprung into action, grabbing weapons, strapping on flak jackets. In passing, he informed us that they were heading to Old Main. There was no way to know which building Creedy was holding the girl, so they had to be careful. But they needed as many cops as they could get to sweep the area.

Skylar sat in Drew's chair, staring at the ceiling.

I was perched on the edge of the desk, my leg jiggling. The anxiety tightened my lungs, and I worked to breathe evenly. I hoped Drew would call us as soon as they found the girl. Once they did, I planned on sleeping for a week straight. I wouldn't need any babysitters, and I could look into my plans for starting a new life somewhere else.

Skylar sat up, and I turned to face her.

"Relax," she said. "I just need to go to the bathroom." She got up and walked toward the front of the station. None of the people left in the room glanced up as she passed.

She'd been awfully quiet the last half an hour, and I wondered if she was thinking of her grandmother. Drew had said they were close. It would be a difficult thing to lose a best friend and your grandma within a few short weeks. I shouldn't have brought her here, making her wait around with me when the weight of her grandma's failing health was at the forefront of her mind.

I turned to Drew's computer and tapped the mouse for want of something to do. The screen woke up, revealing a picture of mountains at sunrise. The screen flickered, like the power wasn't hooked up properly.

I leaned forward and tapped the top of the monitor and reached to jiggle the power cord. The screen flickered again, as did the lights in the room. I looked up and around, but no one seemed to have noticed.

I stood, making my way toward the front of the station. I felt the current on the air, the building pressure I'd almost forgotten about from that first time. I was about to ask the man sitting at his desk closest to me if he felt that crushing pressure when the ringing started.

The pain, I remembered. My hands flew to my ears, just like the last time, the volume increasing, the piercing sound like metal on metal, grating. I was sure this time it was worse, and the lights, one by one, popped. Glass sprinkled everywhere.

Again, it brought me to my knees. Could no one else hear it? I screamed as it grew so loud, so painful, I was sure it was shredding the inside of my skull. My brain would be spaghetti.

That's it. Goodbye for good, Cassidy.

29

Rewind and Level Up

Aretha Franklin was wailing out, breaking it down for whatever schmuck had broken her heart. And I had the pounding headache that decided to rise to the occasion, wailing just as loudly, if not more so than Aretha.

I groaned as I pushed myself up from my prone position, eyes opened only to slits to block out the offending light in the room.

"That you, Red?" a voice called.

It was vaguely familiar, and I forced my lids to open wider to take in the room. The lights were bright, but it was the sun coming in from the window above my head that was a knife into my eyeballs.

I was sitting on a hard, wooden bench, and I swept the room with my gaze. Black bars, brick wall.

There was no forcing it now as my eyes widened with realization. I was still in the police station, but not where I last remembered. The pulsing pressure, the sound. Both times I woke up with a pounding headache like I had a hangover.

I gasped. Did this mean that I was back? What time was

it? What day was it? Panic fluttered through me, my hands tightening their grip on the bench. Did they get to the girl in time?

I looked down at myself. I was wearing the other Cassidy's clothes. The light blue sweater, the dark wash jeans. Even her ankle boots.

I touched the soft knit of the sweater to make sure it was real.

"I was beginning to think you'd sleep all day," the voice said, closer.

My head snapped up. "Keener," I breathed.

"What's got you all riled up?" he asked, shifting all his weight to one leg, arms crossed over his barrel of a chest.

I stood, ignoring the nausea that roiled through me, the headache that clawed at my skull with a vengeance, and flew to the bars, gripping them. "Keener, how long have I been here?"

He furrowed his brow. "Just overnight. Girl, you are a mess. Were you high last night or something?"

I ignored that. If a week there was only overnight here, that meant that Creedy was still out there, no one the wiser. So if it was true, yesterday was the day Drew picked me up for stealing a wallet, the same day Creedy had dumped a murdered a woman. And if it was the day after *that* murder, then he hadn't taken the teen girl yet. I could stop it before it happened.

I lurched forward, and Keener drew back slightly. "You need to find Dre—uh, Detective Seward. I need to talk to him right now."

He shifted again, his hands going to his hips, absolutely zero urgency in his demeanor. "Why?"

"Please," I begged. "Just do it. It's important."

His mouth tipped skeptically. "All right, fine. If it's that important." He turned slowly, eyes narrowed on me.

It was clear from the leisurely pace that he wasn't taking me quite as seriously as I wanted him to. But it didn't matter. We had some time. I turned back from the cell bars, ready to sit down again, to rest my head, make the world stop spinning.

The sound of the door opening was a relief, and I was grateful that Keener was at least humoring me. I sat and placed my head in my hands. One night. Had it been a dream? Was that possible? One super long, incredibly vivid dream?

I touched the soft sweater again, biting my lip. It was definitely not mine, the only tangible reminder of what had happened to me. I stood again to pace, pausing to let the wave of nausea, calmer this time, wash over me.

What happened when I left the other universe? No one seemed to experience what I had. The sound, the lights popping. Had Skylar come back from the bathroom to find me gone? Or was everything adjusted as if I had never been there? I had no idea how this whole alternate universe thing worked.

Soft footsteps announced his presence, and I was surprised that I hadn't heard the door. He was close already, though it wasn't shocking since I was only a couple of cells down, and I turned to face him, my fingers sliding around the bars in eager anticipation.

He caught me off guard when his hand shot out to grip my sweater. He yanked me forward so abruptly I didn't have time to react or stop myself from banging my forehead so hard on the bars that it rang throughout the room.

The echo vibrated inside my skull, and it was only when his face appeared above me in double-vision that I realized I was lying on the floor. But it was not Drew who sneered at me. The green eyes were colder than I had ever seen them, and it became apparent to me just how good of an actor he really must be.

Creedy hauled me to my feet, a process more difficult than he anticipated as I teetered. The world spun and threatened to swallow me whole.

I became aware of the sharp point of the knife tucked under my chin, the blade nipping at the soft flesh.

"You will not make a sound," he growled into my ear.

I didn't respond, not sure that if I opened my mouth only words would come out. He shoved me forward, and I threw my hands out to steady myself, realizing that he had zip-tied them in front of me when I was down. The floor lurched beneath me, but I managed to stay on my feet with his help.

He swiped the electronic key to open the door from the cell block and shoved me forward. He glanced around, and I was dismayed to see that no one was paying attention to this part of the station. Drew and Keener were nowhere in sight.

Despite his earlier threat, I sucked in a breath to scream. The knife jabbed upward. Opening my mouth would drive the blade right through the underside of my chin, so all I managed was a squeak before he was rushing me toward a big door marked "emergency exit." I prayed that he hadn't had the forethought to disable the alarm, but it was short-lived as he pushed me through, and it remained silent.

The icy air hit me, and I sucked in a sharp breath. It cleared my head a little, but only enough to see that we were alone in the back parking lot. Fear replaced nausea in my gut.

But the terror sharpened my focus. No one would hear me scream out here, but I could run. I yanked against his grip on my arm. He grunted but held me fast, tightening his hold. A hard-knuckled hand crashed against the side of my face, knocking my teeth together. I staggered, stunned, and he used the momentum to propel me toward a dark green sedan.

He yanked the door open, and I caught myself before tumbling in, bound hands scrabbling for purchase on the roof of the car. He slammed his elbow against my wrist, and my weak grip slipped. It didn't take much more than a push for me to lose my balance. I landed sideways on the hump in the middle of the floor behind the front seat. I cried out as pain seared through my abdomen, the urge to throw up making saliva flood my mouth.

I swallowed hard, willing the bile back down as he leaned in to fold my legs into the car. I clenched my teeth against the spasms of agony and nausea and kicked out at his face. He jerked his head back so that my booted heel only grazed his chin, and he slammed the door on my ankle. I screamed again, pulling my leg inside.

My mind reeled from the onslaught of violence, a top going round and round, and my only coherent thought was that this couldn't possibly be real. I was asleep at the police station. Or better yet, in Drew's bed.

Please let this be a dream. I squeezed my eyes closed, hot tears rolling from the corners into my hair.

The driver's side door opened and shut, and he started the car, peeling out as he gunned the engine.

Oh, God. I'm going to die.

No! Do something! Move!

I struggled to sit up, stuffed as I was between the seats, dizzy and nauseated, hands tied in front of me.

"Oh no, you don't," he said, reaching back with something

in his hand. He brought it down with surprising force, given the angle.

I screamed as the blade plunged into my thigh, slicing through skin and muscle. My fingernails clawed at his wrist as my scream dwindled to a whimper. I huffed through my teeth to keep from losing consciousness.

He pulled the knife from my leg, and I shrieked in renewed agony. Hot liquid spread over my jeans, visible even against the dark blue of the denim. I couldn't get my hands around the wound and wondered whether he cared if I bled to death.

"I'm guessing I missed the major arteries in your leg. I don't recommend moving from that spot unless you want me to take another crack at it."

I gulped in air, trying not to choke on the sob that built in my chest. Was I destined to be one of Creedy's victims in every universe? Stupid Cassidy! If I'd told Keener what I knew, instead of sending him to go get Drew, maybe I wouldn't even be in this position.

And in this world, Drew was freaking clueless where to look because *I* had given him the idea in the other reality. Stupid, stupid, stupid.

Panic was a hand around my throat, and I was losing my battle against hysterics. I forced myself to focus on breathing since every jerk of my body sent a fresh wave of white-hot pain through my leg. How far was Old Main from the station? How long would I be in this cramped position, my blood soaking my jeans, the carpet of his car? My stomach twisted at the thought that mine was probably not the only blood staining his vehicle.

I whimpered.

God, get me out of this, I begged. *I'll do anything. No more stealing. No more running. I can do better!*

I sensed no answer to my silent plea, and my agony made the minutes feel like hours until we finally stopped. All I could see out of the windows was the gray sky.

Creedy got out, and he was hauling me out of the tight space from the door behind my head before I could do anything to stop him. I did my best to ignore the pain in my leg as I struggled against his grip.

He only allowed me to work against him for a split second before he paused to thump his fist against the wound in my thigh. I cried out, the sound echoing against the buildings that surrounded us.

"If you make this harder than it needs to be, I'll return the favor," he said through his teeth, yanking me to my feet, dragging me toward a back door into a small, plain building.

I limped, unable to keep myself from whimpering every time I put the slightest weight on my injured leg. I tried to locate any distinguishing landmark around me for reference, but all I could see was that we were in a back alleyway, surrounded by trash blown in on the wind or left by vagabonds. Brick buildings loomed all around like indifferent bystanders, silent witnesses to unimagined savagery.

Creedy unlocked the door to the building in front of us and shoved me through into darkness. I stumbled forward, half-dragging my useless leg. I held out my bound hands in case I ran into something, but the echoing sound of my boots on the cement floor told me it was empty.

The door closed behind me, and his hand slid around my arm to yank me sideways. I staggered, forced to put weight on my leg to keep from falling, each time sending a stabbing shock of anguish. I gasped, limping as he continued dragging me with him, and he finally turned on a light.

It didn't illuminate much. Huge, vaulted ceilings loomed above us. Whatever this room once housed was a mystery, now just walls stripped of paint; any carpet that may have existed had been ripped up to expose the concrete beneath. It was only slightly warmer than outside, and I began to shiver. Alone with a killer in a frigid, forgotten place. My chin trembled.

Creedy pushed me forward, and I fell to my knees, forcing back the scream I wanted to release. He grinned as I fought against the urge to sob, then walked back into a part of the room that was obscured by darkness.

I took the moment to move from my knees to a sitting position on the cold concrete. I moved my leg with deliberate slowness, wincing as I straightened it out. In the dim light, I could barely make out the shine of the blood soaked into my jeans. The knife had been sharp enough that it slipped through the fabric without fraying the material.

I tried to maneuver in a way that would help me tend to the wound or at least see how serious it was. Was I going to bleed to death? Could I stop it if I was? My hands wouldn't cooperate, too tightly bound by the plastic, stuck together, useless. I wouldn't have been able to rip my sweater even if my hands were free, so no tourniquet.

Creedy came back, emerging from the shadows like a ghost, his eyes sparkling with malice as he smirked at me.

I scooted back, dragging my useless leg, until my back hit the rough brick wall and stopped me. Its solid presence gave me some courage, and I lifted my chin ever so slightly.

He held something that he shifted back and forth between his hands as he approached.

I cringed away from him when he crouched in front of me, inspecting my leg in the darkness. I didn't think he could see much, given the dim lighting, but I wasn't sure what exactly he was looking for anyway.

With the tip of his knife, its blade blinking when it caught the light, he probed at the wound.

I hissed through my teeth.

He grinned at me. "A little tender?" He tapped the blade against his chin. "I wonder how deep it went." The grin widened. "See, I like to make superficial cuts, but I wondered what it would be like to slice deeper."

He looked down at my leg again, speculative. "It was kind of like stabbing a steak. No—more like a raw pork chop."

I swallowed the bile that rose in my throat.

"I don't think you've lost much blood," he continued conversationally. "But just in case." He held up a rag. It looked clean enough. "Lift your leg."

I had a quick internal debate. Was it better to let myself bleed to death now, rob him of the pleasure he clearly derived from torturing his victims? Or should I let him wrap it and try for an escape later?

His eyes narrowed and the blade glinted in the light again as he twisted it in his hand to get a firmer grip. "Lift your leg."

I swallowed again and did as he said, gritting my teeth against the pain.

He slid the rag under my thigh and pulled it around the top of my leg. He yanked it tight so quickly I gasped at the shock that went through me. He smiled again and stood, looming over me.

"I'm heading out for a bit. Don't go anywhere." His smile grew, and he shot me a wink.

I turned my head away from him then let out a startled cry when he gave my leg a solid kick. I looked up at him, panting, and it was clear that's what he'd wanted.

He crouched down again and grabbed my face, pinching. "Don't you ever disrespect me again. You understand me?"

I nodded, and he released me. I watched him disappear into the shadows again. He unlocked the inner deadbolt and the heavy door echoed out a faint groan as he opened and shut it. Then the outside lock slid into place, the sound a muted *snick* that made my heart sink.

30

Let's Play Therapist

I let out a faint whimper as I looked around the room. Empty warehouse. Screaming would only echo back to me. The closest person was at least a block away anyway. Pointless. But maybe there was some other door.

I shifted, careful not to jostle my leg. The pain still seared through me, and I took long, slow breaths that puffed out in tremulous clouds. How long would I last with blood loss and the low temperature?

The sound of my teeth chattering echoed around me.

Oh, God.

I allowed myself the sob that clawed up my throat, pressing trembling hands against my temples. I squeezed my eyes shut, and the sob became a guttural yell.

Just lie down and die. Give up. The harder you fight, the worse it will be.

I flopped over onto the floor, heaving air in and out while the cement leeched warmth from my body.

The hope of someone finding me here before Creedy squeezed the breath out of me was a dying dream. No one knew where he'd taken me. Hell, I barely knew where I was.

He'd snatched me straight from the station with no one even paying attention. But surely there were cameras all over that building, inside and out. Someone would notice something wasn't right. Especially if Keener got Drew like I'd asked him to. They'd see I was gone and find the cameras. They'd at least search.

I clutched at that shred of possibility. After a beat or two, I pushed myself back up and leaned my head back against the wall, steadying my quivering breaths. What had Creedy been thinking, taking me straight from the station? I remembered what Drew said about serial killers purposely leaving clues when they wanted recognition for their crimes. Was that what he was doing?

I thought back to the pictures Creedy had taken in that other universe. Pictures of me and the other Cassidy, kept in a place as obvious as his work desk. Like a dare. He got a thrill being that close to someone discovering him. The smile he shot at the camera when he'd left the flower on Skylar's doorstep had been so cocky. And dropping hints about where he liked to keep his victims until he killed them.

I lifted my head. Did he always bring them here? Was I sitting where a handful of others had cowered, terrified and terrorized by a sociopath who took pleasure in hurting people?

Just his newest victim.

But I didn't want to be another victim. There was no guarantee that Drew would figure out where Creedy was keeping me, even if they found the security footage of him taking me. I couldn't rely on someone else to rescue me.

I took stock of my situation. The leg was my biggest problem. Any plans I made couldn't involve running or speed. So the first thing I needed was a way to break my bonds. I vaguely recalled watching a video about getting out of zip-ties like the one that held my hands, but I couldn't remember exactly what I was supposed to do. If I could find something, even a scrap of metal to saw it off, I'd at least be in a better position. Hopefully, anything I found could double as a weapon.

The light provided a limited view of what was in the room but, based on what I could see, finding any kind of tool was going to be a difficult task.

How much time did I have before Creedy came back? Was it worth trying to investigate my surroundings? This was probably my only opportunity.

I pulled my right leg up and used the wall to push myself up to my feet, grunting as the movement jostled my injured leg. I wobbled a bit as I put most of my weight on my good foot. The wall remained my support as I turned and limped along its length.

I moved forward and came to another wall. At this point, I was completely immersed in shadows, but I could barely make out the shape of a window that, I was sure, faced the street. Particleboard had been nailed over it to protect the glass. As I moved on, feeling my way along the wall with my bound hands, I came across what must have been the front door. I tried my luck with the knob, knowing it was a slim chance, and found it locked. I felt along the door, pounded with my fist to test its construction. I'd hoped that maybe it didn't have much substance, but it was solid.

I moved on, coming to yet another wall. I followed that one until I came to an open doorway. Whatever lay beyond was dark, and more than just lightless. A poisonous sense of the sinister snaked around my insides. My breath came faster; my palms started sweating. I backed up involuntarily.

There was a crunching sound outside the back door, faint, like footsteps on gravel. My heart climbed toward my throat and nearly choked me.

I broke into a hobbling run to get back to my spot against the wall, trying to regulate my breathing when the door swung open. A fresh wave of frigid air blew in.

He shut the door, the sound of the lock sliding into place echoing throughout the building, and the freezing wind died a sudden death. I tried to track his movement in the darkness as he walked further inside, a toxic cocktail of terror and dread mingling in my gut.

The light caught his face, showing that his cheeks and nose were a wind-bitten pink as if he'd walked from a good distance. He ignored me as he headed straight for the dark room and disappeared into its inky blackness.

He didn't come back for several minutes, and I began to shiver again. The chills cascaded through me, wave after wave, and every muscle spasmed. The ones in my wounded thigh seized and twitched angrily. I gritted my teeth, trying not to make a sound to draw his attention.

Finally, he came back into view, eyes narrowed on me. "How's the leg?"

I said nothing.

He crouched in front of me as he'd done before and inspected the bandage. He held an apple in one hand and brought it to his lips in slow-motion, thoughtful. He took a big bite. "There's an awful lot of bleed-through on this wrap." He looked at me.

I met his look head-on, trying not to shy away from his direct gaze and the way his eyes seemed to go on forever, like endless black pits.

He reached over to touch my cheek, but I recoiled, jerking away. He laughed, and he looked absurdly boyish, dimples appearing in his cheeks, perfectly straight teeth gleaming in the light.

"Did you do some investigating?" he asked, the grin still in place. He took another bite of the apple.

I worked to keep my breathing even. Still, I remained silent.

"I would expect nothing less. Did you see my special room?" He turned his head toward the dark maw of the door.

I suppressed an involuntary shudder.

When he turned back, his eyes were glinting. "It's my favorite place." A soft sigh, as if he were talking about visiting a museum.

No wonder it had repulsed me. That must have been where he did his dark deeds, cruel hands squeezing the life out of poor, innocent women, bleeding them dry. Doing who knew what else. I fought another shiver, but the goosebumps still broke out over my skin.

"You'll get to see it up close soon enough." He winked. "It was so nice running into you at the station. I'd seen you around town, but you were very hard to predict. No routine. You certainly didn't make things easy for me." He pursed his lips thoughtfully, his eyes tracing over my features. "You clearly weren't making permanent plans to stay here.

"I got tired of waiting to figure you out though. It was so. . ." he sucked air in through clenched teeth, the anger making his words come out a growl. "Frustrating. I had to settle for the other girl."

I stiffened. The other girl? Had he gotten the teenager already? But, no. I reminded myself that hadn't happened yet. It seemed so long ago that Drew had picked me up for pickpocketing. And that had been the day of the most recent murder. Was that really only yesterday? He was certainly escalating. Faster here than he had in the other universe.

Creedy watched my expression change with fascination. He must have liked what this conversation seemed to do to me and decided to continue. "She was easy to get to. And I was getting so angry, I needed—" through his teeth again—"*something* to get me by until I could have you."

I battled the terror back. I didn't want to give him the satisfaction of seeing it on my face.

He smiled anyway, like he knew what I was thinking. "You will be my most glorious masterpiece. And such a pretty one, too." He reached out to touch my cheek again, but when I turned away, he grabbed my chin and forced me to look at him. "I'm really hoping you'll enjoy this as much as I will."

I pulled my face out of his grasp, and he chuckled, standing.

"Why?" I asked.

He beamed down at me, pleased that I was engaging him. "Why what?"

"Why redheads?"

He took a bite of his apple again, the sound of his teeth ripping into its flesh like a lion tearing into a gazelle. "Why not?" he retorted. "There's no real reason."

At my expression, he laughed.

"You were expecting some sob story about how my mother abused me? That her hair was that deep, fiery red? That red I find so. . . *enticing.*" He stuck out his lip mockingly. "Sorry, Precious. She didn't. The woman never touched me."

I latched onto his words. There was the slightest edge to the word "touched." Could it be that it wasn't abuse that he'd experienced? But a lack of attention at all?

"You want something to humanize me, make you empathize. Poor little Gavin. No wonder he *snapped*." He waved the half-eaten apple around casually, but it seemed a little too controlled to me. "What about you, Cassidy?"

I flinched at his use of my name, so intimate, almost a purr.

"What sort of damage do you carry around, hidden just beneath the surface? You want to play therapist? Hmm?"

I tried not to react to the condescending bite in his tone.

"Your daddy call you names?" he asked. "Tell you that you were stupid?"

I kept my face stony. He wanted a reaction. Tears maybe. He wanted to arm himself too. Knives weren't his only weapon.

"Or was it your mommy?" The taunt was palpable. "She jealous of you? Not around enough?" He thought for a moment, tapping the apple to his chin. "Did she. . . die?" He said it slowly, and there was no way it wasn't deliberate. He *knew*.

My nostrils flared despite my efforts to remain impassive.

"Ahhh, there it is." His smile stretched slowly. Then he pouted at me again. "Poor Cassidy. Do you want to cry about it? Hug it out?"

Baiting me. I wasn't exactly sure what his endgame was, if he thought I would bawl in front of him. He obviously enjoyed seeing my pain, even the emotional kind. No doubt he had access to whatever information he wanted through the police database. And a cyber genius would have no trouble hacking systems to get deeper.

"What about your daddy? What happened to him?"

I stiffened. It didn't matter how I reacted. He knew this too. His widening grin proved it. A child, eager to taunt.

"Oh, right. You don't know, do you?" He *tsked*, feigning

concern.

Anger slithered through my veins like a drug. Two could play this game. He'd worked to redirect my probe, and I wondered if any of the others had turned the tables on him. Had he punished them for it?

"Why didn't your mother love you?" I asked, using the anger to drive it in like the blade he'd plunged into my thigh.

His eyes instantly darkened, and he took a deliberately slow bite of his apple, working for casual.

"Did she have high expectations?" I pressed. "Never good enough for her? No love for such a disappointment?"

"Tsk, tsk, Red," he said, but the smile he gave me was too tight. "There's no story here."

Gotcha.

I pushed. "No, I really want to know. You wanted a therapy session. Let's play, Gavin. Why didn't she love you?"

He crouched in front of me, and that smile was almost like a rabid dog baring its teeth now. "You want to know how much I like to hurt people, Red?"

"Do it, Gavin. Prove that what she took from you doesn't matter."

His breath was hot and rank against my face. Out of the corner of my eye I saw the knife flash as he pulled it out of his pocket.

"You want to know?" He brushed the cold metal against my cheek, stroking my skin with the flat of the blade. "Normally, I'm very careful about the cuts I make. But maybe we can play a little more, you and me. I'd like to see what sounds you'll make."

I fought the terror that tightened in my gut. Because pushing his buttons was a gamble. But it could make him mess up, feel like he had to prove something to me. I just hoped it paid off.

He skimmed my cheek with the blade again. "You have such lovely skin." Another purr, his eyes trailing down my face, lingering on my mouth.

A garbage truck rumbled by, startling us both, but he was more tense, and he jerked to look in the direction of the street.

I seized the opportunity and grabbed his hand fisted around the knife with both of mine. I caught him off guard and forced the blade into his neck, throwing as much of my weight into it as I could. He screamed and fell backward, hands scrambling to pull the knife from his throat. I lurched to my feet and staggered into a limping run toward the door.

So much for my no running plan.

I barely made out a sliver of light at the bottom of the door, a slice of hope to pull me forward. I pushed myself harder, gritting my teeth against the agony that pulsed down my entire leg.

I was body-slammed to the floor. I threw my bound hands out, managing to save my face from hitting the concrete, but my wrist bent backward, further than it was meant to go. I screamed, the shrill ring echoing around us.

Creedy reared back at the volume of the shriek, giving me enough room to flip to my back and defend myself better.

He brought his weight back down against me, his face contorted by his snarl.

I used my elbow and whacked it against the knife he hadn't managed to pull from his throat. His eyes bulged, the light from the other room illuminating half his face, and he let out an unearthly howl. The blood poured from the wound faster now, coating my hands, warm and slick.

He renewed his vigor, the fury transforming his face into

something terrifying. I kicked my legs, swung my bound hands back and forth. His knee pressed hard into my leg wound, but I fought the pain. I refused to let it incapacitate me, though it threatened to steal the breath from my lungs. I *had* to escape. The door was close, so close I could feel the cold air seeping underneath, just a finger on the back of my neck.

Even with his weight and his desperate hands clawing at me, I could tell he was losing strength. I may not have gotten an artery, but he was still losing a lot of blood.

Just get out, I chanted.

If I could get out of the building, I might stand a chance of running. Adrenaline was an amazing painkiller.

This time, as he grabbed at my face, nails scraping at my skin, I fumbled around his chest, his shoulders, his neck, and felt the handle of the knife. I yanked it free. He screamed again and grabbed my bound hands, knocking them above my head against the concrete. Once, twice, and the knife clattered across the floor.

He scrambled after it, and I flipped, stumbling to my feet. I crashed into the door and groped around for the bolt, yanking it loose. My hands were slick against the knob as I scrambled to open it.

The blast of glacial air forced me to suck in a breath, and I staggered out into the alleyway, muted sunlight revealing that I was still alone and at least a block away from another human being.

He caught me by my ponytail, and I shrieked, the sound reverberating against the stolid buildings, record-keepers of screams that had come before mine. They were unmoved by my panic.

I spun, trying to catch him off-guard, but he was already

stumbling to the ground, losing strength too quickly. So much blood. I batted him away like a mosquito.

I turned to continue my escape, more sure that he wouldn't make it out of the alley. But I could never be certain.

Just get out.

Just get out.

Something moved within the shadows between the two buildings, and the panic clawed its way up my belly, clutching at my throat. Did he have a partner? Had it all been for nothing? Maybe I would die here after all.

The gun came up, and I stuttered to a halt. But it was pointed behind me, and the relief was a warm deluge, soaking me. He emerged from the darkness, the eyes hardened steel as he glared at Creedy.

Drew had come. They'd found me.

Several others came in after him, their weapons drawn. I looked behind me. Creedy was on his knees, white hands pressed to his neck in an attempt to staunch the flow. He looked weak enough to pass out right there, pale and shivering.

The other officers moved in on him, but Drew looked at me and lowered his gun.

"Are you all right?" He asked, holstering his weapon at his hip. He walked forward, cautious, and I wasn't sure what he saw in my face.

He produced a pocket knife, and I flinched as it slid out with a crisp *click.* He paused, his dark gaze softening. "I'm going to cut the zip tie."

I nodded and held out my trembling hands, the adrenaline finally withdrawing, leeching all the energy, all the fight right out of me.

He slid the knife between my palms and sawed at the plastic

until it popped off and fell to the ground.

Drew put his hand to my elbow. "Cassidy."

My name on his lips, spoken in such a different way, almost undid me. This was not the Drew who'd kissed me with abandon. It was simultaneously a crushing blow and a weight lifted.

I met his gaze. "I need to sit down."

He nodded and helped me slink to the ground. I grimaced and straightened my injured leg in front of me, leaning back against the wall.

He crouched in front of me, his eyes roving over every cut and scrape. "I'm thinking most of this is his blood." He tossed his head in Creedy's direction.

I didn't respond.

"I know where you got that knot on your forehead. What about the wrist?"

I looked down at it, bent at an odd angle. "That was during the struggle. Barely feel it."

He raised a brow. "Your leg looks pretty bad."

I shrugged. "I don't think it's bleeding any more."

He frowned as he examined it. His hands hovered just above, not touching.

I winced anyway. "Right after he took me, he jammed his knife into my thigh."

He hissed through his teeth.

I looked over at Creedy, hands cuffed, officers working to stop the flow of blood from his neck. His eyes, feverish, still held the rage. I leaned my head back. In the background, an ambulance's siren screamed.

"You ready for this to be over?" Drew asked.

"God, yes."

31

Fresh Hell

I refused pain meds stronger than ibuprofen. I hated the fuzzy feeling, like having a hazy film over my brain. And there had been enough messing with my head lately.

The ache in my wrist was hard to ignore if I wasn't distracted enough. The leg was pretty negligible when I didn't move it. I dealt with the pain by telling myself it meant I'd survived.

I stared at the ceiling tiles, trying not to let the noise in the hall bother me. How anyone managed to rest in a hospital was beyond me. It didn't help that the police had been by multiple times to go over what had happened. As if living through it once wasn't enough.

My mind wandered to Skylar and Drew, of the life I'd been handed for what seemed like weeks. It was an ache in my heart to be gone, but also a relief so profound that I struggled to put words to it. I'd learned what having friends could really be like. But I no longer carried guilt just for existing. I couldn't say that I'd enjoyed the experience. Nothing had torn at me more. But I was better for it.

I laid my head back. Even though I hadn't gotten any answers for what had brought me to that other universe, I didn't care at the moment. Having survived the last twenty-four hours took precedence. Maybe I would look into it later. But right now, I was grateful to be back where I should have been all along. What I had to face now was what I would make of my life next.

I touched my lips as I thought of Drew, as if I could bring the memory to life. But the last image of him was that steely gaze he'd shot me when he'd jogged out of the station to save the poor girl Creedy had taken. Had they gotten her out safely? I hoped and prayed that Creedy's blade hadn't broken her skin.

"Am I interrupting anything important?"

I couldn't help jerking my head up, and Drew's smile faded.

"Sorry." He held up his hands, palms out.

How could I explain that it wasn't that he'd startled me? That it was the impact of his voice, the memories associated with it? My throat tightened at the knowledge that he didn't share those memories, that I was practically a stranger to him. And that he was likely here to ask me more questions. Or the same ones over again.

"It's fine," I said after a moment. "Come on in."

He walked further into the room. "You seem kind of bored."

I snorted. "I'd rather be bored. I've had more than enough excitement the last few days."

His eyebrows quirked, and he tossed his jacket onto the bed by my feet. "I would imagine so. I'm pretty over it myself."

"And now that you got your bad guy, what's the plan? Party? Vacation?"

He laughed. "I wish. Right now, my life is paperwork."

"Next best thing to a beach in Hawaii."

He laughed again, and the sound was a salve to my stuttering heart. Before I came back, it seemed like laughter had been forgotten. And it was the one thing that really transformed his face.

But the humor shifted to seriousness. "Listen, I have to warn you."

"I know, I know. We have to run through what happened again." I rolled my eyes. "As if during the ambulance ride wasn't enough. And while I was getting settled in here yesterday. That other detective didn't laugh at any of my jokes, so I'm glad it's you this time."

His smile was a little pinched. "It's more than that, actually."

For a second, my heart kicked into a panicked rhythm. He was going to tell me Creedy escaped. Or that he did have an accomplice. I gripped the blankets on either side of me, ignoring the pain it ignited in my broken wrist.

My increased heartbeat registered on the monitor, and his eyes flickered to the machine. He moved slowly around the bed, and his gaze came back to my face.

"Is it okay if I sit?" he asked.

God, that distance, that unfamiliarity. It brought a new wave of emotion that temporarily kicked out my anxiety.

I nodded, unable to make my dry throat produce words.

"You're not in danger," he assured me, his eyes soft. He scooted the chair closer to the bed, lowering himself into it and resting his elbows on his knees. "I'm just giving you a heads up."

"Spit it out already. You're freaking me out."

He winced. "The press is all over this right now. So whenever you get released, they're going to hound you."

I swallowed. "Oh, that's not good." My heart stuttered out my response to this new terror, something he likely wouldn't understand.

But he pursed his lips, and there was a shrewd glint in his eye. "Cassidy, you've been living in your car."

The heat burned in my face. Right. He was not an idiot.

"If I didn't know any better, I'd say you were running from something." He moved his head to catch my eyes. "Or someone."

I thought back to what he'd said about going to the police, letting them handle it. What I'd recently experienced, so fresh in my mind, was beyond anything I'd endured from Callum. So far. Knowing him, the fact that I had run made him angry, though. But could I trust them with this? Stop running and face it?

Drew was watching my face, his expression unreadable. More cop-like again. Because I *was* a victim here.

I didn't know where to start, what to say. How much could I reveal? This was not *my* Drew—a painful jolt shot through my heart. Not mine. That Drew hadn't belonged to me, as much as I wished he did. As much as I missed him.

But who was this Drew, really?

"I get it," he said, interrupting my thoughts. Or perhaps reading them. "We'll get there. Just know that we're here to help you. We can keep you safe."

"Can you?" The anxious thought slipped out loud. "He took me right from under your noses."

He pulled back slightly, sucking in a breath like I'd punched him in the gut.

"Hello?" A different male voice carried to us, and we both flinched.

Drew cleared his throat and stood, turning to shake hands with the doctor who'd entered the room. Hercules was a more apt description now than before. The chiseled Greek god made manifest. Evan, gilded gold. Gone was the pallid complexion, the sagging posture. He stood confidently, smiling like it was permanently etched onto his face, as if the sculptor himself had put it there.

"How's it going?" he asked, grinning at Drew. "I heard you were around here somewhere. Thought I'd stop in and say hi."

Drew recovered and turned to me. "This is Evan, my cousin." As if I didn't already know. Because I wasn't supposed to. "Dr. Henson to everyone else, but I'm sure he'll make an exception for you."

Evan winked, and the charm was unmistakable. There was absolutely no doubt about what had attracted Cassidy in the first place. He glowed with confidence. Not the arrogant kind. But someone comfortable in his own skin. I no longer struggled to reconcile the image of doctor with the football player's build. All of it worked to his advantage.

"You got any problems I need to fix?" Evan asked me, pulling my mind back to the conversation. "I could get you the better pillows, maybe the cherry Jell-O since it's the best."

I smiled, unable to help myself. "I'm fine, thanks."

Drew circled behind Evan, his dark gaze on me, and settled back against the wall to observe quietly. As if he was gauging how we'd interact.

"What's your role here?" I asked Evan, trying to keep my eyes from following Drew. I truly did want to understand what Evan was like when he wasn't being destroyed by grief.

All smiles, dimples set in his cheeks. "I'm in pediatrics. I work directly with cardiology patients. Usually post-operative."

"That must be pretty fun to work with kids," I said. The

word *perfection* echoed through my mind again. Pediatric cardiologist, golden boy. Too bright for me. A match for the other Cassidy, the radiant one who didn't exist in this world. I couldn't help that it still gave me a twinge of bitterness, envy for what I'd seen of that life.

"I enjoy it quite a bit," he replied. He seemed to sense that I had withdrawn a bit, and I tried to play it off as being tired, pressing my hand to my mouth to cover a yawn. "Well, I'll let you get back to whatever you were discussing." He smiled again and turned to Drew. "Come find me when you're finished."

Drew nodded, his eyes following Evan out the door. I frowned, trying to read him. It was hard to tell why he was so silent.

But it was a relief to see Evan whole and to know that my very existence wasn't a source of pain. I longed to know about Skylar, to see her as well. She was someone from that other world that I could picture myself being friends with. I even admitted that she had become my friend against my better judgment.

Drew turned his attention back to me, and I couldn't help but think that he was also measuring me.

"I know you've been let down," he started. "But we *can* keep you safe. I will make sure of it myself. Can you trust me?"

My instinct was to say yes. If any element of Drew was consistent in every universe, this was a man of integrity, even if he could be idealistic and naive. "I can try."

He nodded, placing his hands on the railing at the foot of my bed, and leaned forward. "As you're aware, your testimony is going to be a pretty key element in this case. Unfortunately, these things tend to get dragged out in court. It could take months before it even goes before a jury."

I blew out a breath. Of course, that would be the real reason he'd put forth the effort. It was not personal attachment. My heart ached, and I fought back the moisture that burned in my eyes.

"It's imperative," he continued after my lengthy silence, "that you're available as we build our case." He leveled his gaze on me and waited.

I worked against my hurt, reminded myself this wasn't all about me. I was not the only victim here.

"I can do that," I replied softly. "I would hate for this case to fall apart. Not just for me. But all those other girls."

He nodded and looked down at his hands. The emotion was evident in the muscle twitching at his jaw, the toll in the exhaustion in his face. He lifted his gaze. "I appreciate any effort there. Do you have a place to stay?"

"A social worker has been by. They're finding me somewhere safe to stay until I can get something more permanent." I couldn't help the embarrassment that made my cheeks burn again. As if living in my car wasn't bad enough. Now I was probably going to be at some kind of shelter for the abused. Ugh.

The pity I expected didn't appear. Only acceptance of the facts. "Good. When are they releasing you?"

"They said probably tomorrow."

"Let me know." He waited a beat. "I'd like to pick you up, if you don't mind. Maybe I can take you out for dinner or something. Since, you know, it was basically on my watch that. . ." He shook his head. "I owe you that much."

My answer was almost too quick. "That sounds good. After what I've had here, I could go for pretty much anything.

Bootleg cherry jell-o notwithstanding."

His lips parted into his relieved smile, and I was reminded of what those lips could do. "It's a plan then." He reached out to shake my hand. The gesture seemed so formal, but I lifted the one without the cast.

He took it, and a jolt ran through me, heat that blazed uncontrolled through my veins. His smile seemed to falter. He looked down at our clasped hands, and a question formed in his eyes.

I pulled my hand carefully from his, and the uncertainty in his demeanor vanished.

"Get some rest, and I'll see you soon." He picked up his jacket, making his way toward the door.

"Drew," I blurted.

He spun to look at me, unfazed that I'd used his first name.

"How did you know where to find me?"

He caught his bottom lip with his teeth briefly. "Would it be weird if I said that it was a feeling I had?"

One side of my mouth tipped up. "No. That isn't weird at all."

He gazed at me for one long beat, the question in his dark eyes again. But he said nothing, offering me one last smile, then walked out.

That smile carried me for an hour or more of staring out the window at the dreary sky and what little I could see of the buildings around the hospital. I tried to imagine what sort of future I might have now. The fact that I even still had a future. The press would be a problem, but it was distant enough that I could ignore it for now. This nightmare had to end. I had to get justice for those other girls, if not for myself.

Another voice jolted me to attention.

"Ms. Marchand, your father is here to see you."

I stared at the nurse, uncomprehending until my father appeared behind her, his expression tentative. Not like he was afraid of my reaction, but like he thought I might be asleep.

Nothing like thoughts of the future to dredge up a phantom from my dingy past, from my half-lived alternate life. As if the physical pain wasn't enough.

The nurse hesitated, sensing something was off.

I nodded for her to go, though I wasn't sure it was the right move or not.

I was incapable of forming a word, had no ability to demand what he was doing here, how he found out where I was, who even tracked him down, and where he'd been all my life.

"My God, when I found out, I couldn't even. . ." He lurched forward like he wanted to embrace me, but some unseen force stopped him a foot from the bed. Was it my confused, borderline hostile expression that caused his hesitation? "I'm so sorry it took this long to get here. You know how traffic can be. Your mother. . ."

He looked away and my eyes lit on the hand he brought up to rub the back of his neck—was that shame in his gaze?—but his words finally struck home in my brain, sending a painful stab right into my heart. It dwarfed the pain in my wrist when I clenched my fists.

My mother?

"I'm here, I'm here," she sang, breathless as she rushed in behind him. She stopped too, though my demeanor was anything but hostile now. But she hesitated, hovering awkwardly behind him. No easy greeting from her.

I knew my mouth stood partially open.

My mother. The one who was supposed to be dead.

Just what fresh hell was this?

Acknowledgments

I can't leave without expressing the gratitude I feel toward those who truly deserve it. Many read, edited, critiqued, brainstormed, and encouraged me throughout this process. But some deserve a special shout-out.

Hannah, a brilliant writer, whose friendship has given me so much and whose insight was so critical to this story getting out in the world. Liz, who gave me so many great ideas and will forever be my super friend. Stefanie, who took the time to read, edit, and brainstorm in those early days. Elizabeth, who jumped in later but made sure to truly dive right in with helping proofread and plan my launch. You are all such encouraging, wonderful people, and I could never thank you enough.

Finally, to my mom—the woman who birthed me, laughs at all my jokes, and always reads my books in less than 24 hours with nothing but gushing praise at the end—you are the best.

About the Author

Tracey Barski lives in Colorado with her dreamboat husband and their two adorable and precocious children. When she's not writing or wrangling tiny humans, she works as an editor and proofreader. For fun, she likes to pretend to be eighty years old, crocheting and watching Hallmark movies. She can also be found reading or singing loudly to any song she knows the words to. Find her on Instagram and Facebook, as well as at traceybarski.com, to find out about her upcoming books! If you enjoyed the books, please reach out! She loves to hear from readers! And don't forget to post reviews on Amazon and Goodreads!

You can connect with me on:

- https://www.traceybarski.com
- https://www.facebook.com/authortraceybarski
- https://www.instagram.com/authortraceybarski

Also by Tracey Barski

Resurrecting Cassidy Marchand
Cassidy Marchand thought the alternate reality thing was done. But then the father who abandoned her as a child and the mother who died when she was eight walk into her hospital room, and she realizes she must be in the wrong universe. Again.

Cassidy Marchand Unraveled
Cassidy Marchand has finally taken a stand in directing the way her life goes. Finding the device that enables her to jump when she wants seems to be the break she's been waiting for. She throws herself into the search for answers. Even if that means putting herself and the life she's building in danger.

Heart In Parallel

Luke Pearson and Erin Baylor wake up to a world—and a life—that's not quite right. Desperation and grief mix as they join forces to search for a way to send Luke back where he belongs and to find answers to her brother's murder.

Printed in the USA
CPSIA information can be obtained
at www.ICGtesting.com
LVHW041755160923
758411LV00003B/234

9 781961 707009